STONES
AND
GLASS HOUSES

STONES
AND
GLASS HOUSES

by

Gary Friedman

DEDICATION

To Tracy: for her encouragement, her willingness to listen and provide a sounding board, her uplifting nature, and her love.

The most powerful words in English are 'Tell me a story,' words that are intimately related to the complexity of history, the origins of language, the continuity of the species, the taproot of our humanity, our singularity, and art itself.

~ Pat Conroy
American Author (1945 – 2016)

TABLE OF CONTENTS

ACKNOWLEDGEMENTS

When it comes to transferring thoughts to words, words to paper and paper to pages of a book, I have always said writing a book is the easy part. While I am becoming more knowledgeable on the rest of the dynamics with each book, I also realize how important it is to have qualified people around you to make the dream come true. In that regard, I would like to thank Dr. Sandy Snyder Jensen for her editing skills and her friendship. This is the second book we worked on together and it keeps getting easier.

I would also like to thank Jackie Zimmerman for her work on designing the cover. And finally, a special thank you to Sheila Kennedy and her team at The Zebra Ink for the encouragement and the skills in bringing the whole package together. The author expresses his gratitude for help in the creation of the book.

Gary Friedman

ADVANCE PRAISES

What people are saying...

"Gary Friedman's most recent book, *Stones and Glass Houses,* offers another in-depth look at the emotional turmoil that lurks unspoken and unseen in a typical modern family. The tale is a web spun from equal parts of conceit and deceit. With a vivid cast of fleshed-out characters, the reader can readily relate to the familial damage caused by routine absences, habitual reticence, lingering resentment, and hidden desires that permeate the plot. Through an intricate concoction of coincidences and unforeseen consequences, two families are flung asunder only to be joined as they both find redemption, peace, and purpose. This story reflects entwined family entanglements and interwoven friendships twists and turns throughout a succession of first-person narratives. Friedman has written a tale that is destined for the silver screen!"

~ Bruce Mitchell, MS
Adj. Prof., SUNY at Buffalo & Canisius College (ret.)

—— • ——

"Humanity—the quality or state of being human—can be demonstrated through simple acts of kindness and compassion or conversely, identified via a more complex, intertwined "situation." In his latest novel *Stones and Glass Houses*, Gary Friedman explores the voice of Humanity through an engaging story of six characters' points of view and their collective yet varied experience of the same event. With a pinch of intrigue helping to turn the pages, Friedman personifies Humanity in this clever and thought-sparking tale of the grave consequences of truth and lies. Ultimately relatable and relevant."

~ Caris Vujcec
Actor/Producer/Director,

———— • ————

"Make sure you have a cleared schedule when you start this novel; it keeps you turning the pages and surprises you at the end that you won't see coming! Written in a style similar to Liane Moriarty; a must read!"

~ Althea E. Luehrsen
CEO Leadership Buffalo, Inc.
And an avid reader!

———— • ————

"This is a poignant story, which weaves interpersonal relationships about love, family, and truth or lack thereof. This riveting novel reveals what it means to be with the needy in their worst times and to take them forward in recovery. Consider this read! The surprising ending will leave you wanting so much more. Hopefully, this talented author has a sequel in the works."

~ Dawn Mirand
Executive & Community Leadership
Former Superintendent of Schools

STONES
AND
GLASS HOUSES

Gary Friedman

CHAPTER ONE
JESSE

———•———

I lie. I lie a lot. I have been lying for thirty-two years, non-stop. It started out rather innocently at first, and my lies have mushroomed into creating a life I did not choose, but one I wear on my back like a hair shirt. Each and every day of those years, I promised myself I would unwind the world I have created, bare my soul to the people I continue to hurt, and live just one day at peace.

It's been said that telling a lie is like sticking a shovel into the ground, turning over a clump of grass and starting a small hole. Each subsequent lie digs the hole a little deeper. Each attempt to cover that lie digs it deeper still. Yet, the series of holes I have dug are too big, too winding, too entrenched to wave off with a simple *Mea Culpa*. The Grand Canyon's got nothing on me.

As the sun's rays reach down for the horizon, late on a summer's evening, I'm at the one place where my twisted soul can find a small moment of peace...walking the bike path at Delaware Park in the heart of the city of Buffalo. The path is a 1.8-mile track that circles around softball diamonds and soccer fields, surrounding a nine-hole golf course and drifting past the underappreciated Buffalo Zoo. Nothing gets your pace increased more than the drifting aroma of the bison exhibit. This verdant pasture is all a part of the Buffalo Olmsted Park System, one of the true jewels of my hometown.

As the sun drops, I am close to violating another law. The park closes at sunset and I'm pushing my limit. My plan is three laps and that will extend my walk past dark. Going to my home in Amherst tonight without this walk would be just too much to put my mind and body through. I simply want to get through the night and get some sleep without turning over one more shovel full of deceit. Each lap takes a half hour to complete and I need every step of it to ease the pain.

How did I ever get myself in this position, living every moment as if a guillotine's blade were poised and ready to drop just above the collar of my Under Armor shirt? I had good jobs, gained enough experience in manufacturing to be in a position to travel the country as a consultant, finding myself on the road as many as five nights a week. That travel has enabled me to create my cover, live my life one step ahead of the executioner. Crimes? By most standards they are minor but not so minor that being exposed wouldn't destroy my life from so many different angles. Any attorney worth his or her salt would have a field day, like vultures picking at a carcass. Do I deserve that fate? Absolutely, but none of my crimes were committed with intent. I'm not really a bad person. I told a lie, one of arrogance, not meanness; you can say that it was minor manipulation for personal gain, not wanting to cause anyone in my life any pain. But the hole was dug, then another, and another and the canyon widened.

As I pass my car for the first time, the sky has turned from dark blue to glowing red. The sun has slipped below the horizon, leaving a colorful memory of itself across the wispy clouds above. I try to take this walk as often as possible. It's one of the few consistencies in my life. Despite the quality of my work, I avoid the spotlight at all costs. My picture will never appear on the news, in the local paper or in trade journals. It is certainly in my best interest to remain anonymous. If I get involved in a golf or tennis tournament, events I could win with ease; I will drive serves into the net or nine irons into the water on purpose to avoid winning and the notoriety it would bring.

My choices require two vastly different cars as well as two distinctly different wardrobes. Two separate doctors send bills to two different addresses, addressed to two different names. Not only do I live two diverse lives, but I am two different people with two different birthdays and I always celebrate them with my family. My craving is to be just one inhabitant of this skin but not sure how to get there or know how I would ever consolidate. My whole life is documented on Google calendars, coded in seven colors, designed so that no one but me could ever decipher it. I spend little time with a spouse or children despite adoring them all. For the most part, I am a ghost in their lives, and we are ships passing in the night. They can, however, reach me at any time on one of my two separate cell phone numbers that are both forwarded to my one device. Life is a balancing act and I am the master juggler, the guy with six long sticks balancing spinning plates. There is no time off. Should just one of those plates shatter to the ground, so would the juggler.

Is it possible that yesterday was the fall of the first plate?

Age is becoming the enemy. The first thing to go is short-term memory. I have noticed minor hiccups starting to form. Forgetting keys, walking into the next room to find them, and forgetting why I walked into the room in the first place. Calling people by the wrong name saying the wrong things in the wrong company. For a man living life on a tight rope, any slip of the tongue is a slip of the noose. I can be no less than perfect at all times with absolutely no room for error. Living with that form of self-created pressure is, at times, unbearable. I wish this life on no one, least of all me.

The second lap is not much different than the first. The attendant at the snack bar had been racing through the process of closing for the night. When I approach the stand for the second time it is dark, and all evidence of customers and server has disappeared. Cars parked around the outer ring of the path have dwindled to one or two. As I glide along the parkway, it officially becomes nighttime in Buffalo. Rounding past the starters shed at the golf course, my car comes into view in the distance. It is decision time. Do I climb into my car and head home or do I break the law and try to squeeze in one more lap?

The hardest choice, do I make a decision on what I came here to contemplate?

Every single hour of every single day is spent in search of a way out of my predicament. What purpose would one more lap serve in that search? One doesn't survive a lifetime such as mine without a small bit of optimism. Maybe one more lap will provide the answer that has eluded me to this point. At the very least, it will delay a return to my life for another thirty minutes. How's that for optimism? One more lap as I pass my car on the right, parked along Ring Road, near the soccer fields. As I go by, I glance into the driver's window and see the envelope containing my admission of guilt. It awaits me like rifles at a firing squad, aimed at me for one last goodbye.

Ahead of me, a line of vehicles is inching forward, each one waiting to pull out of the zoo parking lot and then onto Parkside Avenue. One guard stands at the exit but doesn't see me stride by. The only cars still in the lot belong to employees left behind to clean up for the next day's crowds. As the zoo passes out of my view, the silence of the now-empty park surrounds me, bringing a modicum of peace to the end of a hectic day.

Having returned to Buffalo this morning, I went to Spot Coffee on Elmwood and set up my office there. Traveling as much as I do makes paying rent for an office space pointless. Hiring a secretary to keep track of me would be dangerous in the life I have chosen. I maintain just this mobile office, but despite the dangers, I was fortunate to find Emily. She has truly been a lifesaver for me. She is loyal beyond any definition of the word and seems to understand me better than anyone else on the planet. She helps coordinate my lives between appointments and emails and personal plans. She always, *always* has my back. I honestly don't think I could have survived all these years without her help. Working from her home, she is able to bring sanity to my beyond-crazy existence. She remains the only person on the planet who knows all of my secrets.

Circling the park is my only true me-time, my sanctuary. More than once I have dreamed of dying and having my remains buried here along the path with no headstone, no trace of my life, no monument to my stupidity. Just peace and tranquility, surrounded by the footsteps of those seeking answers to questions far less complicated than mine were. Whispering to each passing soul, "Don't worry. Look at me. It all works out in the end."

In an effort to get out of the park under my own control and not that of flashing police lights, I pick up the pace. I notice my increased pace in my calf muscles, but I try to ignore them so I can keep up my momentum. I have all night to rest. I push past the next exit, leaving the zoo behind for good. The path starts to follow along Amherst Street as lights start to illuminate the interiors of the beautiful homes that grace the street. I push past the Colvin Boulevard entrance then the beautiful Nichols High School campus and its athletic fields. The path swings to the left as the park intersects with Nottingham Terrace, one of Buffalo's elite neighborhoods. My mind leaves its never-ending troubles behind as I try to carve five minutes or more off my average lap time, partially for the health benefits and partially to avoid the Buffalo Police Department. Only one car is visible along the pathway as I near the snack bar for the third and last time.

One foot in front of the other, walking shoes slapping at the pavement, half a lap from the end. It feels as if I am running away from a life that has become more than I can bear. I am haunted by a feeling of dread, like my world as I have constructed it, is about to disintegrate at my feet. My walk doesn't wear me out anywhere near as much as the executioner's song that plays over and over in my head. It's not my own demise that saps my energy, it's the thought of the pain that will crush the people that have trusted me all these years, moored their lives to mine, ones who saw me as a man of integrity, someone they could trust and count on no matter what happened. I can see their smiles ahead of me as I walk. Will I ever see those smiles again?

As I circle the park for my last lap, the snack bar is dark and deserted. The signs and menus have been pulled inside. I move along the tall clump of bushes just past the snack bar. Two strides later, I can feel a stinging sensation in the back of my neck, like a wasp or a yellowjacket taking out their vengeance on me. Did I step on a fallen nest, disrupting their twilight meanderings? I try to lift my right arm to fend off my attacker, but it won't respond. My left arm falters as well. Both have dropped to my side. My momentum keeps me moving forward but my legs no longer hold up their end of the bargain, causing me to fall forward to the bike path, face first. My body flips over once, leaving me flat on my back and looking straight up into the tree's upper branches. No matter how hard I try, my limbs won't respond. I am totally paralyzed. Only my eyes seem to move. I am feeling no pain and couldn't scream out if I did. The dark limbs of the trees sway slightly. Bats are darting back and forth above the branches, catching their share of winged breakfast food. I can hear footsteps running but can't tell if they are coming towards me or running away.

Air. The frustration of it being so available...yet my lungs seem incapable of drawing it in. This is not the death I had imagined; my life ending by a small bug instead of at the hands of the ones I have deceived for so long. I hear the sounds of the night...the birds singing their twilight song, the distant traffic...the light dims as each breath becomes more and more labored. I feel a slight sensation of blood trickling down my face. My thoughts slow. A pair of eyes look down at me, but I can't form the words I intend, "Don't worry! Look at me! It all works out in the end!"

Gary Friedman

CHAPTER TWO
HUMANITY

———•——

I am not Me. I am more Us. Defined as a collection of Us, a collection that began as a population of one and has grown to colonize the world. I represent the best of Us. I represent the worst of Us. I am the source of the greatest discoveries this planet has ever known yet I continue to disappoint. My artwork ranges from the most majestic masterpieces the world could imagine...to graffiti on the side of a railroad car. My music stretches from the greatest symphonies ever created to street musicians beating on empty pails. All well-meaning and all for their audiences to appreciate.

I am no longer a physical being, more so a conscience, a soul, an observer of what I represent. I am beyond vision, sound, and touch, yet I have experienced every sensation, every emotion relished by those I observe....and I observe all, sometimes with great pride, sometimes with great sorrow. I am not a god, a deity in any form. I am more a history of what has been; a measuring stick against which change is arbitrated.

I am Humanity.

I do not judge, get involved or interact. I am known by all, but my legacy seems to carry little weight. The eyes of humans appear to have turned inward, focused on themselves, while empathy has dwindled to the status of lost art. During my existence, some individuals, some movements, have come along that changed the view of me, altered my reputation. Those aberrations tend to balance out over time. Despots come and go; reason settles the score. History has less effect on my members than does its own misguided actions, fueled by a shallow heart or confused brain. The examples are endless.

Rather than provide a timeline or a roster of lost souls, I would prefer, instead, to share with you one story. A story of a small collection of my compatriots who have lost their way. It has been said that members of my kind can barely get through a day without a juicy reorganization. The subjects of this story may have set a new rational standard by creating their own paths, rejecting all measurements of reason, believing in their compromised head and heart that they can break every single rule of logic and still escape consequences. If I have discovered any truth, the truest may be that all behavior, no matter its importance or triviality, is accompanied by equivalent consequences. There is virtually no escape from that truth. The only variance is the length of time between behavior and its ultimate result. Sooner or later, time catches up.

A word of caution. Despite the fact that I willingly share this story with you, absorb it as you might as the member of an audience. Be respectful. Smile if so motivated, laugh if moved, cry when touched. All I ask is that you be respectful. Do not look down upon these lost souls and judge them from On High. Do not scowl and wag a finger in their direction. Save your wagging for the mirror of life before you, for all of humanity has a reflection. Remember that most have fingers to wag and reasons to be wagged at by others. Stones and glass houses, such as it is.

This is the story of one man, but it touches upon the lives of many. Two families in particular, linked by the choices of one man and known only to him and one innocent observer, one so distraught by what he saw that he felt a need to intervene. He viewed himself as a hero, one determined to save all of the people involved. His belief is proven folly. My history is laced with such heroes, those who violate the laws of Humanity in pursuit of some noble cause. My history is also fraught with examples of those who further the cause of revolution, of assassins, traitors, and gossips. They act in such ways as to save an injured party but in truth, they are more interested in their fifteen minutes of fame, a few moments on center stage. The reality is that they do far more harm than good when they attempt to fix one problem because it can leave twenty more egregious upheavals in the wake. From my lofty view, such is the path of self-appointed heroes.

I am offering you a story and will share it with you through the voices of the participants. Since they will tell their story via their own myopic view, I may drop in from time to time to give you the vision of Humanity. What my involvement offers is a moment of clarity to see through the clouds of rationalization. Don't think for a moment that this is a unique story. Tales such as this happen all over the world on a daily basis. My goal is to educate and possibly supply a point of reference for your own decision-making. You may also find some relief in knowing that you are not the only one to choose a path that leads to obstacles you can't overcome. Maybe this story will allow you to laugh at your personal misfortunes, knowing that as bad as things may get, it could always be worse. So, consider my offering, created with a goal to educate, to console and possibly to entertain. To entertain you ask? Why, of course! Such entertainment lifts us up and momentarily takes us away from the daily doldrums.

I am not me. I am Us. I do not judge. I am simply a standard by which the world compares its current state of affairs.

I am Humanity.

Gary Friedman

CHAPTER THREE

ADAM

— • —

A perfect sunset: the kind of moment you would want to share with the woman of your dreams, snuggled tightly in your arms as you look to the west and simply sigh together in contentment. No words spoken; none are needed. Just two people deeply in love and committed to a future together creating moments, sharing the memory of, "Hey, remember that sunset we shared on that perfect evening?" The scent of her perfume fills my senses, her head on my shoulder while her hair flutters against my face. The total breadth of the horizon fills my windshield.

Windshield? Where did that come from? Call it a reality check, I suppose. The sunset is real, but the moment isn't. There is no girl of my dreams. In fact, every one of those potential dreams have turned into nightmares. No hair brushing my face, no memories worth holding onto. Just the view from the passenger seat of this WNY Response Service ambulance. No perfume filling my senses, just the ever-present antiseptic cloud that floats through the air along with the after-effect of our last call; the soiled remains of a human being in crisis, hanging onto her life with every ounce of her being. I have been riding in this rig for twelve long hours and there is another twelve to go. The life and existence of a paramedic, where time becomes irrelevant and the only one to "snuggle" with is Devon, my EMT partner and the full-time driver of this rig. He and I have been together for eighteen months now, not because I want him as a partner but because no one else will take him off my hands. He is a nice enough guy and all, but as incompetent as the day is long and an encyclopedia of every conspiracy theory known to man. Just when I think I have heard them all, he pulls three more out of his hat from websites that surely have no more than three or four followers. We sit along the road entering the Albright-Knox Art Gallery awaiting our next call while Devon, with his long, not-so-clean hair covering his face, stares down at his phone while espousing his latest theory. He makes no eye contact, never turns his head to look at me. I don't think he notices or cares that I am studiously ignoring him.

It has already been a long shift. There have been five calls: three major ones and two false alarms. The day started out with a four-year-old child who probably broke her arm after taking a bad spill off her bicycle. That was followed by a two-car accident caused by a man going into cardiac arrest and drifting head-on into traffic. My professional best guess is that the other guy will be fine, but the cardiac case will be hanging by a very thin thread. Then after two non-emergency calls, we ended up on Elmwood Avenue in the heart of Buffalo, gathering a homeless woman for what may be her final ride anywhere. I will never get used to those calls. Forget the decaying condition of her body or the offensive-doesn't-cover-it condition of her clothes with the absence of any personal hygiene. For me it's...the sense of a lost soul, the "there but for the grace of God" aspect of it all. What choices has a person made in his or her life to end up in such a state? Is it simply giving up once, or is it a series of surrenders? Exactly how many bad choices are any of us away from inhabiting that corner on Elmwood? Even after trying to rid the aftermath of that call from inside the ambulance, the physical aura and the emotional confusion stay behind. No other kind of call upsets me more. Devon not so much. Despite the aroma of death hanging in the air, he is chowing down on the peanut butter and jelly sandwich he made fourteen hours earlier while explaining between chews why Abraham Lincoln never really existed.

I continue to ignore him as best as I can while I ponder, and not for the first time this week, how I ended up here. By here, I don't mean this empty roadside or in this seat in this rig. More, how did my road, my path in life bring me here? Is it the result of the good or bad choices I have made along the way or is it simply my destiny to be Devon's main man?

I'm certainly not past my prime, being only twenty-five. No choices I have made in my life, to this point, have to be permanent and none of those choices were even close to being immoral or illegal. I could use the age-old excuse that I am the product of my environment, coming from a family where material goods were everything and time spent together almost non-existent. A family where my father travels the world and is never home and my mother is so wrapped up in her social world that neither her husband nor I am a priority. Maybe it was that lack of affection or closeness from my family that has left me more comfortable being alone than in the confines of a relationship, I have yet to find a woman who motivated me to change. I plunge all my free time into work and school. Don't get me wrong, I am probably as much of a romantic as the next guy, maybe even more so, but I didn't grow up with parents who modeled a close loving relationship, so I have had a hard time making love a priority. Most of the women I dated caught on early. I simply was never long-term-relationship material. Maybe I was avoiding it, or maybe I was afraid of it. Either way, the girl of my dreams has remained in dreamland.

Despite all that, I love my parents, but it's almost as if I raised myself, taught myself my own lessons. If it's true that only children are spoiled rotten, then I am the exception to the rule. I

17

would call myself intelligent but seriously unmotivated. I never saw a class that didn't scream "skip me" from the highest rafters of the student center. My original goal was to be a doctor, but I was never that committed to the classroom. I entered the University of Buffalo with my eye on medical school but didn't have the discipline in my studies to make it work. I always wanted to help others but had a tough time helping myself.

After floundering around from menial job to menial job, I began a process that to date has been foreign to me. I started to grow up. Not necessarily enough to commit to ten years of med school but at least one year at Erie Community College to get certified as a paramedic.

I did a ride-along once with WNY Response and loved it. And they loved me, it turns out, and I did much of my early training with the company. They assured me that when I completed my course work at ECC, I would have a place with them. I found myself blossoming in their confidence in me and worked hard to be sure they knew their confidence was a good investment. As a result, I moved up quickly. I enjoyed being part of a team and finally found myself making new friends with relative ease. I enjoyed the comradery, the shared experiences, shoulders to lean on when the scenes became too gruesome to face. For some, the horror of the job turns out to be more than they can handle, and their debriefing turns out to be an exit interview. For me, that has not been an issue.

The twenty-four-hour shifts are the worst for me with no time to myself, meals grabbed on the run, and of course the endless blabbering from Devon. When the calls come too close together, I can't help but become callous to the idea that these are human beings with families who depend on my professionalism and to a large part, my empathy. Some days my bedside manner stays in bed. If I was motivated by money, I chose the wrong career where the shortness of mealtime is only exceeded by the shortness of pay. My family is pretty comfortable financially, so money isn't the great motivator. I don't call them for money often but it's good to know that I have my own personal bank if the need arises. For me, my motivation is in helping others, feeling like that adds significance to my life. My bills manage to take care of themselves.

I developed a decent reputation for thoroughness. As a paramedic, we are required to make snap judgments and decisions based on the symptoms in front of us. I take the time to circle back to the emergency room staff to find out how the people I helped had fared. It is important for me to know if my on-the-spot diagnoses are accurate or even close. I would even go to the point of asking to observe autopsies to see where I might have made a mistake. I don't have the training to be a hundred percent right all the time in a profession where I can't afford to be wrong very often. Just as it is for the highly trained doctors, people's lives depend on my every action. I take that seriously.

The sun has passed through its rendezvous with the horizon, leaving behind a cotton candy blend of pink and orange sky. This is one of my favorite parking hang outs. It's close to the city without being in the middle of it while still leaving easy access to the northern suburbs of Buffalo. Romance is in the air as couples, young and old, walk hand-in-hand around Hoyt Lake. A lilting tune drifts into the window as a couple of troubadours serenade the passers-by from the steps of the art gallery. A typical summer's evening in my hometown. Not a tough way to spend work hours.

I let my head drop back against the cushion. It's not with the intent of taking a nap. I'm not saying I have never fallen asleep during work hours, but it was never with intent. You use every trick in the book to fight it off but sometimes the body just takes over against your will. You can feel your head start to bob but can do nothing about it. Maybe it's the acoustic music or the gentle breeze wafting in though the same window. Maybe it's the peace of the sunset, the ever-darkening sky as night falls. My eyes become heavy as they give in to the moment. The light and music fade. Even Devon's pontifications become white noise aiding my drift from reality. Visons begin to dance against my closed eyelids, angels with harps, flying in formation across the fading sunset. They are joined by bathing beauties busily coating their bodies with sunblock. Hey, it's my dream, right? Suddenly, the bikini-clad ladies stop with the sunscreen application, turn to me, and start to yell, loudly, persistently, tapping me on the shoulder.

"Adam, wake up. There's a call coming in!" It is Devon doing the touching.

"ALL UNITS, ALL UNITS—MAN DOWN ON JOGGING PATH IN DELAWARE PARK AT NOTTINGHAM ENTRANCE NEAR SNACK BAR."

"UNIT FIVE RESPONDING. ONE MINUTE OUT," Devon replies.

Reality snaps back into place as if my chest had been hit with our own defibrillator. I'm not one to panic during emergency calls. My reputation among other paramedics is that I'm unusually calm when the stuff is hitting the fan. This call is no different. Suddenly awake and alert, I bark out commands to Devon, not willing to leave the route up to him, based on previous experiences. "A right on Elmwood and a right on Nottingham is the shortest route. The only hard part will be getting across Delaware in one piece."

The gorgeous and monstrously expensive homes on Nottingham Terrace fly by like pickets on a fence. Stop signs are ignored for the most part, followed by inching cautiously across the five lanes of Delaware Avenue. The park is in full view on the right, guarded by the naked statue of David. The snack bar comes into view in the distance. Our siren brings noses pressed against the windows of the homes we speed past, our flashing lights reflecting off buildings and trees and our sirens drown out the voices on their collective cell phones. A matching set of lights comes into view from the Buffalo Police cruiser, already on the scene. A Buffalo fire department unit arrives ahead of us.

Despite the darkening sky, the scene is illuminated by the collection of law enforcement head lights and spotlights. One police officer is in the street keeping cars away from the park entrance and is waving a flashlight in our direction. Employees leaving the zoo for the day have gathered along with local residents, almost all of whom have various-sized dogs on various-length leashes. This is obviously the local neighborhood's main event. We turn into the short drive with our headlights shining on the deserted snack bar. The jogger is on the ground to the right of the snack bar's benches. Another police officer is giving the jogger CPR with ferocity. Knowing that the victim is getting some attention tells me I can focus on gathering the necessary equipment. For me, this is where time usually starts to click into slow-motion. I start to jump out of our rig before it comes to a full stop. I spin quickly toward the side of the ambulance and start jerking open doors to the storage compartments. I pull my medical kit out of one and the defibrillator out of another. Meanwhile, Devon circles around the back of the ambulance and pulls out a stretcher and wheels it along the blacktop walkway.

As I walk quickly along the sidewalk, I recognize the officer directing traffic as a friend that I have come to know and appreciate while on the job. We have even gone out for drinks when our shifts end. We also went golfing together a couple of times. Now he follows me up the sidewalk and fills me in on what they found. "Hey Adam. This guy was discovered by a zoo employee who was driving home. His 911 call found us on the other side of the park near the golf course. It wasn't thirty seconds after the call that we arrived. When we got here, he was barely breathing, and his lips were turning blue. His eyes were open, but they were staring straight ahead; I mean straight up. We have been here about two minutes and my partner has been doing CPR since we arrived. At first glance, we didn't see any injuries that would have caused his condition. You need anything else from us?"

"Not much, Gerry. Just keep the park entrance clear so nothing delays our exit and maybe keep the onlookers back," I reply.

"We just got called out to the other side of the park," the officer continued. "There is a detective on site, and we will be back as soon as possible."

"Not a problem," is the best I can muster under the circumstances. Police policy is his business. This injury is mine.

I approach the jogger and set my bag down next to him. He seems to be in good physical shape, wearing summer running gear. The officer has the runner's nose pinched and is in essence breathing for both of them. Onlookers surround us, some holding hands, some in prayer, all hoping for some sudden movement, waiting for the jogger to sit up and continue his run. Devon rattles up next to me with the stretcher, the breathing apparatus strapped to the top of the cushion.

"I got this," I tell the officer on the ground. What was slow-motion before now becomes even slower, living the moment almost frame by frame. The officer pulls up and pushes away from the victim, dropping to his own backside, dizzy from the experience of breathing for two for so long. His movement gives me my first full view of the jogger. It takes a moment to realize who is before me. Frame by frame grinds to a full stop as in that moment; the world stands still. I try to speak but only one word comes out.

"DAD!"

CHAPTER FOUR
ANNIE

———— • ————

Bright white lights are so unfair. Why did we ever replace those warm yellow lights with these? The white lights show off every line, every shadow so sharply. Every change that age has worked across my features show up so violently. Every line and wrinkle come to life, every sag is pronounced, every blemish is more defined. I really don't need to be reminded that I'm closer to the end than the beginning. With my thirty-fifth high school reunion coming up soon, I'm well aware that lines and wrinkles are to be expected. I just don't need daily reminders. I've got to put "buy softer light bulbs" on my to-do list.

I have to admit that the rest of the view in the mirror doesn't give away my age. I have worked hard for that. The few gray hairs that do appear don't last long; they are either colored or plucked. I'm very careful about what I eat. I run five miles every day and go to the gym three or four days a week. I play tennis twice a week, and I'm on my way there as soon as I can get ready. On nights when I am alone, which is darn near all of them, I replace any exercise a husband might provide with riding my Peloton before bed. Like I said, I work hard.

I'm pleased with the results. Not even the color of the light bulbs can deny what my hard work has done for me. The naked view in the full-length mirror shows no ill-effect of the birth of my son twenty-five years ago. My tummy is still flat, my hips the same width as when I got married. My breasts have always been small, so no noticeable sag has affected them. My arms have not developed that mid-fifties fleshiness I see on women my age at the gym. No stretch marks, no scars, just a few drops of water scattered on my skin from my just-ended shower. No one looking at this image would ever guess my age. The only place the years gather is upon my face. Another reason to change the light bulbs.

Anyone looking from the outside would consider me blessed. Afterall, I have a beautiful, lavish home, a loving son, a husband who works hard to maintain the material aspects of our lifestyle, two luxury cars, a full walk-in closet, the ability to travel at will, and friends to travel with. Certainly, more than my share of blessings. All that is from the outside view. From the inside...not so much.

We have worked hard to earn this place in life and that has come with some costs. Professionally, it has been a long road. I started out in my own little cubicle at Libracon Health Care Systems. From there I worked hard and moved to service manager overseeing others' cubicles. Then I jumped to the third floor and the corporate offices, and finally landed on the fourth floor in my own corner office as CEO of Libracon. The good news has been that I didn't have to compromise my values to move to the top. It just took hard work and the respect of my co-workers. You must know I'm proud of my accomplishments, but there have been a number of sacrifices along the way. Many of my closest friendships didn't survive my climb to the top. My free time became scarce and there were petty jealousies, which were created by my climb to the highest rung of the ladder. The work friendships that remain are tethered to the influence I have over their careers. I'm not unaware of that dynamic and it leaves me distrustful and wary of many I call "friend." My family, both original and in-law, are scattered around the world and are no longer central to the choices my husband and I make as a couple.

And that brings me to the couple thing. That is the saddest part of my life, such as it is. Between my travel schedule and his, we are lucky to share the same bed once or twice every other week. Even special events and holidays are hit or miss. Nothing seems to alter the amount of time we spend together. When our calendars do mesh, however, we are still like a young couple very much in love. Maybe it's the absence of "quantity time" that forces us to treasure the "quality time," and the nights we spend together contain the same passion we shared when we first started dating. We both work hard to please the other, but at times it feels as if we are just checking off one more of our obligations, making sure we accomplish all of our goals. Sometimes sex feels rehearsed or staged, where the depth of emotions dwindles quickly. Then there are the times where we lie together after our obligations are met, and he seems to be a thousand miles away, a place I'm not welcomed and don't belong. I can almost feel his body drift away to parts unknown. Despite the vast amount of time we spend apart, I never feel more alone than when he drifts off to his own Neverland.

Yes, I love him, and I have no doubt he loves me. It's just that we no longer seem to be priorities in each other's lives. As much as we make the best of the time we do spend together, it almost feels that if we should never cross each other's paths again, we would both be fine, even to the point that it would take months for either of us to even notice.

That's not to say either of us would ever consider divorce. I don't even believe in the concept. It's not a religious thing, which is something that is not a part of our lives. It's just that I'm a firm believer that once that word enters into your vocabulary, it takes on a life of its own, and I refuse to give it life. I do dream of the days when we will inevitably slow down and in doing so, consider retirement. And then we can re-evaluate our relationship, maybe travel together instead of on our own and live what most would call a normal life. That, however, is years away, if not decades. I just hope there is enough left of us to be able to survive just being a couple and not individual hard drivers in our own corporate worlds.

The things that we used to enjoy doing together I have learned to do alone. Where we once competed in a couple's tennis league; I now do as a single player. One doesn't rise within the corporate world without being competitive and one doesn't leave that competitiveness in the office. It follows me onto the tennis court. Like in all things, I hate to lose. I tend to dominate this league and have climbed into the rank of the top ten women players in my age bracket in Western New York. When each match counts in those rankings, it tends to take most of the fun out of it, where winning is again, just one more chore checked off my list.

How long have I been staring at this mirror? I hate when my mind drifts off like this. It tends to be such a waste of time since all the daydreams in the world rarely, if ever, change reality. The beads of moisture that were left on my skin after my shower have evaporated thanks to the air conditioning. I turn off the lights above the mirror, leaving only the fan light to illuminate the room. It's funny. The observations that I made only a few moments ago, and my reflection staring back at me, seem to have missed one important feature. It's the sadness in the eyes that look back at me. How could I have missed that? How long have my eyes been just a bit less shiny? The corners droop just ever slightly more. How could a woman with all my "blessings" show the slightest signs of sadness? Am I ungrateful for all I have?

I have always been proud of my home, all I have accomplished, my son and my husband. I step back from the mirror and inhale deeply, shoulders back. I exhale and shake my head quickly to rid myself of the negative energy. What in the world have I got to be sad about? I am successful and I'm grounded. Honestly, I can't imagine anything that could undermine that. Stop all this! I need to get to the courts before I end up defaulting my match. That won't help the rankings.

I walk from the hard granite of the bathroom floor to the plush grey carpet of our oversized bedroom. The peaked ceiling contains two skylights and two ceiling fans, hard at work. Sliding glass doors lead to a small private balcony on the back of the house and massive floor to ceiling windows dominate the wall to the front of the house. The setting sun leaves some patches of light behind as stars start to decorate the darkening sky. The draperies are open on both windows. The price of modesty doesn't compare to the beautiful view both windows offer. If anyone makes the effort to look in so be it. I haven't worked so hard to keep my figure just to scurry around to conceal it. I guess you could say I'm extremely comfortable in my own skin and don't care who knows it.

My bedroom drawers are just as compartmentalized as the rest of my life. I pull out my tennis drawer and select my outfit for the match. Thank goodness the boring white skirt and top days are long gone. The tennis courts have become the same fashion show as the rest of my world. I pull out a printed multicolor Under Armor top with matching skort. My socks, shoes and wrist bands are with my racquets in the back seat of my car, so I slip on some flip flops to get me to the courts at the tennis center. I grab a gym bag and toss in a fresh towel and some toiletries, slide in my purse, sling it all over my shoulder and head down the spiral staircase. On my way out the door, I stop in the kitchen where I grab two bottles of water, one for now and one for after the match.

Setting my bag on the kitchen island, I walk into my office, the heartbeat of my home life. I switch on my laptop and jump to my tennis schedule to glance at tonight's competition. To be honest, there isn't much to worry about. This will be the third time I have played her and it was 6-0, 6-0 both times. I don't even think she will qualify for our division next session. I look to the bottom of the screen and see I have an hour to go before the scheduled match. That leaves me a small window in my crazy night to check my email. My work email contains little that I would consider critical. A couple of resumes to check out for new hires and lists to review for possible promotions. Tickets for my travel next week are there as is my itinerary covering conference topics. It will be another busy week.

With time still left, I jump over to my personal email to skim through the inbox. Again, nothing earth-shattering. Junk mail, bank statements, two birthday reminders, three shipping confirmations of stuff I have ordered online and one personal note from my husband reminding me he will be home in forty-eight hours and that we have a dinner to attend this weekend.

I stare at the message for more than a few moments. No "hi," no "how are you," no "I miss and love you." In fact, no greeting at all. Just words you would send to a secretary or business associate. Another itinerary. I will be home Friday night, jump your bones, have you on my arm Saturday night and fly out the door again midday Sunday. How did we get here? When did all the air escape from our collective sails? This, right here, this is where the sadness in my eyes comes from. Is this how it feels to settle? Wanting so much more? It didn't get like this overnight...and it would take just as long to get back to where it was. Neither one of us would ever walk away, but neither of us has shown an inkling to reclimb the mountaintop our relationship once glowed from. There was so much love, so much passion.

Maybe this weekend we can find some time to talk, explore where we are and see if we are still on the same page. There are still fleeting moments like this one where I miss him so much, but like everything else in my life, those moments have become assigned slots on my busy schedule. When those moments are over, I move on to the next item on my list. Somehow, I survive in this life without letting pesky emotions like love get in the way.

Once again, I glance at the clock and to my surprise, thirty minutes have disappeared. Now I have to rush just a bit to make it to my match. I close my laptop and jump out of my office chair, grabbing my bag as I jog through the kitchen. I reach the back door that leads to the garage and hit the button that will send the double garage door riding up its rails. Just as I am about to pull the door closed, I hear a song playing from my cell phone, a very distinctive ring. I drop the bag off my shoulder and dig through its contents to find my phone, but it's not there. I look up toward the kitchen and can see it skittering on the counter. It must have fallen out as I tossed the overflowing bag over my shoulder. I dropped the bag in front of the door to keep it from closing and race back to the kitchen. I pick up the phone and see a familiar face smiling back at me.

"Hi Baby!"

"Hi Mom. Look..." he starts to reply.

"Honey, I'm off to a tennis match and I'm running late. Can I call you back later?"

"No, Mom, you can't!"

"Adam, what's wrong?" I reply as I feel my heartbeat increase.

"Mom, it's Dad."

"Adam, Dad is in California and won't be back until Friday," is my response, somewhat less confidently than I would have stated two minutes ago.

"No, Mom, he isn't. He is in the back of my ambulance and I'm heading for ECMC in full lights and sirens. I should be there in two minutes. There is a double door next to the emergency entrance. I will wait for you there."

I can feel the blood rush from my head as what must be shock settles in. The calm and normal world of only seconds ago seems to have gone up in smoke. It can't be him. I just got his email. What is going on?

"Adam, is he going to be OK?" I ask.

"I don't know, Mom. Just get here. And Mom…"

"Yes, son?"

"You better hurry."

CHAPTER FIVE
DYLAN

———◆———

Toothpicks. Maybe that will help. Anything to keep my eyes from closing involuntarily. I have been awake now and mostly on my feet for forty-four hours. How does any of this even remotely make me a better doctor? One would think that in my second year of residency, I would have proven myself to a point where these two-day shifts wouldn't be necessary.

I have pretty much decided that trauma is where I want to start my medical career, and I know that means being on call for some long periods of time, but I'm looking forward to having more control over those periods than I do right now. I firmly believe this marathon-man-mentality does not develop better doctors, but I guess it serves the hospital to fill the weekend hours that staff doctors have no interest in filling. I vow, at this moment, exhausted head in hands, not to do this to my residents. I will take some of these off-shifts so they can get more rest and, in the process, be better doctors. Of course, this will earn me the scorn of my fellow trauma doctors who will think they have paid the price of residency and have earned more sleep. My view, of course, is that I'll be giving back to my profession and creating better doctors. We shall see how things work out.

Maybe a shower will help, followed by a fresh set of scrubs. The first twelve cups of coffee didn't help so I doubt a thirteenth will do the trick. I just have to make it another three and a half hours. When the clock strikes 12:00, I can race for the parking lot with the few drops of energy still crawling through my body. I can do it. I have no choice.

To think this was my goal in life. Becoming a doctor was all I ever wanted to do since I achieved undefeated status on the board game of Operation. I got so good at it that none of my friends, few as there were, would play with me anymore. It didn't stop me from playing in solitaire mode. I moved up from there to Squishy Body and anatomy models. By the age of twelve, I knew every bone, muscle and organ and their functions. One might say I was ready to open my own practice at age fourteen. Needless to say, my obsession did not make me the most popular kid on the block. Even in a world of ultimate geeks, I was in a class all onto myself. Even the geeks thought I was too geeky.

Such was my life growing up. No real friends, a father who was never around, a mother who crawled out of bed in the morning and directly into a bottle. Not even a dog to chew up my homework. My schoolwork was my everything. It's where I excelled. It's where I gained what little self-esteem I could muster. I either got an "A" or I argued why I should have gotten one. I didn't go to social events, football games or any other athletic competition. I never had a serious girlfriend, although I got close a couple of times. It didn't really change after I went to college. Higher education was simply the next steppingstone to my predestined life course. I took my studies very seriously. If an assignment was due on Friday, I turned it in on the preceding Wednesday. If the professor said write five pages, my last sentence ended at the last line of the fifth page. I read every word of every chapter assigned and usually did so twice, writing out questions for anything I didn't understand or disagreed with. I was the academic boy scout; "Always Prepared."

I was raised in a small suburb of Buffalo and when it came time to go off to college, the University of Buffalo was my only choice. Being number one in my class and scoring a perfect 1600 twice on my SATs, (yes, I took it again after scoring 1600 just to prove to myself it wasn't a fluke) I had enough award money and grants that I could move out of my house and travel the five miles to campus and move into the resident halls for free. I went through my share of roommates since I openly objected to partying in my room or to any activity that would get in the way of my studies. I tended to speak my mind and was not the most tolerant of other people's opinions. I ended up with a single room, not because I demanded one but more because no one wanted to put up with my attitude. In high school, no one wanted to sign my yearbook, and I have no doubt that if I had invested in one in college, the number of signatures would not have increased.

I was dedicated to my plan. Four years of college meant four years of college. I could have graduated early but chose not to. Instead of graduating with the customary one-hundred-twenty credit hours, I managed to squeeze in one-hundred-sixty-three hours. I didn't choose between electives; I simply took them all. When it came time for the School of Medicine, I didn't change campuses, only buildings. I saw no point in going anywhere else. Call me a creature of habit. Even though I went from undergraduate to post graduate, my general perspective on education didn't change. Classes still came first. What did change was the power and influence my classmates had over me. We were all top students and high achievers and for the most part, dedicated to our studies. What was different was that this class had a small collection of guys dedicated to dragging me into the world kicking and screaming. They invited me out and didn't take no for an answer, even to the point of carrying me out to the bars. They explained that it was academic; assured me I couldn't possibly save mankind without at least a minimal understanding of what mankind looked like and how they behaved, even at their worst. It took most of half of the first semester to convince me to at least see socializing as an experiment and the rest of that semester for me to start enjoying it.

Grudgingly, I changed. I slipped quietly into the human race. I didn't do a one-eighty, becoming the life of the party, or a screaming maniac. What I did do was make some friends and begin to develop a personality, generating a life outside of the classroom. It was the only phase of becoming me that I didn't anticipate. There was no remorse that I didn't find my humanity sooner, I just saw it as another part of the education I needed to acquire over time.

As for my emergence as a doctor, I couldn't have timed it better. The city of Buffalo had developed a medical campus second to none. It gave me a great opportunity to explore every aspect of a potential career in medicine. Despite all the opportunities, nothing got my blood flowing quite like trauma. Life in the emergency room was dynamic and immediate. It was me battling against Death. Not the long war of oncology, but the battle at the wall of the castle, the defiant attack, the now-or-never action, the win or lose of it all. I saw my patients on the worst day of their life and consoled families with no preparation for the news that I was delivering.

I know it makes no sense. What is this confirmed geek with a limited social life doing? My limited experience with the human race outside of a hospital might have made it seem that there was no way I would be able to provide comfort to a scared or grieving family, but over time, I eventually got it; something not all doctors can say. Some doctors blithely travel through their career incapable of seeing through the eyes of their patients or families, never escaping the cold confines of the classroom. To my good fortune, I climbed out of that hole...all as a result of a few acquaintances not giving up on me and dragging me into the world. Their attention served to make me a better doctor, a better friend, and an overall better human being. It didn't extend to making me a great son, probably because that ship had sailed and most likely sunk, but it did start the process of turning me into the man I am today.

I have learned a lot about myself during my months in the emergency room. I have come a long way from being the guy who excelled at Operation. I have become good at my job, a man that other newer students and residents turn to for advice or a shoulder to cry on when the war has been lost and the sight of the carnage left behind is too much. When it comes to breaking devastating news to families in the waiting room, it always seems to fall on my shoulders.

So here I sit, exhausted head still in hands, counting down the seconds until I can breathe in fresh air, leaving behind the unforgettable stench of death. ECMC is the number one trauma unit in all of Western New York. We are the location of choice for every emergency response team in the area. We are on a first-name basis with the members of almost every one of those teams. Our waiting room is rarely empty, and the line never ends. Our ER draws everyone from concerned parents of newborns to the bloodbath of the gang activities. And because of that, triage is the greatest challenge. Who is most critical? Who goes directly to an examination room without waiting?

The doctor's lounge is quiet and empty except for me. The only light in the room comes from what passes through the opaque glass of the door that separates the lounge from the insanity of the trauma center. Since it is an early evening in the middle of the week, the crowd has not yet formed, and the relative quiet affords one of the two trauma doctors on duty a chance to catch up on some rest. Even though it was my moment to do so, I'm never able to totally relax while here. Maybe it's the anticipated knock on the door, the sudden vibration of the pager on my belt or the muffled distant sound of an incoming siren, my body always seems poised to jump into the fray.

I spin on the couch and swing my shoeless feet up on the cushions. My head hits a pillow that I am convinced is designed to discourage rest and relaxation. I close my eyes and hope for a few seconds of sleep. It's not to be. Instead, my mind wanders again to home, wondering what stage of sobriety my mother achieved today; what far-flung country my father's plane landed in before taking off for some other important location, way more important than wife or son. His visits home seem few and far between, and it seems all so unfair to my mother. To her benefit, when he shows up, she does everything she can to make the visit worthwhile. She saves all her smiles for him, dresses up for him, never complains or nags, just makes him feel like the king of his occasional castle. To his credit, not that he deserves much, he returns her attention full force. When I was younger, I would feel deserted in his absence but even more so upon his return. When my father was home, I ceased to exist for both of them. It was almost like a whirlwind love affair that lasted the full forty-eight hours of his visit. There was virtually no room at the inn for me. Their passion for each other was constant and far from quiet, leaving me to feel like a perverted intruder in my own home. Awkward doesn't begin to cover it.

When Dad packed up his bright red suitcase on Sunday afternoons and flew out the door it seemed like Mom's personality left with him. She would immediately slide back into the garden of her depression that she kept well-watered by tears and vodka. It would break my heart to watch her backslide and was the biggest reason why I hated his recycling home. I didn't hate the man, I just hated the condition he left my mother in and the little he seemed to care about what this life was doing to her or to me, for that matter.

Why do I do this to myself? Why do I let my poor excuse for a family take over what little peace I have? Maybe this is why I try to fill every waking hour with my career. Maybe medicine has become my hide-away from reality. The old saying goes: *fear not death, fear instead an unlived life.* So, do I live as a doctor or hide from life as one? That may be the greatest medical discovery of my career, assuming someday I actually find the answer.

Until then, here I lie staring at the textured ceiling, a style you don't see much anymore. The light forcing its way through the glass and highlighting the ceiling makes it look more like the moon surface. Bodies moving past the door constantly alter the amount of brightness reflected on the ceiling, making it appear as if it were an animation dancing just for me. Come on sleep, put me out of my misery.

A distant siren sings through the night, automatically putting me on alert. The result is two wide-open eyes and one more glance at the stained face of my wristwatch. I'm not the only doctor here. Maybe my partner cleared his cases and will be available to take the next one that rolls in, leaving me a few more moments of peace. The damage, however, is already done. Any hope I had of sleep is dashed by the thought of incoming.

The siren continues to get closer. No question it is coming here. Lights of an emergency vehicle start to flicker through the closed blinds. Jumping off the couch, I gingerly step across the darkened room, sliding my fingers through the slats of vinyl blinds and peering out. It's a WNY Response Team rig. One of their better paramedics, Adam, jumps out of the passenger side door and circles around the back of his vehicle. He is met there by his very strange partner. If memory serves me, I think his name is Devon. He rarely speaks, letting Adam take charge of every arrival. They rip open the back doors and pull out the stretcher, which appears to contain an adult male. I can tell by their body language that this one is critical, that they need to get the cart inside quickly. I go back to my couch and sit down, assuming that if they need me, I will know in seconds. No sooner does my body hit the cushion than the door flies open, and my pager lights up.

"Dr. Dylan, we need you!"

"Kathy, how many times do I have to tell you, it's Doctor or Dylan but never Dr. Dylan. It makes me feel like the sheriff on Gunsmoke." That is the best response I can muster as I pull on my boat shoes.

"Sorry, Doctor. Doctor Riley is tied up and you're on deck. Better hurry! Exam room two."

The adrenaline supplies the energy that gets me back on my feet to follow Kathy back out the door. I can see Adam and Devon emerge from exam room two. Adam races off down the hall, leaving Devon as if he were standing guard.

"Where is he running off to?" I ask Devon.

"Best as I can tell he knows the family of this one. He told them he would meet them outside," is Devon's reply and longest sentence I have ever heard him utter.

"Okay, so what have we got?" I ask as I reach the door of the exam room.

"A jogger we picked up in Delaware Park. Barely conscious, not communicating. The pulse and respiration are negligible. The fire guys got there ahead of us and did CPR. I'm guessing heart attack. I think this one is circling the bowl."

"Thanks for your medical opinion, Devon," as I push through the curtain and into the exam room. Inside, Kathy and Sarah are working frantically to get monitors attached to the patient. At first glance the vitals are horribly low. I stop to pull on a pair of gloves then turn back to the gurney. Kathy backs away, giving me full access to the patient for the first time. I reach up instinctively for his eyes to check his pupils. My hand freezes enroute as my whole body locks up. This can't be. How?

"DAD! Dad, can you hear me?" I yell.

Gary Friedman

CHAPTER SIX
MARY BETH

———— • ————

Sluggish. That is the kindest way to describe the current state of my afternoon, my evening, my life. One moment grinding slowly into the next. This is not the life Mr. Rogers promised in his neighborhood if I was a good little girl. And I really was. I never gave my parents a moment of trouble. I cleaned my room, helped out Mom in the kitchen, and always did my homework on time. I was the model child by every standard, so how did I end up here?

I followed my life plan to the exact letter. I was the valedictorian in my high school graduating class and I did the same in college. I got some scholarships and grants, worked two jobs through college and managed to graduate without an ounce of debt, which is a fact of which I am extremely proud. I got a great job after college, got a perfect apartment in Elmwood Village, a new car, and a tight circle of friends. I never had a serious boyfriend, and I was fine with that. My plate was very full, and there was no room for the kind of things my friends battled with like dating, boyfriends, and ex-boyfriends. It's not that I felt superior to them, it's just that my plan and my priorities did not include the hassles and unnecessary pain most of my group found in relationships. I never felt I was missing anything.

Then it happened. I agreed to meet some friends out for a few drinks. We arrived at the bar on Allen Street well before the late-night crowds and got the table of our choice—one in an alcove near the entrance. There we were, five fairly carefree women in their mid-twenties with an opportunity to get out, relax and laugh like we rarely did throughout the week. By the second pitcher, I was feeling no pain. I was sitting in the corner of the alcove, facing the front door when he walked in. He was in a group of three guys, well-dressed in a suit and a long camel coat, definitely a class above the other men in the bar. My eyes followed him as he walked down to the far end of the bar and turned to face my direction. He had an amazing smile and appeared to have a truck-full of confidence. He was obviously the focal point of his intimate small group and he gave his friends his undivided attention. He wasn't like most guys in a bar whose eyes wander over every lithe figure in the room. He was there for his buddies and I could tell he made them feel important.

I was absolutely mesmerized, my eyes glued to his every movement. The conversation around our table seemed like it was three bars away. This really doesn't happen to me, getting all google-eyed over some guy, but this wasn't just some guy. He was the only living being in the room and I was smitten. So much so that I didn't notice the conversation at our table had waned or that my four girlfriends were all looking pointedly at me and then scanning the room to see what had stolen away my attention.

"Mary Beth."

"Mary Beth!"

"MARY BETH! Come back to this planet, girl."

I looked up and around the table and everyone was looking at me and laughing. "What?"

"Where did you go, Mar? Who is that guy? Do you even know him, or do you just drool at strangers?" asked Patti.

"I don't quite know what you're talking about," I replied, trying to hide my embarrassment.

As the laughing increased, I tried hard to gather my composure. I looked back across the bar one last time, but now, the object of my drool was staring back at me with a very slight smile on his face. Neither of his friends had noticed that they had lost his attention. He briefly spoke to his two buddies then moved away from the bar. Was it my imagination or was he crossing the room in slow-motion as if in some starry-eyed movie scene, his eyes never leaving mine? He walked over to our table, excused himself, and reached his hand out, palm up, to me.

"I'm sorry to bother you, but do you have a minute?"

I smiled and stood up as I reached for his hand. I followed him off to the front door and out to the sidewalk on Allen St. Our time together that night was surprisingly brief.

"I know you are here with your friends and I am with mine. I don't want to steal you away from them, but I would love the chance to get to know you." He pulled two business cards and a pen out of his pocket and handed them all to me. At his suggestion, I wrote my number on the back of one card and kept the other. He smiled, said thank you, kissed me softly on the cheek and then walked back to join his friends...leaving me frozen in place in some sort of cosmic trance. I went back into the bar and rejoined my friends physically, but my mind was stuck on the vision of him, his voice, and his soft, gentle lips on my cheek. Though our time together was brief, a fog had settled in my brain that stayed with me the rest of the night.

That was thirty-one years ago, and I seem to have been in that fog ever since. I have been earth-shatteringly in love with that man all this time. James became the focus of my life. Even though he traveled quite a bit for his job, we spent every moment that we could together when he was in town. That time amounted to only one or two days a week but in those couple of days he was capable of making me feel that I was the center of his life. Within six months, I was pregnant with his child and we were married by a Justice of the Peace a few days after we found out. Jay and I bought a home in Orchard Park, south of Buffalo and raised our son there. I continued to work at my job, but for the most part, I was a single parent. Gratefully, my husband always provided for us financially. I didn't have to work; it provided me with a break from raising my son and a diversion while waiting for my husband to come home. When he did, he made me feel loved and desired. He cared about me, listened to me like no one else ever had and our love-making was unlike anything I had ever expected. The joy of being with him made his walking out the door each week harder and harder as the years went by.

The wonder of our forty-eight hours together left the rest of the week hollow and empty. Jay paid little attention to our son, and never took me to any social functions. Our date nights were always just the two of us. I had friends at work but that's where they stayed. Since we were financially secure, I eventually gave up my job and stayed at home, focusing on the needs of our son. By the age of eight, our son stopped asking for his father and when he was coming home. It didn't seem to matter to him anymore. As our son got older and more focused on his schoolwork, which turned into almost an obsession for him, I found myself more and more alone, leading a life of profound emptiness. Over the years, phone conversations with Jay became less frequent, leaving only our two days every other week to keep us connected. Yet even those were fading away in intensity. He seemed more distant, more pre-occupied. His leaving no longer had the same effect. It was almost a relief when he drove away.

It started slowly. A glass of wine at night with dinner and maybe an occasional glass at lunch if I was in the mood. Then a glass at night before bed to help me sleep, but it rarely did its job. During the glorious months of summer, a bottle of beer might slip into the mix, then two. Before I knew it, I was buying both my beer and wine by the case, every couple of weeks for a while, then weekly. On those nights when I knew I would be alone, I filled in the space with alcohol. Some nights I would make it to bed, some nights I would fall asleep on the couch and some mornings I would wake up on the floor.

Control, peace, and happiness were soon all things of my past. I lost interest in my life as I knew it. My son drifted away from me as his schooling and career took priority. I did my best to hide my drinking from him as well as from Jay. When I knew he was due home, I tried desperately to gain control of my drinking and my life. I would hide the empties and take back the returnables. I would pour half bottles into former vinegar bottles or water jugs. I would pay cash at liquor stores so the receipts wouldn't show up on my statements. I became incredibly good at covering my tracks.

I knew my condition was getting worse but the motivation to stop waned as my depression deepened. Tears were never more than a mirror away. One look at myself and my failures surrounded me. My youth and my looks were gone and with them, my confidence. I felt like I had lost the interest of my husband. I had come to feel that coming home and spending time with me was the last thing he wanted to do, that he purposely extended his trips just to avoid me. Maybe there was another woman somewhere stealing away his interest. Could anyone blame him? Yes, the mirror is my enemy.

There are days when I think about stopping. Not my drinking, my living. When getting out of bed is the last thing I want to do. The loneliness envelopes me like a bath towel. I struggle with just creating a plan for my day. My eyes open, I look at the clock next to my bed and immediately start to calculate how many hours left to the day. The loneliness has a best friend—silence. I used to leave a television on or turn on the radio just to fill dead air, but both would bring back memories of happier times when we watched movies together or he would take me for a spin around the kitchen to a big-band tune. Eventually I stopped that as well. I decided that I needed to get out, to exercise or to take walks. It worked for a short while, but I always came back to the empty silence that had become my life. The thoughts of suicide grew more frequent, but then I found that just the thoughts weren't enough.

I started to formulate a plan. I began to arrange my life so that the ones I left behind would have no difficulty tying up my loose ends. Who would find me? Who would tell my family? Would anybody say they saw this coming or would they pretend to be shocked?

So here I am, at what one would call a turning point in my life. It's a beautiful summer evening. The sun has retreated for another day leaving a purple sky behind. I have managed to get through the entire day without taking a drink, a challenge I made to myself while in the shower this morning. If I can just get to sunset, maybe I can make it through the entire day sober. I get these brief moments of clarity where I can see my dilemma and can genuinely seek an exit ramp. Today is one of those days. I'm sitting on a chaise lounge on my patio, watching the sky darken. Listening to the song of the cicada as it calls out for a mate. I can see bats circling above the trees seeking out their next meal. Clinging to nature makes me feel less alone. An occasional rabbit or squirrel dares to approach my chair. I try to strike up a conversation but that scares them off.

My laptop is resting on my thighs as I browse through the last five years of pictures. Family, friends, a bathroom remodel and a couple of our weekend getaways. All good memories warming up an already-warm evening. Maybe my life really isn't all that bad. Maybe I can make some changes in my life, changes that would brighten my future. I know I can no longer depend on anyone other than myself to make it happen. Maybe counseling?

Maybe an AA meeting? Something has to help. I lay my head back on the lounge and make an honest effort to slow my breathing, to relax, to find the remnants of my life that may be calling out to me. My eyes start to grow heavy as my head starts to drop to one side. No! Don't fall asleep, focus on your breathing, focus on the good things worth living for! Please, don't give up Mary Beth! Don't let the loneliness win. I can't let the mistakes I have made in my life remain wrapped up in a bundle of despair that I carry on my shoulder.

Human beings need companionship. I have made my husband my first priority when I am no more than fifth or sixth from the top of his list. I have a son who has followed in his footsteps. My friends have drifted away through no fault of theirs. I simply don't make the effort to keep them close. Instead of doing anything about my loneliness, I seek solutions staring at the bottom of an empty glass while pondering how it got so empty so quickly.

I can't just make a commitment to stay sober. I have to rebuild my social world, and pry myself out of this house, this stone fortress blocking those who seek entry. I recall a saying at an AA meeting I attended once, "If it's going to be, it's up to me!" I really do believe that. I have to believe that. If I wait for someone else to fix me, I'll be in the bottom of this glass forever.

I am surrounded by the darkness of a new night. My patio lights are on a timer that I haven't adjusted to the earlier sunsets. The dark settles on me like a blanket, making me feel secure in the moment of living the entire day sober. It's a quiet victory to say the least, knowing there will be many battles to follow, but you can't achieve a second victory until you celebrate your first. My pat on the back for my day of sobriety cheer is like every other moment in my life, alone and celebrated in silence. I look down at my laptop and cruise through my list of friends on Facebook, looking for someone yet to judge me or give up on me. I need a partner in this tough fight, someone to be accountable to, someone unafraid to call me out when I'm giving up on the fight. There must be one person among this list who will care enough to join me on this journey.

Reality comes knocking in the form of a ring from my cell phone, brightening its screen. My phone is on the table close by, but far enough away to get me out of the chaise. I swing my legs over the side of the lounge and lift myself up, stable in my sober stance. The caller ID is familiar but surprising.

"Hello."

"Hi, Mom, it's Dylan."

"Of course it is, no one else calls me Mom."

"I really don't have time for a clever reply. I'm at the emergency room at ECMC tonight. You need to get down here as soon as possible. Are you okay to drive?"

"Do you mean am I drunk? No, I'm very sober. What's going on? Are you hurt?"

"No, Mom, it's not me. They just rolled in a new patient for me. You really need to hurry!"

"Dylan, you're scaring me. Who is it?"

"It's Dad."

"That's not possible. He's in Seattle until Friday."

"I don't have time for a debate. It's Dad, and if you want to see him alive again you better get moving. I'll see you soon."

The light of the phone disappears in my hand just as the patio lights come on. How can this be? He didn't tell me he was coming home early. In fact, he never has come home early. He lives more tightly to a schedule than any human being I know. Dylan said hurry. Why am I frozen in space? He said if I want to see him alive again. Of course, I do.

I run into the house, leaving the sliding door open; sprint up the stairs, letting my robe drop in the hallway. I throw on some leggings and a top, grab my purse and run back to the staircase, almost tripping on my robe. I fly down the stairs and back to the kitchen. I frantically search for my keys and find them on the counter next to the sink and an empty glass. I reach for the keys and stare at the glass. My hand brushes against it, almost knocking the glass into the sink.

I am frozen again.

Maybe a quick drink before I go, just to settle my nerves. I can't let him see me this scared. I will be able to function better when I get there. I won't get through this without at least one sip, a shot, something. I have to. I'm so not good at this. I can't do this alone. I can't. My hands are shaking.

I reach out for the glass but this time I succeed in knocking it into the sink, sending shards of glass flying. My hand is still extended but empty, open as if holding the former glass. The sound brings me back to the patio and my resolution to sobriety. The glass becomes a symbol of my broken life, my shattered dreams, everything I have done wrong for the last thirty-one years. My arm slowly withdraws to my side. My husband needs me. My son needs me. I have to be strong. If I can get through this, well, it will be a turning point. I can do this. I throw my shoulders back and rid myself of my drunken slouch. I throw my purse over my arm, pick up the keys, ignore the shattered mess in the sink and stride for the garage door with only one thought, *God, don't let him die. Please. James, my Jay, needs to see me strong.*

As they say at every AA meeting I have ever attended, "If it's going to be, it's up to me."

Gary Friedman

CHAPTER SEVEN
WILL

———— •————

The tears are running down my face, dripping off my red beard onto my t-shirt, with some falling to the grass and others soaking the front of my t-shirt. I didn't think it would be this hard. When I first made this decision, it made so much sense. But the closer I get to that moment, the harder it becomes to follow through. I covered all my bases and calculated the risks. I have to do this. I have to follow through. People I care deeply about are counting on me even if they don't know what I am doing. They will understand.

How did I get here? How has this burden fallen to me? It's been a week since the awakening...since I faced this problem. I have never broken the law, never even gotten a speeding ticket. And yet here I sit, ready to violate all the principles I have ever believed in. It's not out of revenge, since technically, I haven't been wronged. It's not out of hate; I have grown up with this family since my first day in kindergarten. I act out of obligation, like someone has to fix this problem and since I'm the only one who knows about it, it falls to me.

Kindergarten. I recall that's when Adam and I became inseparable. Best of friends sounds too weak, more like brothers. I went to his house every day after school, staying for dinner most nights. My parents both worked, so they were thankful that Adam's family paid me so much attention. My parents were unable to have kids, so adopting me as a newborn seemed like a good idea at the time. It was another box to check off their life plan. Once I arrived, however, their lives always seemed to get in the way of being decent parents to me. I became more of an obligation.

I was grateful for the third chance at a family because without Adam and his parents I would never have felt love growing up, or how it feels to be part of something bigger than myself. Adam and I shared everything together all the way through high school. We managed to get the same teachers every year, the same schedule, as if it were meant to be. Kids at school called us Siamese twins. Adam was way smarter than me, so he helped me with my schoolwork. I was more athletic than he was, so I helped him with getting in shape and in gaining the skills he needed to make the teams we both tried out for. We put in good words for each other when it came to dating, encouraged each other, and cheered each other on. We experienced our first kisses days apart. We got drunk, smoked weed and passed out together for the first time. We built snow forts together; got in fights together and took on the world together. I called his mom, Mom and his dad, Dad. They were all family, and more than my own family could have ever been. I loved them. I owed them.

Most things in life came easily for Adam, maybe too easy. He really is brilliant and wanted to be a doctor, but he let his social life and partying get in the way. When he went away to college I stayed behind, getting a job with a local landscaping company instead. I would leave early on Fridays when I could and went off to spend the weekend drinking with Adam. College academics were easy for him but it was never a priority. Taking the easy way became his curse.

It was different for me. I knew if I was going to be a success at anything it would take hard work. I had worked part-time with the same company during high school, so when I graduated, I stayed with them full-time. During the winter I would take over the snow-plowing part of the business for my boss, Steve. He was pretty smart but not a hard worker and certainly not a people person. He yelled first, and if he ever got around to listening or asking questions, his guys would tune him out and tell him as little as they needed to, just to get away from him. If anything ever went wrong, and it did often, he first found someone to blame. Then he would tell his customers that an employee messed up and lamented to them how hard it was to find good help. The crews changed constantly as guys got tired of his act. The summer guys would quit, and the regulars would hook up with other landscape companies. I would never let the nonsense get inside my head. I stayed focused on my plan at all times.

I saw this company as an opportunity. I would sit up late at night and talk with Adam about my plan. First, I would become my boss's most trusted, go-to guy. I would never argue or complain. I would follow his orders to the letter, be on time, work late, and never stop until the work was done. Some of the other guys called me an ass-kisser, but it didn't bother me. I stayed true to my plan. My second step was to keep detailed records of every job I worked on, every driveway I plowed. Before long, I had a thick file on all of Steve's customers. I knew them all and they all knew me.

That was the third part of my plan. Every customer I came in contact with, I killed with kindness. If I plowed their driveway, I would get out and clear their porch as well and then move on to their sidewalks. If it was a decent hour and I knew the owners were home; I would knock on the door and tell them what I had done and asked if they needed anything else. When it was a lawn job or more extensive landscaping, I would do it perfectly and would thoroughly clean up after myself, leaving the yard spotless. Then I would walk through the job with the customer and let them know the little things I had done above and beyond the contract. My reason was simple. Let them get to know me and the quality of my work. Let them see me as the face of the company. Sometimes it would garner big tips, but that wasn't the reason I did it. I wanted to make an impression.

After five years of persistence, my hard work finally paid off big time. Steve crossed a line. He was arrested for slapping his wife around. The article and his mug shot made the local papers. I knew the negative publicity would scare away loyal customers, both his regulars and his new referrals. I also knew this was the chance I had been waiting for. I pulled together all the crews for a meeting and told them what happened and what I thought the result of his behavior would be legally and business-wise. I told the crew I was going to start my own business and I invited them all to join me. I told them we would take nothing physical from Steve's business, not his equipment or his office staff, but that I would reach out to all of his customers. I told them I would give them all a slight raise in their pay but more importantly, we would be a team, working together for the same goal, building something for the future. I told them I would treat them with respect, without the ranting and raving that had been part of the deal when working with Steve. I would treat them all positively and all I asked is that they do the same for me and our company.

The vote was unanimous. They all moved with me. A personal loan from Adam's mom helped me to buy the equipment I needed. A face-to-face visit to every customer resulted in all but three of them signing on with me; those three were Steve's family. Even Steve's in-laws moved with me. When he got out of jail, Steve found he had an office and tools but little else. No business, no customers, and no wife. Needless to say, I was not on his Christmas card list.

The company grew rapidly. Within eighteen months, I had paid back all of Mom's loan. I didn't waste money on office space and leased barn space for the equipment from a local contractor. I took the calls and referrals myself. My crews all stuck with me and I had enough business to enable me to add more crews and more equipment. My business plan, actually Adam's and my business plan, succeeded masterfully. I was proud and so was Adam. I had offered him a chance to join me after he bailed on his education, but he refused. He was taking a paramedic course and he wanted to make that work.

Most of my business is in the northern suburbs of Buffalo. Adam's family is still in Amherst and they are my number-one customer. My parents drifted out of the area, and we are rarely in contact anymore. One day I took a call for a referral in Orchard Park, a southern suburb. It was from a woman whose husband traveled a bit and wasn't home to keep up with the yard work. She needed someone on a regular basis. I don't normally work in the Southtowns, but I felt sorry for this woman, so I agreed to come out and look over the job. It appeared to be little more than basic maintenance with a few major projects; I agreed to take it on. I asked for payment upfront for the first month like I do with all new customers, and also because I questioned this woman's sobriety. She seemed more than a little shaky.

On my second visit, on an exceptionally hot day by Western New York standards, I was riding my mower for my new client. While coming around the side of the property, I saw a vehicle pull into the driveway. A man got out and pulled his bright red suitcase off the back seat. My customer was standing on her front porch smiling broadly. When the man stepped back, bag in hand, he looked up at me. My heart froze. I could feel ice water flush through my veins as if I was going into shock. I stopped the mower and watched as the man strode up to the porch and kissed my customer, rather passionately. With my mouth frozen open,

55

my head dropped into my hands when I realized what I had seen. It took every ounce of control in my body not to drive my mower up its ramp on my trailer and get away from there as quickly as humanly possible.

There was absolutely no doubt in my mind that I was staring in the face of Jesse, Adam's father. Why was he here? Why was he kissing that woman? I gathered all my senses and finished my job. Just as I was securing my mower on the trailer, I saw the same man come out of the garage with golf clubs over his shoulder. He threw them in the trunk of his car and backed out of the driveway. As he drove past me, he looked at me and seemed to linger in the process. When he was gone, I went back to the door and asked my customer if she wanted to do a walk-through to see if my work met her satisfaction. As we walked, we struck up a conversation.

"So, that guy in the driveway, is he a friend of yours?" I ask.

"No," she laughed, "that is my husband. He travels quite a bit and isn't home as much as I would like, so his visits can be a bit of a whirlwind. Why do you ask?"

"Oh," I stammered, "he just looked familiar, like another customer. Kinda caught me by surprise." I was stunned by her response and felt incredibly awkward. She smiled at me and handed me a twenty-dollar tip for my efforts.

"Thank you. The yard looks great. See you next week?"

"Yes ma'am. I'll be here. You have a good night." I walked slowly to my truck. I started it up, turned into the driveway, backed out and headed through the development. My work for the day was done. I headed north back into the city. I was driving with both hands on the wheel, but my mind was a thousand miles away. I saw what I saw, and I know what I know, but what do I do about it? I have to tell Adam, but how? Before I say anything to anyone, I have to be sure, beyond a doubt.

I park my rig in our lot outside the contractor's barn and jump into my Jeep Cherokee. I head over to McDonald's drive-thru, load up on burgers, fries, and the largest drink they offer and head back to Orchard Park. I stop along the curb just past my customer's house facing their driveway and wait. Four hours later, with the sun near the horizon, Jesse's car pulled back into the driveway. As the garage door opened up, my customer came out of the garage and greeted her husband warmly. He pulled his golf clubs from the trunk and disappeared into the house.

When the garage door hit the ground, I got out of my car and walked toward the house. I pulled down the front of the mailbox and found newly-delivered mail. Pulling out the top envelope, I read the electric bill and find it made out to the last name of my customer but addressed to James. I took a picture of the bill with my cell phone and walked slowly back to my car. It was time to head home and start my research.

Once settled in front of my laptop with the half-empty McDonald's cup on the table next to it, I typed Jesse's name into Google Images and found a professional picture of him. Next, I typed in James' name and the same picture came up. Not a look alike, not similar, the exact same picture taken by the same photographer with the same backdrop. My stomach sunk. I could feel my shoulders sag with the weight of what I had discovered.

How? How does a man do this? How does a man maintain two separate identities with two homes, two wives and two families? Does he have two separate social security numbers, two credit ratings? How does he do his taxes? How does he keep it a secret for what appears to be an exceedingly long time? Sure, he might not be the father of both sons, but by appearances it sure looks like it. They could be twins. Even his two wives have similar features. What about holidays and special occasions—Christmas, Valentine's Day, his birthday? He hasn't just been playing around, he has been carrying this on for decades. Jesse had always been a good father to Adam and was always attentive to his wife when he was around. I witnessed the same affection in my customer's driveway just a couple of hours ago. He had to know that sooner or later he would get caught. He had to.

Well the hell with him. I have no sympathy for that man. Like with anything else in life, he made his choices. He put himself in this position, I assume, voluntarily. Whatever happens to him he has coming. But what about his two wives and his two sons? What did they ever do to deserve this? They are victims. They had no choice. Sooner or later, they will all come to find out what I now know. They will be crushed. If Jesse cared about them, how could he let this happen?

And now the big question, what about me? How fair is it that I have to deal with this? What am I supposed to do? Do I confront Jesse (or whatever his real name is) or do I break it quietly to Adam? We have been friends for over twenty years. He needs to know, but how will he react to me as the messenger? I can't just keep it a secret, but how do I break up a family I care so deeply about? I have no doubt I will be one of the victims too, cast out through anger and embarrassment. No one will be able to look me in the eye. This is so unfair.

I stared at my computer screen. The feeling that had begun as a rock in the pit of my stomach had morphed into sadness and dismay. Those feelings are now starting to bubble, like boiling water on a stove. My hands start to shake, almost violently. My reflection in the mirror above my desk shows my cheeks reddening, my eyes narrowing. I can't ever remember being this angry. What do I do? This is all Jesse's fault. He needs to be punished severely. No, he needs to die. That's it. He doesn't deserve to apologize or make amends. No collection of words can make up for this.

I have to do this. Not for me but for the families. I need to find a way. Any way to keep myself clean, take him out in a way that no one will ever know and where I will never come under suspicion. I have never thought about taking a life but if there was ever a justification for murder, this would be it. Killing someone is the ultimate selfish act, but so is keeping two families in the dark. This is the only way I can bring an end to this charade and not become the enemy. I need to keep anyone else from knowing about my decision, so I can keep from losing the only family that has ever really mattered. Doing nothing is not an option.

I stayed up the rest of the night and poured over the internet, looking for a possibility, a way to carry out this bleak task. This was not something I ever imagined doing, nothing that is in my DNA. All I knew was that I need to find a way to complete the task and that would allow me to get away from the scene without making noise or leaving a mess behind. That meant no guns or knives. I started to research injectables. I needed something I could get to put in a needle that would immobilize him immediately while other drugs that took longer to take effect could do their job. I found on the internet that Methohexital or M99 would put him down quickly while another drug, succinylcholine, a slower-acting sedative, could paralyze most of his vital systems.

Getting a needle would be easy but not so the drugs. My best hope was an old high school friend, Rick, who had become a nurse. I remembered him having an overactive justice gene. I knew that if I could activate that gene, he would understand my desire to right this wrong. My only question was would he risk his career and his freedom to aide me in my quest? Equally important, would he keep our conversation just between us, no matter what happens.

After a long sleepless night, I called Rick and asked him to meet me for lunch. Since he works afternoons, he would most likely be free. He agreed to meet me at Panera Bread around 12:30. After small talk and getting our food, I laid out what I had discovered about Jesse and his philandering. As I share my plan to right a wrong, including a few tears rolling down my cheeks, I can see his eyes begin to light up and a sinister smile snuck onto his face. I told Rick that if he could get the drugs to me safely, I would never do anything to implicate him. Surprisingly, it didn't take long to convince him. Rick has this love for superheroes and Marvel movies, so he sees himself as an Avenger on a mission. Whatever it takes is fine with me. He tells me to meet him at a bar on Elmwood at midnight and he would provide me with drugs and two needles. We met later that night, and he didn't disappoint.

It took me two days to catch up with Jesse. Once I did, I started to follow him around the city from a coffee shop on Elmwood and finally to Delaware Park. It was late in the day and the sun was starting to set. I parked near the snack bar and watched him pass by. I noticed a small clump of bushes just past the snack bar that was hidden from the path.

Once Jesse was out of sight, I loaded both needles just in case I somehow messed up with the first one. I waited until another walker passed by, then I hurried from my car and settled in behind the shrubbery. From my lair, I could see all the way around to the zoo entrance. I could see the runners, but they couldn't see me.

So, if this is what has brought me to this moment then why the tears and the anxiety. My mission is clear but the vision is clouded by one thing that surprises me: my love for Jesse. In all ways but biological, he has been my father. He helped raise me, encouraged me to be the best I could be, and approved of my business plan. How could I take the life of a man who has done so much for me? Yet because of him, because of the man I am, how can I not?

Finally, I see Jesse come around the curve. Sweat is dripping into my eyes while my hands begin to shake. The reality of what I'm about to do is right before me. I start to question my motives, to wonder about the consequences of my actions. I am furious with Jesse. I feel sorry for both families. I believe I'm making things better for everyone, but what if I get caught? Is fixing this worth the rest of my life in prison? Someone said once if you don't stand for something, you will fall for anything. Is this my time to stand up for what I believe in? There is no way I can quit now.

Jesse approaches the snack bar, his pace steady. As soon as he passes where I'm hidden, I stand up. When I get a clear shot at his back, I pounce. My left hand grabs his shoulder while my right hand drives the needle into his neck. I fumble a bit with the needle when moving my thumb to the plunger, but it finally connects, sending the cocktail into his veins. He reaches back with his right hand as if he is swatting away a bug then tries to turn his head but can't. I pull the needle from his neck and walk deliberately back to my car. I drive out the Colvin Avenue exit and slip into the evening traffic.

It is over. I look back once and see Jesse on the ground. I don't look back again.

Gary Friedman

CHAPTER EIGHT
JESSE

———•———

Justice is such a fleeting thing. Yet, riding in this ambulance seems to fit the bill. "The best laid plans of mice and men." I suppose if this is to be my end, so be it. Not what I had planned for the end of my day but not far behind.

My senses are dulled. My eyes are open, but my vision blurred. I'm trying to focus but failing miserably. I can hear but most words are drowned out by a constant buzzing, like power lines humming. Words are mangled due to the noise in my head and I can barely hear the ambulance's siren shrieking. My body can sense the bumps in the road and the hard turns that would toss me off the gurney if I weren't strapped down. Unless the hospital is nearby, I get the sense that this chariot will become my funeral pyre with flames licking the evening sky. So befitting of my Viking ancestry.

It feels like my body is shutting down one cell at a time. I'm losing contact with the world as I have known it. Do I really deserve such a peaceful death? I have counted on the worst ending at the hands of one of the many I have betrayed, a justifiable homicide if ever there was one. Little did I know that a common wasp would be my Angel of Death. Nature's messenger sending my body off to its final resting place.

What of my secrets? My loved ones deserve a better fate. They deserve to hear it all from me, all my lies, as well as my apology. They need to know that I loved them all, maybe too much. They all consider me a strong man, a leader in my field. But no, I am the weakest of beings, afraid of the punishment I have coming, afraid to be alone with nothing but the memories of how it felt to be loved. How will I be remembered? By what name will I be identified on my death certificate? Which of my pastors will give my eulogy? And what of my estate? Who will get the treasures I have left behind? What a mess I have created. That doesn't even include the human suffering that will follow, mourning not only my death but the death of a fantasy family that never existed. I deserve all the things that will be said about me when I'm gone.

We hit another bump in the road as the ambulance slows. My head bobs to the left just enough to change my perspective. The blur clears momentarily but just enough for me to get a glance at my attendant. Oh no, it's Adam, my Adam, my beautiful son. He is trying to concentrate on his task but even with my dusty vision, I can see tears course down his face. He is so handsome, mostly with Annie's good looks. He appears worried, desperate, like the task of pulling off a miracle rests on his athletic shoulders. I want to tell him how much I love him, but I'm unable to make my lips form the words and any sound I could utter would be smothered in the mask wrapped around my face.

What would I say if I was able? Would I remind him that I am his father and that I adore your mother and everything we have shared is real? Should I confess that I'm not the man I have pretended to be, that I have failed badly in my life. Not a failure of strength but an exposure of weakness. I failed to make the right decisions, not that I have known what those decisions should have been, even now, in this moment of judgment. Yet, any decision not made is essentially a decision in itself. "When all becomes known," I imagine telling Adam, "please understand that I'm deeply sorry for my weakness, for my inability to give you the attention you needed and desired." I was right to address the envelope to him. I will have no better advocate after I am gone than Adam.

My thoughts are halted by more rapid movements of the gurney being yanked violently from the ambulance and shoved though glass doors. Ceiling tiles fly past above my head. I hear as Adam speak briefly to someone...who? The attendant? A nurse? ...then runs out the door. My journey continues through another set of doors and I'm suddenly surrounded by more voices. I'm shifted from one cart to another, hooked up to machines, nurses running around like a polished pit crew at a NASCAR race, each fulfilling their responsibility. A tube is forced down my throat, needles shoved in my arms, clothes cut from my body. Another garbled voice takes control, demanding numbers, ordering actions. Because of all the things being done to my body, my head is turned enough to see the doctor's face. Is it really Dylan? Both of my sons in the same location?

As careful as I tried to be, it never occurred to me that they might know each other...or interact within the medical field and yet here they are, feet apart from each other. Maybe my arrogance made me careless. My son Dylan looks significantly older than he did at our last encounter, but just as angry. The first major consequence of my lying was the loss of a relationship with my older son. He was always a bit of a loner, so our dwindling relationship was somewhat of a natural by-product of the way I neglected his mother. He hated that she drank and blamed it all, and probably rightfully so, to the lack of attention I paid to her. He will most likely judge me the harshest when the truth comes out.

Our relationship is not one of words; no apology would suffice. Dylan is a man of action; "Don't tell me you will be a better father or a better husband. Promises are weak. You want to convince me? Show me." Act the part. If my families ever come together, his voice, the loudest, will also be the harshest and most unforgiving. No justification for my behavior will assuage him. If a blade were being swung toward my neck, it would be in his hands. Yet with the quick glimpses I get of his face, I can see the same concern in his eyes. Tears—held back by the violent blinking as he struggles to maintain his professional demeanor while trying to save my life—run down his cheeks. There is no time left to find another doctor. Hidden below the tough exterior is a son who loves his father, loves him for giving him life. Angry as he may be, he will not shirk his responsibility. He will try to save the unsavable.

As the emergency team works over my body, my head is again shifted, this time to the right. As my eyes slowly adjust, I can see Adam and Annie with their faces nearly pressed against the glass, trying desperately to peek through the mostly-closed curtain at the work being done on me. Adam is looking anxious, Annie not so much. She appears more angry than concerned. Then I see him, just past Annie's shoulder. He is nowhere near the glass. He is pressed back in the far corner of the room, almost hidden. Tears stream down his face, soaking his red t-shirt

It is Will. Why is he here and why is he crying? He is more responsible for my being here than he realizes...or does he? He must know I saw him at Mary Beth's house. I recognized him just as he surely recognized me. The vision of him staring at me from his mower unnerved me. I knew from that moment that my chaotic personal life was about to be not-so-personal. I called and cancelled my golf outing and went down by the Niagara River. I sat on a bench as I watched the boats drift by, pondering my future, weighing every option. Despite the fact that I had practically raised Will, I knew his allegiance was to Adam and not to me. I love Will like a son, but I knew, based upon what I knew of the man that he had become, that he would act on his discovery. I could try to reach out to him, but I knew in my heart that he would reject any plea I could offer. I briefly considered hurting Will but my conscience...Ha! What a joke—*my conscience*—wouldn't allow me to go through with that. Then I considered talking to Adam to try and make him understand. He would be furious with me and would be unable to hide his anger from his mother. Truth be told, even after three hours of soul searching, I saw no easy way out. No way at all.

It had to happen sooner or later. Someone from one of my lives would see me at the wrong place, the wrong time and with the wrong family. It wouldn't take much to put the pieces together. It has been weakness, maybe cowardice, that has kept me jailed in the life I chose. I have no one to blame for my circumstances and no one to look to who could get me out of my cell. If weakness got me into this, maybe it could get me out. I have considered every option, looked behind every door of escape. Maybe I could run away, gather what belongings and savings I could muster and hit the road, creating a new existence on my own. However, what would that leave behind? Mary Beth would be left without an income, no way to support herself. She would lose everything and hate me 'til her death. The bottle would become her only friend. Dylan would hate me even more if that was the case. No matter what choice I make here, nothing will change that relationship for the better. Adam will do fine either way. He has a great support system and a good job where he is respected. He will survive. Annie has a successful career of her own. She might have to cut back her lifestyle a bit, but my disappearance will not set her back much. It's Mary Beth who is at greatest risk. So, my choices are staying and facing the music...or run.

And what of suicide? I have heard it called a coward's final act. Could I do that? Is taking my life a viable option? Taking my own life takes me out of the equation, an equation where their pain and grieving will no longer touch me. I will have gotten the end I deserve, the only end that I had anticipated, and the only reasonable exit strategy. Of course, suicide would mean that my two life insurance policies would go unpaid. Whatever financial protection I would have provided with those policies would be gone, which is a hardship Mary Beth would endure intensely. What about leaving; starting over somewhere else? Honestly, my heart wouldn't be into creating a new life elsewhere, despite all the real options I have. Crazy as it sounds to most normal folks, I adore both Annie and Mary Beth, yet I know there is no exit where they will not be hurt once my secrets are revealed. From that pain there is no escape, no matter what I choose. But maybe...if only there was a way where my death could be an accident, where suicide would be harder to prove, but how?

Either way, I knew I had to say my proper goodbyes, write letters to my family members, so I could at least try and explain the choices I have made, how each decision I made was out of my deep and endless love for each and every one of them. But sending letters would be proof of the suicide. So, four hours of contemplation on a bench watching boats drift past on the Niagara River led me back to the beginning with no concrete answers. Will could divulge my secrets at any moment, and still I had no answers.

Somehow, I had to find a way to explain myself, and to share my heart. While Mary Beth slept soundly, I spent the entire sleepless night writing goodbye letters to my family. Sealed each letter in an envelope with their names on the front except Adam's. I put his name on a large manila envelope where I placed all the other sealed letters along with the letter I wrote to him. Because of his connection to Will, (who also got a letter), Adam would be able to put the pieces together and distribute all the letters to the rest of my family members. Sealing that last envelope brought me a strange sense of peace. It was at least a beginning to setting the record straight.

I found my father's old gun, which had long been hidden in MaryBeth's house. I had fired it every so often, so I had no doubt it would work for my final act. I tossed the gun under the passenger seat of my car and Adam's envelope on top of the passenger seat. I had no formal plan in place, I just wanted to be prepared, in case the final solution showed itself. In the end, the gun was never needed. How fortunate for everyone that the wasp happened to come along when it did.

Wait just a second. I have heard of killer bees and wasps but never knew them to be this far north, where winter gets in the way of their life cycle. It makes no sense that killer insects would find their way to Delaware Park...so scratch that idea. Maybe I had an allergic reaction to the sting? Yet in my life I have suffered bites and stings from every insect that finds a home in Western New York and never experienced even the most minor effect. The reaction that I experienced tonight doesn't come out of nowhere. What if it wasn't a sting? What if it was a human sting from someone who wanted to kill me? Why me? I have no enemies, not a soul that would want to...

Slowly, the vision of my last few steps comes back to me, reliving the moment for the first time. One stride after the other in slow motion, approaching the snack bar, dark and quiet. Next come the bushes on my left, hiding a dark shadow that I see and ignore. As I move past it, I hear a rustling. Next moment, a hand settles on my left shoulder and a heartbeat later, I feel a stinging sensation in my neck. I try to reach for it but can't lift my arm. As I start to fall, a second hand grabs my right shoulder and attempts to ease my fall. When I land hard, I hear a voice whispering in my ear, "I'm sorry, Dad." A broken voice but one I know. I am facing the middle of the park but can make out a reflection in my watch, the bottom half of a torso walking quickly away toward the solitary car parked along the roadside. Will looks back once, then drives away. For some reason, my heart breaks for him, knowing that whatever comes of his action, he will carry it with him for the rest of his life. If anyone knows the effect of carrying a secret for a lifetime, it's me.

My eyes slowly drift back to Will, cowering in the corner. Those aren't tears of grief or sorrow, those are tears of guilt. It was him! He did this to me! Though my face is numb, I could sense a tear sliding down my cheek. Oh Will, thank you, thank you, thank you. Little do you know how you have solved all my problems, how you have enabled me to leave this world while still providing for my loved ones who would still receive the letters I had written them. You put all this in motion and ended it at the same time. It was such a courageous act, borne out of your love for Adam and Annie. Surely the authorities will find the needle mark and know I didn't do this to myself. The insurance companies will be forced to pay out my claim. All of us, me included, will get the most we could possibly deserve.

How do I let him know that I forgive him, that his unselfish act, to some degree, saved a family and ended my pain; two things I could never do on my own?

The room begins to darken and the buzz in my ears grows softer. There is no way to run, no way to scream out, no way to say I love you one last time to all those I couldn't say goodbye to on my own. The air grows colder. I'm surrounded by a peace like I have never known. I get a dim view of Dylan's face above me, frantic in his efforts to extend my life if even for one more moment. I can make out the beeping of the heart monitor as it continues to slow, can feel the oxygen being pumped into my lungs. The methodical beeping becomes a long tone then nothing. Brief flashes of intense heat across my chest as Dylan tries in vain to bring me back, then another and then nothing. Dylan leans down, his lips close to my ear and whispers, "I did love you Dad. I am so sorry I couldn't show you more. Rest well."

CHAPTER NINE
ADAM

———•———

The bedroom was dimly lit by a night light that masqueraded as a lamp. It was lit every night, not to illuminate the room but to alleviate the fears of a young boy and his dislike of the dark. The boy is snuggled down under the covers while his father sits on the edge of the bed closest to the lamp with his back against the headboard. The young father is trying to steal enough light from the nightstand to read to his young son. Tonight, it is from Dr. Seuss' *The Lorax.* Reading had become a nighttime ritual on those nights when Dad was actually around, which were few.

Most of my memories of my father were like that, darkened by time. If someone asked me what my father did for a living, all I could offer was a shrug. Despite my asking several times, the answer never made the picture come into focus. To this day, I have no idea what my father's company does. Some kind of manufacturing is the best I can do. It could be widgets for all I know. The only emotion I could tie to his work has been frustration because it served to keep him away from me way too much. I cherished the man as much as I did his presence. Growing up, when he was gone, my mom was always there for me. She was strong and hard-working and did well at her job, but she never missed a sporting event or an open house at school or a teacher's conference. We celebrated special events and big wins on the field exuberantly. She was always happy and upbeat but never more so than when Dad was around. Their love for each other was as clear as day. On those days she was on cloud nine, clearly excited to be a family. We took every opportunity to make those moments become memories we could hang around our necks like gold medals in Dad's extended absences.

We did weekend family getaways, trips to the local fairs, camp-outs in a nearby park or just in our backyard. Dad would take me to the playground and push me on the swings while Mom snapped picture after picture. He swam with me in our above-ground pool in the summer and build snow forts with me in the winter. Yet it always seemed frantic, like we were trying to squeeze two weeks' worth of living into one crowded weekend. When I woke up Monday morning he was gone again, and life went back to Mom and me as if he had never been there and like we both didn't miss him like crazy.

Growing up in my world was unlike what any of my friends experienced, but it seemed good enough for me. I never lacked anything I wanted because my mother didn't want me to be unhappy or to blame the absence of a father for the lack of material goods. We lived in a nice house in a great neighborhood and for the most part, life was good. My mother took care of all the chores or hired someone to do them, thus I was never burdened with responsibilities. Looking back, if there was a cause for my lack of motivation for college, that was probably it. I was always able to avoid hard work and when it came to my studies, if it got hard, I would procrastinate, waiting for Mom to hire someone to do that too. I can't say I'm proud of my performance, and slowly but surely, I am figuring life out.

My back is up against the wall just outside of the emergency room entrance. The warmth of the day has not eased; it has turned into another beautiful Buffalo summer night. I have always considered this doorway an entrance and not an exit, as many of the people I wheel through these doors never come out again, at least not alive. It is so much more difficult when the patient on the gurney is one of the most central figures in my life, a man I truly love. His long disappearances never diluted that love. Doing what I do and with as many trips here as I have experienced, I don't have a good feeling about what the next hour will bring. Based on the vitals tracked, Dad's chances of survival are slim. Mom is only minutes away and I have to be strong for her. While it's true Dad wasn't around very much, we both lived with the eternal count down to his next homecoming. The anticipation of his arrival kept us going. I never doubted that he would come back, until tonight.

Being a weeknight, the emergency room is quieter than usual, quieter than a typically insane weekend battle zone. No ambulances, no co-workers stopping by for a chat; just the sound of traffic from the city streets. The relative silence is shattered by the sound of tires squealing and an engine roaring. Seconds later, Mom's car turns into the ramp seemingly on two wheels, screeching to a halt directly across from the entrance. She leaps from her car like she had just won a set and was jumping over the net to greet her opponent. She sees me immediately and runs directly into my arms, her body clearly shaking. Seconds, many of them, pass without a word.

"How is he?" she asks.

"Not well, Mom. You better prepare yourself for a tough night," I reply.

"What does that mean?"

"Look, I'm not a doctor, okay, but I think he is fighting for his life. It may have been a heart attack or a stroke but either way, his vitals aren't good, and his responses are worse. I'm scared, Mom, so I want you to be prepared. We will get through this."

"Of course, we will, Honey. Take me in there."

We keep our arms around each other's waist as the automatic doors swing wide open. I guide her up to the window that overlooks the emergency room operations. The examining area, encircled by curtains, is the only one in use, and Dad is behind them. There is a small gap in the curtains that allows us only a brief glimpse of the activities within. Every few seconds, a nurse comes running out, surely following an urgent request by the doctor. That would cause a brief, wider gap in the curtains for us to peer through. The activities we can see are frantic. We catch flashes of instruments reflecting light, tubes being connected, and people jockeying for position around the table on which my dad lay...dying? We can barely make him out through all the people around him trying to save his life. Mom's arm tightens around my waist as she sees that Dad is looking right at us, acknowledging our presence, maybe even forcing a grin and perhaps a wink. Certainly, more our imagination than reality...right? A nurse wheels in another cart that contains an AED, a defibrillator designed to send an electronic charge through a patient's heart. This is not a good sign.

The curtain has hung up on the cart, giving us a view of the nurses stepping back in unison, followed by my father's body being jolted by the paddles. No one moves. A second jolt is applied. Again, no movement. Mom clutches my hand tightly. The air seems to escape from the examining area as the nurses' heads droop at the close of the frantic dance to shock my dad's heart back to life. Then a sight I didn't expect. The attending doctor leans over Dad's body as if he were whispering in his ear. He then takes the man on the gurney into his arms and hugs him. The curtains close on the scene as Mom turns to me and buries her head in my shoulder, her body reacting to the sobs that feel like they are exploding from her soul.

Say what you want about the number of days they were together, Mom loved Dad as much as one woman could love a man. She cherished every moment they spent together, and she was devastated at the impact of realizing that the love of her life is being ripped away from her. I walk her over to a set of chairs in the waiting room, fearing she would collapse in my arms. I hold her until convulsions reduce to smaller shudders and then longer...until she falls quiet. She shows no signs of a willingness to let me go; I will hold her as long as she needs me.

My eyes scan the room, not sure what else to do. My fingers are running through Mom's hair as I look back at the glass that just held our attention moments ago. The rest of the room has been deserted. No, it actually hasn't. Hidden in the dark recesses behind a coat rack is a man that is bent over a in chair, elbows on his knees and hands covering his face, crying just as hard as Mom is. He slowly lets his hands drop away and I'm stunned. It is Will. My best-friend-growing-up Will, a brother close enough to call my mom, Mom and my dad, Dad. How did he get here? How did he find out? He is the last one I expect to find here. He can see me looking at him and he knows I recognize him. I wave at him and gesture for him to come sit with us. He takes the invitation hesitantly, walking across the room like he is being dragged.

As he nears, I try to sit up taller. "Mom," I whisper. "Look who's here. It's Will." She slowly lifts her head from my shoulder and looks up at him, her face and eyes reddened by tears.

"Hi Will, dear." She looks at him for a moment and forces a smile. Then she turns back to me.

"Where did you find him?"

"He was standing over there in the corner."

"What?"

"I said he was standing there in the corner, just now."

"No, not Will. Where did you find Dad?"

75

"Oh, I'm sorry. I was called to the bike path at Delaware Park. There were witnesses there who said he was walking around the park. He was wearing his jogging clothes, so I assumed they were right."

"I don't understand. How could that be? He wasn't supposed to get back into town until tonight. He called me today and said he was waiting at the airport in Los Angeles for his flight. How could this be, Adam?"

Will puts his hand on her shoulder as he starts to cry again. I slide over to make room for Will to sit down and hug Mom too. "I loved him too, Mom. I'm so sorry." With that they both start crying again and fall into each other's arms.

I get up from the bench and bend over with my hands on my knees, trying desperately to catch my breath. I didn't realize how much I had been holding it since the crash cart was wheeled in. While looking down, I can hear the emergency room doors swing open. I slowly stand up and glance at the door. Standing in the opening is Gerry, the Buffalo Police officer I had spoken to at Delaware Park. He wiggles a finger at me, calling me to him. He is holding a large manila envelope in his left hand. He turns and walks back outside, signaling he wants me to follow him. I turn back to Mom. "I'll be back in a minute, guys. A friend of mine just showed up and he needs to talk to me."

Mom looks up briefly and nods. Will, on the other hand, has become white as a ghost and is staring at the still-open entryway. I have never seen a look like that on Will's face and I thought I had seen them all. I'm sure he's just shaken by all that is going on. I turn and walk slowly outside. Gerry's back is to me and he has put his right foot on a planter, looking straight down at his feet.

"Hey Gerry."

He turns slowly. "Adam. How's your father doing?"

"He didn't make it."

"Oh man, I am so sorry. Is there anything I can do?"

"Not at the moment but thanks for asking. So, what's up?"

"Remember me telling you at the park that I had another call to go on?"

"Sure."

"Well that call is tied to your dad."

"In what way?" I ask, taking a step closer to him.

"We got called to the other end of the bike path where a walker had spotted a gun on the floor of a car."

"What does that have to do with my father?"

"It was his car, Adam. I ran the plates and they came back to him. I took a Slim Jim to the door and got it open. I took possession of the gun. He doesn't come up as having a permit. Did he carry it often?"

"A gun? Believe me, Gerry, I have never seen a gun in my house or ever seen him handle one. My mother wouldn't allow it. She's dead set against them."

"I believe you, Adam. I'm going to take it back to the station and lock it up as evidence. If you find out anything more about it let me know. There's one more thing."

"More than a gun? What else is there?"

"Sitting on the passenger seat was this envelope. It's addressed to you. Listen, I could get in a lot of trouble over this so please tell me you have my back."

"Trouble over what?"

"Since I found it in the car with the gun, I should probably take it in and let the detectives check it out. Based on our friendship, I didn't put it in my report. Take it. Just don't tell anyone where you got it. I could get in a world of hurt for doing this, but I'm riding single tonight so no one knows. I really am sorry about your loss, Adam. If you find anything in that envelope that I need to know about, call me. Remember, no one else knows about this."

"Don't worry, Gerry. It stays between us. I appreciate you doing this."

"Let me know if you need anything, anything at all. I will see you at the wake."

With that, he turns and walks quietly away into the night. I look down at the envelope in my hand. It had weight to it, as if it had more than just a few pieces of paper. My name was written in my father's controlled handwriting, with large letters in a dark black heavy ink. The flap was sealed by two metal silver clasps holding it down. I pull the clasps up and open the envelope, looking down into its darkness. I can make out four white envelopes with writing on them and three sheets of paper. I pull the sheets up and again recognize Dad's handwriting. It is a letter addressed to me. I pull it closer, but my vision is blurred by the tears once again returning to my eyes. I can't read this now. Mom needs me to be with her. I push the flap down and reseal the clasps. I turn back to the sliding doors and into the waiting area.

Mom's back is against the wall as she stares up into the ceiling tile. Will is bent over with his head in his hands, his sobbing drifting across the room like a sad melody. He gets up and gives me a hug that pushes all the wind of my lungs then walks quickly through the double-doors. I sit back down on the bench and place the envelope on the seat next to me as I take Mom back into my arms and hold her as tightly as I can, far tighter than I have in years. Time ceases to exist as images of us as a family, time spent together, race across my mind's screen. No words seem appropriate. The only syllable belongs to Mom as she utters over and over again, "I just don't understand."

The moment is broken by the sound of the emergency doors flinging open again. A woman walks in alone, looking somewhat lost and disheveled. There is no one at the reception desk to guide her. She walks slowly to the wall of glass and looks inside for a sign of what to do next. As she does, the door to the examining room opens. Out walks Dr. Dylan, the one who had worked on my father. His eyes scan the room and stop on our bench. I assume he is about to bring us the news of Dad's passing, reporting to us what happened. Instead, his eyes keep moving until he finds the woman looking through the glass. He looks back at us, seemingly confused by our presence, but continues to walk to the disheveled woman. As he strides toward her, his pace quickens. She turns and sees him coming and begins to meet his stride until she falls into his arms. Her body nearly collapses into his as her tears seem to explode at once. He holds her close, consoling her with a familiarity greater than any doctor would have for just any patient's family. His face is etched with pain, but no tears follow.

I am frozen in the moment of time, unable to respond or to speak in any way. I'm a video camera recording the scene around me. Understanding isn't only avoiding me; it has run from the room. I stay on the bench, consoling my mother over the passing of my father while the attending physician, who moments ago was whispering in my father's ear before taking him into his arms, comes to the waiting area and ignores us while consoling another woman for her loss. It's like someone telling me a story in a language known only by the speaker, invented for his own amusement. The doctor, the woman, the envelope, Will, all floating in a moment of time. A tabletop with jigsaw puzzle pieces from vastly different puzzles where nothing fits, and no picture comes together. It begins to feel like a dream, a very bad dream.

CHAPTER TEN
DYLAN

———•———

I remember sitting by the living room window as a kid, waiting, watching for my father to come home. It was usually on a Friday afternoon. The visits were always brief, maybe a weekend, rarely longer. Seeing his car pull into the driveway would send me running to the back door off the garage, hoping to watch him unload two bags from his car instead of just one. That would mean a little bit longer stay. In his absence, Mom would always call him her Greek God. For me, he was more like the mail man, here one second, gone the next. I would get a quick hug and a rustling of my hair. Then he would greet my mother like the long, lost lovers that they were.

He made no effort to make this a family reunion. He was there to reconnect with his wife. I was the second thought. We might spend a little time together on a Saturday afternoon, while Mom was doing his laundry or possibly a Sunday visit to church or family, but despite my nose-against-the-window greeting and my ever-growing high hopes, nothing ever changed. After many years of keeping my fingers crossed, I gave up hope. His brief visits became more of an interruption than a reunion. They interfered with my social life and with my relationship with Mom. Not only did he ignore me, but he took her away from me for the length of his visit. I never blamed her for his absence. Her loneliness for him and the reconnection of marriage took control during their brief encounters. Even as a kid, I recognized that she needed him. I knew, however, just based on the lives of people around me, that this wasn't normal. I also recognized that I had no control over the situation, that this was just the way things were going to be and that I had better get used to it. My chosen method for getting used to it was to stop caring about his visits and concurrently about him. The distance between us was a progressive thing, always growing, never shrinking, never a glimpse of what a father and a son should be.

And now, tonight, looking down at the gurney that holds his body, I'm pulled apart by the emotionless responsibilities of a doctor along with the aching pain of a discarded son. Both parts want to save him but for entirely different reasons. The first is because it's my responsibility as a physician and the second because...as long as he is alive, I dare to hope to gain his love. Either way, the doctor in me has to win. The personal emotions needed to stay on the back burner where they have resided for so many years.

As the ambulance driver had mumbled, his vitals are in a dangerous range. There is some responsive movement in his pupils, and he is drifting in and out of consciousness. His pulse is weak and slow, and his blood pressure is dropping. I'm following the protocol that my training and experience has taught me, but with limited results. I can feel his life slipping away. The team of nurses work quickly and efficiently as always, having no idea that this man was in some way related to me. I call for the defibrillator cart, hoping I can shock his heart back to life. One nurse runs for the cart while another holds back the curtain surrounding the work area. In that brief moment, I lean over my patient, my father, and whisper into his ear, "Come on, Dad. Don't give up. Mom needs you. I need you and...I love you. Come back!"

His head is turned slightly to the right and he appears to be looking out the window to the waiting area, a tear forming in his eye. Then his head is rolled back toward me and he smiles just slightly, enough for me to know that it is for me; his eyes slowly close and the line on the heart monitor goes flat. The AED is charged, the paddles are applied, and the resulting shock sends my father's body arching off the gurney. The line remains flat. A second charge, then a third getting the same results. My head droops and my arms go limp. I know I need to communicate to my team but the words, "Let's call it," won't form. The only sound in the room is the steady trill from the heart monitor. This time, the tears in the room are mine. Confused eyes peer at me; no one understands what is happening to their resident physician on call. I bend over one last time and kiss my patient on the cheek. "Good-bye, Dad," is all I can utter. I hear gasps as the nurses realize this case was special. They try to console me, but the moment is awkward at best. After a few hugs, I ask for a few moments of privacy. They quickly exit and close the curtains around us, leaving my father and me alone for the first time in years.

"You know, Dad, I really did get it. If I climbed out of my little boy heart, I knew how much Mom needed you, and saw how lonely she got when you were gone. I think you knew it too. You gave her all the attention you could when you came home. Even though I needed you too, you saw me as the stronger of me and Mom. You knew that I could get through the weekend and the time you would be gone without the extra attention. So, you gave it where it was needed most. It's easier to understand now than when I was a kid, but I really do get it. I always held out hope that someday we would have this conversation together, but it never happened. I suppose you were right. I will be fine. It doesn't mean that I love you any less or didn't miss you when you were gone. I love you, Dad. You can finally rest now." With that, my head drops into my hands as I cry softly next to the man I never really got to know, holding his hand in mine, crying tears that had been held back almost thirty years.

A hand settles on my shoulder. "I'm so sorry, Dylan."

"Thank you, Kathy. I still can't believe it's really him lying here."

"I'm sorry to bother you at a time like this, but do you want to hold off on the death certificate?"

"To be honest, Kathy, I'm not sure I should sign off on it at all, considering. Ask Dr. Riley if he wouldn't mind. If he is reluctant, I will take care of it."

"I will. Can I get you anything?"

"No thanks. I'll be okay." I hand the medical chart back to Kathy and stand up, looking down at my father one last time. I turn and pull back the curtain, only to see my mother standing at the glass watching me. Her skin is pale with a look of panic in her eyes. I slowly pass through the double doors leading to the waiting area. To my left is the EMT named Adam, consoling another woman. I nod to him but keep moving toward my mother. It all feels like a dream, like I'm simply drifting in space. The sounds of the night fade away to a low hum. Despite being only a few feet from Mom, the walk seems to take hours. Her arms reach out for me and mine to hers. We connect in silence at first before I can utter any sound at all. "I'm sorry, Mom. He's gone."

I can feel her knees give way as she falls into my arms. Her sobs turning to wails as reality sets in. She feels so thin in my arms, as if a slight wind could blow her away. I guide her toward a set of chairs along the wall, holding her closely as her tears mix freely with my own. Her entire body shakes next to mine. All the years spent waiting by the window for him to come home, the lonely nights wondering when our lives would become more normal, the years raising her son on her own, all the doubt, all the pain is now pouring from her body. All I can do is hold her, be there for her, let it drain from her. "I got you, Mom. I got you." Time seems to pass blindly around us.

After what seems an eternity, a new hand rests on my shoulder again. It belongs to Lisa, another nurse from my team. "Doctor, may I have a word?"

I raise my hands along my mother's arms and pull away gently. "I will be right back, Mom." She leans her head against the wall while wrapping hers arms around her frail frame. I step away and lean down toward my nurse. "Yes, Lisa, what is it?"

She stands on her toes to get closer, "Doctor, that's the family of the man we just had in room one. They are asking what happened. I told them you might be able to talk to them for a minute or two."

My eyes move slowly across the room as my body straightens. Adam and who I assume is his mother are watching my every move, staring at me. What do you mean his family? I am his family. I barely know Adam and have never met this woman. I don't understand. I look back at my mother who is still lost in her grief then back at the waiting scene before me, then back at Lisa. It's as if my world as I know it is about to shift, that the next step I take will lead me down a road I have no map for. I'm frozen in place.

"Doctor? What should I tell them?"

"Lisa, would you stay here and keep my mother company for a few minutes?"

"Yes, of course, whatever you need."

I move slowly, looking over at my mother. "I'll be right back, Mom. Lisa will call me if you need anything." The waiting area isn't that large but the walk across the room seems to be miles long. Halfway there, I stop, every bone in my body wanting to turn and run straight out the door. I turn back to my mother and see her watching my every step. At the other end of the room, a woman wearing tennis clothes waits with her son, Adam, still in his uniform, watching my movement as well. It feels like I'm walking along the top of a dam, trying to get from one side to the other in full awareness that I could tumble down the side into the murky water below. Most of me wants to get to the other side while a small part of me hopes the collapse, or the tumble, comes sooner rather than later. It doesn't feel like there will be a good outcome, however it goes.

After a few more steps, I freeze. Like being struck by lightning, all the pieces drop in together. All of my life, all of my mother's life suddenly makes sense. More importantly, the life of the man lying dead just a few yards away becomes crystal clear and the picture of the man makes me both angry and nauseous at the same time. I know, without a doubt, that my suspicions will become reality in the moments to follow.

As I approach the couple, they both stand. Adam reaches his hand out to shake mine. "Hello, Doctor, this is my mother Ann."

"Hello, Ann." We shake hands as well. "What can I do for you, Adam?"

"Can you fill us in on what happened with my dad?" he replied.

"The last patient you brought in?"

"Yes, Doctor."

"He was your father and your husband?" I ask, turning from Adam to Ann.

Adam's head cocks as he looks at me strangely. "Is there something wrong, Doctor?"

"Possibly," I reply, slightly stammering. "Well, first, you have my deepest sympathy, but it appears as if the patient you brought in suffered a heart attack while jogging. I'm sorry to tell you he didn't survive. We did everything we could to save him." My head is spinning as I turn my body, facing my mother once again. She has stood and appears to be waiting for me to say something. I spin back around.

"Ann, you say this man is your husband?"

"Doctor!" Adam yells, taking a step toward me.

His mother places a hand on Adam's arm to pull him back. "Yes, Doctor. My husband for thirty years. Why would you ask that, at a time like this?"

I spin again. My mother is now standing fully erect and appears to be a step closer than at my last glance. I shake my head to clear the ever-growing cobwebs.

"Excuse me, Ann, for the questions but please tell me, did your husband travel a lot?"

A surprised Ann begins to look alarmed. "Yes, he did, if you must know."

"I'm not asking to be disrespectful in any way, please believe me. This is very difficult and is only going to get worse. One last question, did he travel so much that he was only able to come home about every other weekend?" The slot machine inside my head is spinning as the cylinders slow and as they do, click into place on the screen. Questions left unasked or answered suddenly appear to have solutions I never expected. The why and how of his life becoming clear.

Adam again steps forward, anger burning in his eyes, "Doctor! I demand to know, right now, why you're asking all these questions."

I stare at Adam, absolutely sure that the next words I speak will shatter the worlds of almost everyone in the room. I hesitate, stumble and stutter, looking for what to say next.

"Please answer my question first, every other weekend?"

"Yes, every other weekend," Ann said softly in anticipation of my next words.

"Now my question," demanded Adam.

"Because for every *other* weekend," my hands start to tremble as my mouth goes dry," the weekends when he wasn't your husband and your father, the dead man on the table in there was my father and her husband," pointing back to my mother, "for the last thirty-one years...the last *thirty-one years.* That son of a bitch!"

Silence. Absolute dead silence. Everyone in the room wears frozen looks of shock. Adam's eyes scour the floor, head shaking, looking up at the glass that separates all of us from the body of the man that caused the shock wave. He looks to be seconds away from sprinting for the door of the trauma room, ready to pummel his father's remains. Ann drops back into her chair with a kaleidoscope of emotions swirling across her face. Her sad blue eyes are highlighted by her reddened skin, her lips tight with anger. Her hands begin to shake. Behind me, my mother stops in her tracks, leaving Lisa far behind. Her face is blank, impossible to read. Her hands hang by her side, her eyes lock on mine, searching to find some meaning to what she just heard. I slowly look back at the pair before me.

"Did you know?" Adam asked quietly.

"Honestly, Adam, I had no idea. It just all came together at this moment. I know it's shocking but suddenly everything in my life makes sense for the first time. Why he was never around when I needed him, why I knew so little about his business, why we would go days without hearing from him. The monster juggled two families and not for a short period of time, not a year or two but for over thirty freakin' years. It all makes sense now."

"You know what, Doctor?"

"Please call me Dylan."

"You know what, Dylan? I understand that his heart gave out, but I don't think it was his intention to live out the night under any circumstances."

"I don't understand," I reply.

Adam turns around and goes back to his seat. He picks up a manila envelope and pulls out what looks like a letter and four envelopes. "He left these on the driver's seat of his car. There is a letter to me and these four envelopes, one for my mom, one for you and I'm guessing this one is for you." Adam reached out and handed an envelope to my mother who had joined our group.

"I believe he was planning on ending his life tonight and that I was to become his mailman. It looks like fate took away his choice. I'm sure these are goodbye letters. Maybe he knew his heart was failing, maybe he wanted to say goodbye, maybe he was just nothing but a coward and couldn't face anybody with the truth. You are right, Dylan. We have all been making excuses for him for years. Now, all the trips, all the absences, all the excuses piled on top of excuses make sense. I simply can't believe it. I don't want to have to believe it, yet I know it's true."

I remain locked in my place. My mother puts her arm around me as her eyes focus on the terrazzo floor. I reach to extend a hand to Adam. He takes it as we shake hands for the second time. I attempt to smile; awkwardly at best, not totally sure I have pulled it off. Adam shakes my hand again and returns a smile as forced as my own.

Mom brushes slowly past me and moves toward Ann, who turns to stand face to face with my mother. Mom takes a step closer and reaches out to Ann. They gently, awkwardly, wrap their arms around each other. Not a word, not a smile or a tear. Just the two wives of one man, holding each other, offering support to each other. Neither blamed the other; there was no anger or shame. Both were victims, both duped by a man who had mastered the art of duplicity, who was able to maintain two lives with two families for three decades without ever having any of them cross paths despite living only miles apart. Each woman devastated by the loss of a loving husband, reaches out to comfort the other for her loss. It's a shame he couldn't take his eyes off of himself long enough to realize what a lucky man he was to have been loved by two such souls. He certainly didn't deserve what either of his wives offered.

I look down at my letter, my name scribbled on the outside by his some-what familiar hand. The envelope shakes slightly as I hold it. I stuff it into the back pocket of my scrubs to be read later. Despite my familiarity of the workings of the human body, the working of the mind continues to amaze me. Had I not been the victim of such a ruse, I never would have believed it possible. I look up at the glass divider and watch as the nurses roll my father's death bed down the hall. Closing my eyes, I can visualize taking control of the gurney and pushing it out through the double doors, into the parking lot, down the street and into the traffic on Route 33. Certainly, a more fitting end.

My eyes reopen to the sight of the nurses disappearing down the hall. My fists are clenched as the rage boils inside of me. I want to scream but I can't, not here. Any respect I have ever had for the man is gone, with the last ounces of my love for him not far behind. How? How did we get here and how did he pull this off? How did the truth escape me? Escape all of us? Who was this man I called Dad?

CHAPTER ELEVEN
ANNIE

———•———

Numbness. My hands are on the steering wheel, but they seem disconnected from my arms. My foot is jammed down on the accelerator, pushing my car forward as fast as it is will go. There is sound coming from my stereo system that should be words and melody...but it is all a faint background buzz. I feel like an astronaut strapped into my seat awaiting blast off with no control over the outcome of my voyage. Yes, Houston, we do have a problem.

I am confident of my ability to handle crises either at home or at work. In truth, however, I have never faced the loss of a loved one, someone on whom happiness and my grounding depend. Adam sounded scared, more frightened than I have ever heard him. I have no doubt at all that this is serious, profoundly serious. The weight of the moment has served to unhinge me in a way I didn't think was possible. It's true that my husband and I spend less than a hundred nights together per year. It's true I don't need him financially to survive. It's also true that my social world would also survive just fine without my marriage. But to lose my husband, to wake up without the anticipation of his next arrival, to not feel his skin against mine again would tragically end a part of who I am. Despite multiple opportunities, I have never strayed on my marriage vows, never even imagined another man's touch.

I would still be a CEO, mom, and tennis champion, but those parts of me are mere satellites to the woman who loves her man.

His appearance in my life was unexpected, and I'm still taken aback at the memory of the sudden appearance of his handsome, smiling face, and more so by the mutual connection that I know we both felt. I never had a shortage of suitors, but none of those dates ever became serious or lasted more than a month or two. Jesse was a whole different creature. He was older than me by a few years. I was still a senior in college and Jesse was already making his mark in the manufacturing community. He was extremely busy and in high demand professionally, but he always made me feel like I was the center of his universe.

I was a tennis player even back then, playing for the Niagara University team for three years and I also played in every singles tournament I could qualify for. I was good but not good enough to earn the chance to play professionally. It was during the annual MUNY tournament, probably the most prestigious event in Buffalo, that he first caught my eye. I was playing an average opponent in the second round at Delaware Park. Jesse seemed to be watching my every move, even during breaks. His ever-observing eyes unnerved me, even to the point of helping me to lose a set to an opponent I should have been crushing. Losing that set woke me back up and with new focus I went on to win the match. As I packed up my equipment, he came over and introduced himself. He pulled out a pen and two of his calling cards and asked me to write my number on the back of one and to keep the other.

It took less than twenty-four hours for him to call and less than another day for our first kiss. It was almost magical. We became inseparable and following my graduation from Niagara the next summer, we were married. The arrangement was never ideal, with his traveling as much as he did, but we made the best

92

of every moment together. With his job and me starting a career at Libracon, there was a constant demand on our time, we quickly learned the value of quality over quantity. Four years into our marriage, our first and only major bump in the road came with my pregnancy. With a child on the way, I knew my life would change drastically. I assumed Jesse would change his as well to accommodate his growing family. He didn't. His travel didn't diminish a bit and, it may have even increased. I was hurt and confused. For his part, while Jesse didn't decrease his travel, when he was home, he went out of his way to make his presence focused, more romantic, maybe even more attentive if that was possible. I grew to accept this as our permanent way of life.

When Adam finally arrived, I couldn't have been happier. Jesse took a week off from work and helped us get settled with our new addition. Following that week, he was back on his every-two-week schedule. I adjusted. I learned how to manage my new roles as wife, mother, and employee. As has always been my way, I excelled in all three. Through our thirty-one years of marriage and the twenty-five years since our last fight, I have never, not for a minute, regretted marrying Jesse. He is the source of my greatest joy and he has always treated me as his queen, pampered me, loved me, and never failed to make me smile, even laugh out loud. The gap caused by his long absences was more than compensated for by the wonderful son that we share. Adam being Adam made up for his father's busy work schedule.

Surely this won't be the end. Maybe Adam is just being dramatic. He will meet me and escort me in to talk to Jesse, sitting up in bed waiting for me to take him home. All the rest doesn't matter. Not even the, "What are you doing in Buffalo?" question. Plans change all the time. Maybe he caught an early flight home. Maybe the email was sent to set up a surprise he had intended for me. Maybe I'm worrying over nothing. Calm down, Annie. Take a deep breath. Nothing is ever as bad as it seems at first glance.

My car curves up the ramp to Route 33, taking no regard for the drivers who seem to feel that they have as much right to the road as I do. My peripheral vision is shrinking down to the tunnel directly before me. I see no signs or buildings as they fly by me. My eyes glance at the road while searching the horizon on my left for any sign of the Erie County Medical Center. I have lost track of time and distance, existing on the hope that the ten or twelve stories of the hospital will stand out among the houses that fill the neighborhood, enough to grab my attention and direct me to my family.

There it is, emerging from above the trees. I cut hard across two lanes of traffic and bounce up to the exit ramp to Grider Street. I ignore the red light at the top of the ramp and make a hard left onto the city street. The bright green letters, ECMC, are high above me on the right. I see the sign for the emergency area and turn into the ramp, seemingly on two wheels. I pull in the first parking space directly across from the double-glass-door entrance. I sit frozen behind the wheel with my sweat-soaked palms still wrapped around the wheel, not wanting to move, wanting to maintain the fantasy of life that was familiar for just one more minute. Maybe if I just sit here this will all go away, like a bad dream. A man in a uniform, probably security, looks in the driver's side and knocks on the window.

"Lady, you okay?" All I can do is turn to him and nod. My fingers reach for the door latch as he steps back to give me room to stand up. The door opens wide as I slowly swing my legs out and set my feet on the pavement. He reaches out a hand to help pull me up and out of the driver's seat, but I ignore it as I lift myself out of the car. Over his shoulder, I can see Adam leaning up against the wall of the emergency room entrance. As soon as he sees me stand, he moves quickly, jogging to my side. Seeing him, the security guard steps back and watches our embrace before returning to his station.

I hadn't noticed my lack of tears to this point but no sooner do I feel Adam's arms around me than my guard drops, and the water begins to flow. While his hug is reassuring, his words are not. All he can say is to brace myself for the worst, that things don't look good.

The world seems out of focus, as if I'm wearing someone else's glasses. Adam guides me across the pavement and up the curb toward the door. The glass doors sweep to welcome us on our slow march. The waiting area is empty. Even the receptionist has left her desk. It feels like I am drifting, like my feet never touch the floor. Gliding along from glass door to glass wall, I notice is that all the activity is focused on a small area behind the glass wall that is surrounded by a curtain. Doctors and nurses are racing around in some choreographed dance. The curtain slides back and there is my Jesse. He is surrounded by white uniforms. Naked from the waist up, his arm falls off the table and hangs limply, almost lifeless until scooped up by a nurse and placed softly back on the gurney.

His head is turned slowly, and our eyes connect. Is that the beginning of a smile forming on his handsome face? It's a look I have seen so many times before, usually in the morning when I wake before him, watching him slowly leave dreamland behind. He would look around at our bedroom as the memory of our lovemaking the night before lights up his face with the same smile I can see now. It is a smile of contentment, satisfaction and what I believe is his love for me. Why can't this be every morning? What is so important that draws him from my arms for such long periods of time? He slowly looks back at me and our eyes lock, his arms drawing me closer, feeling his skin against mine. His hands begin to pick up where he left off the night before. My eyes close at his touch.

When they open again, I'm back in the emergency room at ECMC, looking through the smudged glass at where the strangers are trying to save my husband's life. A new piece of equipment is rolled inside the curtain. Jesse's eyes seem to fade, but still reach out to me, not wanting to close, to leave me behind from his next journey. The nurses in the room step back as paddles are set against my husband's chest. His body leaps violently then drops back. Nothing. He leaps again in response to another jolt. Same conclusion. A third time and then nothing. No movement, nothing but silence. The doctor leans over and hugs my Jesse. Why would he do that? Adam's sobs fill my ears. I turn to him and we emotionally collapse in each other's arms. Adam pulls back and leads me to a small bench where we sit and hold each other for what feels like an eternity.

My mind returns to the burning question that drove with me along the 33: What is Jesse doing here? He was supposed to be on a plane coming home from the West Coast, not lying on his death bed. Why did he lie to me? I have never found a reason not to believe him about anything in our marriage. Was this just a small glitch? Is there a simple explanation?

The moment is broken by Adam moving away from our bench. I can't comprehend what is going on until he comes back with Will. Oh, poor Will. He is crying even more than we are. I know we have been like a family to him, but I never would have expected a reaction like this. He settles on the bench next to me while Adam stands in front of us, bent over with his hands on his knees. I keep my arms around Will as his body continues to shudder from tears that show no sign of slowing. How is it that he happened to find us? Did Adam call him too? Like every moment of this evening since my phone rang, nothing is making sense. All forms of communication seem to have abandoned me, making me lose hope of understanding any of it.

The moment is broken by the sound of a deep voice, calling out my son's name. Adam acknowledges the stranger and tells me he will be right back. As I nod acceptance, Will turns his head, and sees the man in uniform walk out the door with Adam. Almost as if someone flipped a switch, Will's heaving sobs end, followed by him sitting up straight while watching Adam and the officer walk away. I can feel Will's whole body stiffen as he pulls away from my arms. The grief has left his face and is replaced by what almost seems to be fear. I have never known this boy to be anything less than self-confident, almost cocky in his self-assuredness. To see him frozen by fear in a moment like this seems unnatural. There have been many times that I wished that Adam had Will's strength, and yet here we are in a crisis and Will seems to be jumping from grief to fear. I look through the glass doors, anxious for Adam's return, suddenly unsure of the young man sitting next to me.

Minutes feel like hours before the doors slide back open and Adam walks back in alone. He is carrying a large manila envelope that has his full attention, moving it up and down like he is trying to judge its weight. He walks slowly back to me. Next to me, Will is trying to look around Adam toward the door. Is he looking for the police officer? As he looks, he sees a police car drive past the window and down the ramp through the parking lot and back onto Grider. Will appears to relax, an invisible weight seemingly lifted from his shoulders. He stands, leans down to give me a kiss on the forehead and then turns and hugs Adam, crushing the envelope between them. He whispers something in Adam's ear and walks slowly through the glass door and into the night.

Just as the glass doors close, they slide back open again. Through them walks a woman, unsure of her next step. She has a timid nature about her. She glides slowly to the window where we stood only moments ago. She looks around, unsure of what to do next. She looks into the cubicle where Jesse still lies. Then she looks back at me. Something strikes me, like she is familiar to me in some way, like we have crossed paths before. I can't put a finger on it, but I know that I have seen her in some other setting. Maybe in a picture or online somewhere. Maybe even in a dream. She walks slowly to the windows and looks around the working area of the emergency room. She looks up as if she recognizes someone. She offers a slight smile and a nod.

The door to the inner rooms opens and the doctor walks out, the one that had been hugging my dead husband moments ago. He shares something with the woman, and she breaks down in his arms, falling against him. Her sobs grow louder until they fill the waiting room, each one cutting through me. He guides her to a set of chairs along the wall and holds her closely.

The confusion that rode in the car with me continues to grow. It has now reached full blossom, all the questions a new petal all its own. Why is my husband home so early and why didn't I know that he was in town? Why is the doctor who tried to save his life so passionately now offering his support to another woman? Was there another death here earlier and his family member just arrived? Did he mistake her for me? The doctor appears as distraught as the woman, tears decorating the front of his hospital garb. I don't understand any of this. No, not at all. Losing the man of my dreams, moments ago, only to have to watch this scene unfold before me? It's like a nightmare.

The door to the examining room opens again and a nurse walks into the waiting room. She steps in slowly and looks around the room, looking first at the doctor and the woman and then at Adam and me. She walks over to Adam and gives him a hug.

"Adam, I am so sorry for your loss. I know how much your family means to you," she says.

"Thank you, Lisa. This is my mom. Mom, this is Lisa, we used to work together," Adam replied. "Can you tell us what happened?"

"You know what, let me get the doctor. He should be the one to share the details with you." She puts her hand on Adam's arm then walks over and gives me a gentle hug, which I return as best I can. She turns and walks slowly across the room to the doctor and the woman he continues to console. She gets close, then puts her hand on the doctor's shoulder. He turns his head and looks up at the nurse, tears streaming down his face. She whispers a few words in his ear and steps back. The doctor places his hands on the crying woman's arms and speaks to her softly before standing up and away from her, his back to us and now alone with the nurse.

The nurse begins to talk to him and as she does, points across to us. Adam has rejoined me on the bench with his arm around me. The doctor's head snaps around, and he stares at us, a look of total confusion coming over him. He uses his sleeve to wipe his wet face. He turns slowly back to the nurse, who then repeats her motions, pointing at Adam and me. She looks up at him unsure of what else to say. The doctor puts his hands on the nurse's shoulders and his head drops between his arms before slowly straightening up. He looks over at the woman who has turned her face away from the room, still sobbing. He steps over and takes the woman in his arms and leads her to a chair nearby. He gently sits her down, whispering something into her ear. He then straightens up, looking at the nurse first, and then back at us. He turns his body to face us but hesitates, seemingly not willing to take the next step.

At that moment, everything around me changes, absolutely everything. The world seems to stop spinning as my soul drifts upward and away from my physical body. Adam still holds me, but I can't feel his presence. The people across the room have frozen in place, like in a piece of art, with one woman holding her head in her hands, a woman in a uniform still pointing at us while another man in a uniform stands still, growing in stature by the second, facing us as if he is about to charge across a bull ring. I don't see a weapon in his hands, but I have no doubt that whatever he wields will alter my body, my life, maybe even my will to live. He won't be attacking the walls of my castle, but he will remove its foundation, causing everything as I know it to collapse. I am floating above the scene, distant and apart, not wanting to know what happens next. I sense what is about to happen and fear has taken control of me. I want to run from the attack, never to know the outcome to the battle. I want to cease to be.

The room begins to spin at an increasing rate. Adam turns with a concerned look, calling out to me. The words lack meaning, garbled beyond recognition. He grabs me in his arms again as my eyes begin to close; my head begins to drop backwards against the wall as the world turns to black. Then nothing.

Oh Jesse, don't leave me. Please come back. I need you now more than ever. Help me; protect me. Don't let them take away the image of what we have shared all these long years. It's bad enough that you are gone, don't let them turn my memories of you to dust. Somehow, I know what's coming, what he is going to say, who that woman is...and I need you to be here with me to reassure me that none of it is true, that they are making a huge mistake. Please, Jesse. I need you. Please, my darling. Please.

CHAPTER TWELVE
MARY BETH

———•———

Despite all you hear about Buffalo winters, summer couldn't be better anywhere else with its moderate temperatures, cool evenings, reasonable amounts of rain. It is easily my favorite time of year. This night is like so many others with a bright moon and light breezes and temperatures still in the seventies. Sitting in my BMW with all the windows down, what little wind exists moves slowly through my car. Traffic drones quietly in the background.

I'm doing what I can to stay calm, trying not to over-react to what I am about to face. It could be nothing. Maybe Jay just passed out, got dehydrated while jogging. Dylan did say to hurry but that doesn't mean the worst. Maybe it just means that Jay wants to get released from the hospital, and they are waiting for me to arrive. None of that explains why he is in town jogging when he just left two days ago. He is not supposed to be back for another ten days. Come on now Mary Beth, don't jump to conclusions here. He will have a simple explanation. He always does.

The light from the hospital parking lot shines through my open windows. A moth flitters in then flitters right back out again. A horn honks in the distance. A siren disrupts the quiet of the night. My knee accidently brushes against my key chain looped around the gear shift, sending it falling to the floor. I'm stalling; mostly out of fear and a lack of confidence. I have a horrible sense about what I'm about to find. I need to go inside and find out what is going on. Dylan will explain it all. He is such a good son. I just wish he could find some peace with his father. It's not too much to ask. Can't he have peace with his father and peace in our family? Okay, Mary Beth, get moving.

I close all the windows one at a time and pull the latch to open my door. I swing my legs out and stand upright on the pavement then bend over to give my hair a once-over in the car's side mirror. I take a mint out of my purse to freshen my breath and then turn toward the emergency room door. As I move toward the glass doors, I can see two men saying goodbye to each other outside the double doors, one in a police uniform and the other in some other kind of uniform, maybe a fireman or an EMT. The police officer leaves and the EMT turns to go inside. I begin my walk, slowed by a building fear. The waiting area is mostly empty with just one woman about my age, sitting on a bench in the waiting room crying. Next to her is a younger man who is also crying but much harder. The EMT appears to be with them. Whatever news they received, I'm glad I'm not them. The only staff I see are nurses moving in and out of a trauma area that is enclosed by blue curtains suspended from a track in the ceiling.

There are no other hospital employees around, so I walk up to the row of windows along one wall of the waiting room in hope of finding a staff person to help me. As I wait at the window, I see a nurse rolling a cart with machines on it out of the trauma area. As she does, the curtains stay open long enough for me to see Dylan bending over his patient. He looks upset, as if he is crying. Oh, please God no, tell me that isn't my husband on that table. My shaking hands move up and cover my mouth and what must be a look of horror on my face. This can't be happening. Another nurse passes through the curtain and this time, Dylan looks up before the curtains close again. He sees me. I know he does. The curtains part again and this time my handsome son emerges, looking in my direction and giving me a quick nod. He walks out through another set of double doors, moving quickly in my direction. He takes me in his arms and holds me tight.

"I'm sorry, Mom, he's gone."

The words cut through me like a chain saw. My knees start to give out and Dylan responds, holding me up before I can fall. I let out a wail that I would not have recognized as my own. I can't catch my breath; I am gasping for air. Dylan leads me to a set of chairs and helps me sit down. Then he just holds me, lets me sob. I don't have any questions…all I know is that my husband is never coming home again, not next weekend, not ever. How will I survive without him? How can I even live a life that doesn't include his smile, his laugh, his calming touch?

Time becomes a stranger. I can't begin to guess how many minutes pass in my son's arms. Every memory stored away of our family time together comes rushing back. Jay's deep love for me, the day we met, his proposal, our marriage, the day Dylan was born. All moments flying across the screen in my mind, one sweet memory after another.

Dylan starts to pull away, breaking me from my trance. A young nurse taps him on the shoulder.

"I'll be right back, Mom."

I watch him intently. The nurse whispers something in his ear and points across the room at the woman I had noticed before, except now she is sitting with the man in the EMT uniform. Dylan stands up straight and stares at the couple, then he looks slowly back at me with a very strange look on his face; one I have never seen before. Then his gaze turns slowly back to the couple across the room. He turns to the nurse, responding to her.

"Mom, I have to go take care of something. Lisa will stay here with you until I get back. Are you okay with that?"

"Go, honey. I will be all right."

Lisa smiles and sits down next to me. She puts her hand on my arm where it rests upon my lap. I acknowledge her, but my attention stays on Dylan. No matter what was wrong with our marriage, we sure produced an amazing son. I'm so proud of the man he has become. He starts to move confidently across the room until he once again stops and glances back at me with the same look on his face. This time it affects me so deeply; I feel compelled to stand up with Lisa rising with me. Whoever these people are, and whatever Dylan is doing, somehow, I know...this has something to do with me, with my family.

As Dylan starts to talk to the couple, I can sense an electricity between them. The EMT appears to be getting angry, shifting his weight from foot to foot. Once again, Dylan looks back at me, confirming that my instinct was right. This does have something to do with me. I pat Lisa on the hand to assure her that I'm all right while thanking her for the attentiveness she has shown me.

"Go on back to work, Lisa. I'm really fine."

"If you're sure. I don't mind staying."

"I'm good. I'll tell Dylan I sent you away." I pat her shoulder this time and take two steps away from her. I look back to watch her disappear through the double doors then turn my focus to the conversation across the room. I'm magnetically pulled toward this family, closing the distance between us. After several more steps, I'm close enough to hear every word of the conversation.

"Because for every other weekend," Dylan begins, "the weekends when he wasn't your husband and your father, the dead man on the table in there was my father and her husband," pointing back to me, "for the last thirty-one years...the last *thirty-one years*. That son of a bitch!"

The words strike at me like a hammer. Can this possibly be true? The man I adored, the man I waited for, pined for, the man who said he loved me, who told me I was the perfect wife, shared himself with another family of his own creation, not just for a month or two but for the entire *thirty-one years* of our marriage? I was a good wife. I raised our son on my own, kept his home for him and all this time I only had half of him. When you add in his business, far less than half of him.

And to think that all this time I saw myself as the problem, a woman not worthy of his attention, incapable of being enough to keep him home, to adjust his life to his family's needs. I felt like such a failure throughout my marriage, like I simply wasn't good enough. I found a way to medicate my pain. I drank to feel worthy, to bolster my confidence, to fill my loneliness. And for what? For him?

I look back at the woman across from me. She is standing so tall, so confident. Stunningly beautiful and in such great shape. She is the woman he went home to on my "off" weekend. What I wouldn't give to feel half as strong as she looks. And yet, every other weekend he left her alone to be with me, so in the end it didn't matter who I was or who she was. If we were both strong and beautiful or both weak and unsure of ourselves, he still would have bounced back and forth between us. This was all about him and never, *never* about her or me or our successes or failures as wives. It was his inability to be a husband and a father. I didn't deserve this and neither did she. Neither did my son.

Wait. Is that her son? My husband's son? My Dylan's half-brother? Oh my God! Not only did James cheat on his wives, but he also cheated on his sons. He couldn't have been there for his children any more than he was for his wives. The enormity of this realization floors me.

"It was never about me. I was a good wife. I never failed," I said out loud to no one in particular. I felt my arms go ramrod-straight at my side; my fists clenched. Standing as tall as I can with my head tipped back and my eyes closed, I professed the truth out loud. "There was never anything wrong with me except trusting the wrong man."

At that moment, standing as alone in the world as any one woman can feel, I sense an adrenaline rush starting in my head and spreading heat throughout my body. I feel a powerful wave of light filling every cell, filling me with a sense of warmth and relief unlike anything I had ever known. Then, as quickly as it had started, it's gone. Standing alone, a mere five feet behind my son, I suddenly feel something I hadn't experienced in the last three decades. I am at peace. Totally at peace. No anger, no loss, no mourning. It's as if my soul had somehow been cleansed by the surprising revelation of Jay's dishonesty, the awareness of my blamelessness and strangely enough, by his death.

I step up next to my son and put my arm around his waist. The young EMT is speaking, but I'm really not listening closely. The next thing I know, the EMT is handing me an envelope with my name on it written in my dead husband's handwriting. How unusually thoughtful of him. There is nothing in this envelope I care to read, nothing he can say that would allow me to forgive him, no excuse possible to justify anything he has done to my family. In my newly-found peace, I have absolutely no interest in explanations or apologies. I only want to look forward and not backward even for the time it takes to read this letter. Any control he had over me is over.

What I can do is help the woman across from me who is in so much pain. She has been looking at me as if I'm some sort of monster, the creator of all her agony. She reads her envelope then dramatically tears it into small pieces, throwing the scraps on the ground and stomping on them. I step forward and toss my unopened letter in a nearby waste basket and then move gently forward and reach out to her. She looks up at me as tears refill her eyes. I take one more step and open my arms to her. "I am so sorry for all of this," are all the words I can find.

"Me too," is her soft reply as she falls into my arms, weeping against my shoulder. For my part, there are no more tears. I hold her tight while she sobs, stroking her back with one hand while the fingers of my other hand run through her long hair. Her body is stiff at first then slowly softens against mine. Neither of us is in a rush to end our hug as more reality awaits on the other side. That, plus neither of us want to be the one to end it. The EMT comes over and puts his hand on his mother's shoulder. The woman gently releases herself from my arms to be in his.

I walk slowly over to the glass wall and look in at the blue curtains surrounding the lifeless body of my husband. Dylan walks up behind me and places an arm around my waist. "Do you want to go in and say goodbye to him?" he asks.

"You know what, honey, I have already said enough goodbyes to that man to last me a lifetime. I don't really think one more will matter, do you?" We hug again and I kiss him on the cheek. "Thank you for understanding, Dylan."

"I understand completely. I think you are being far more accepting of what has happened than I ever could if I were in your shoes. Let's go say our goodbyes." We walk back to my husband's other family and go through another round of hugs. Dylan and the EMT make arrangements for the four of us to meet for breakfast the following morning to discuss final arrangements. I doubt whether any of us will get much sleep between now and then, but we set a time for ten in the morning. Dylan and I remain arm in arm as we watch them walk out the door holding hands.

"Mom, they will call in another doctor to replace me, but I can't leave until he gets here. Why don't you wait in the doctor's lounge until my replacement comes in? Then I can drive you home."

"You know what, Dylan, I think I'm fine to drive home on my own. I really am. Why don't you finish up here then come home? We can go to the restaurant together in the morning."

"Are you sure you're okay to drive? It won't take long for the next doctor to get here. I don't want you to be alone right now."

It's hard to hide my smile. "Don't be silly, Dylan. Your father left me alone through most of his life. Being alone in his death means nothing. I promise you I'll be fine. If I feel any unexpected emotions sneaking in, I promise to call and wait for you to rescue me, but I don't expect any."

We hug one last time before I turn and stroll through the double automatic doors. I nod to the security guard as I step off the curb and across the marked pavement to my awaiting BMW convertible. Back in the driver's seat, I lower all the windows and recline the seat back just a little, dropping my head against the cushion and taking in a deep breath. The night is quiet, leaving me alone in my thoughts. I arrived here tonight a concerned wife and mother, my thoughts on everyone else, as usual. Now, I am here for me, secretly enjoying the moment, feeling free of the woe-is-me elephant that has hunched on my shoulders for decades, free of the high mountain of low self-worth that I have been forced to scale on a daily basis ever since Jay began his bi-weekly visits.

The shower of peace I felt in the waiting room returns to bathe me in comfort, one I hadn't felt since the days of being courted by my husband-to-be. I have no idea what my future has in store for me, but I'm surprisingly excited at the prospect of setting my own path...for me, just for me. I should hate Jay for the time he stole from me. I should be just as furious as his other wife, but I'm not. There is nothing I can change about the past or about my marriage. All I can do is move forward and get on with my life, without a husband (or a bottle) to lean on to get me through the next hour or the hour after that or the hour after that.

No more, never again.

The quiet night is shattered by a screaming siren as an ambulance explodes into the ramp servicing the emergency room. In my side-view mirror, I can see the attendants racing around the ambulance, tearing open the back doors and dragging a gurney to the concrete slab. Nurses run out to meet them and trailing the nurses by a few feet is my Dylan. He has moved onto his next patient and left the previous one behind. Good for him, good for me.

I reset the seat to its driving position and back slowly out of my parking space and continue down the circular drive back on to Grider St. Looking in the rearview mirror, I reach up to adjust it and get a quick glance of myself looking back at me. The edges of my mouth are turned up just a bit, just short of a smile. It's not a smile of happiness, simply one of peace.

Gary Friedman

CHAPTER THIRTEEN
WILL

———— ·❖· ————

The distance from Delaware Park to my house can be measured in single digit minutes. I don't think I blinked more than twice. Each time I did, all I could imagine was the sight of Adam's dad watching me walk to my car. I can't say that I have ever been in shock, but this must be what it's like. More likely what a zombie feels like. Once I make it home and the door closes behind me, I begin pacing. Back and forth, from room to room, avoiding every mirror or reflective surface that might just force me to look at myself. What have I done? That wasn't me in the park, it couldn't have been. I don't do things like this, hurt another human being. I could go to prison for the rest of my life no matter how righteous I felt doing it. I just wanted to help people I loved, people who gave me a life, a family. I wanted to put them out of their misery. It was a noble act, right? What that man did to those two families was despicable. He deserved punishment. So, if what I did was a good thing, why do I feel so afraid and awful?

Shock is slowly giving way to panic. I really hadn't thought this thing through. I have to cover my tracks. Did I leave anything behind at the park? No, I'm sure I didn't. I took the needle with me and I wore gloves, just in case, so no fingerprints should show up anywhere. I didn't eat anything while I was there so no wrappers were left lying around. I didn't even spit while I was there. I'm sure no one saw me, not walking to or from my car; no cameras where I parked, I'm sure of it.

What about at my apartment? I put on another pair of gloves and scan everywhere for any clues that I might have left behind. I grab a plastic grocery bag and begin to fill it with anything that might be incriminating; the needle and the backup needles; the empty bottles of the drugs I used. I shredded the receipts for the stuff I bought and deleted my computer search history. I know there might still be incriminating evidence on my hard drive. I hope it doesn't go that far since all my landscaping business stuff is on that computer. I can't wipe out all my records; that would be just as suspicious.

But wait, what if Jesse didn't die? What if the mixture wasn't as foolproof as all the bragging on the internet claimed it was? What if he pulls through and remembers seeing me walk away, then what? More pacing, more sweating, even more pacing. I have to get out of here. They probably took him to ECMC. Maybe I should go there to find out if he survived the injection. I grab the plastic bag of evidence and start driving. I glance over at the bag on the passenger seat. What do I do with it? I scan the homes and businesses that line the street on the way to the hospital and spot a large blue Modern Disposal dumpster behind a Subway shop on Grider Street. Perfect. Plenty of traffic, so my car won't be noticed. Plenty of business so the garbage will be collected regularly. I pull close to the bin, leap out as fast as I can and throw the bag inside. OK. That task is done. On to ECMC.

Pulling into the circular driveway, I find a parking place as far away from the doors and cameras as possible. Wearing a dark pair of shorts, a plain t-shirt, equally plain wind breaker with sandals and a baseball cap pulled down over my eyes, I walk slowly through the double doors into the waiting area. Annie and Adam are standing by the window looking into the examination room. I move slowly into a darkened corner near the empty receptionist's desk. I want to console them, but I can't explain how I knew to be here, so I remain in the shadows.

Then, like a bolt of lightning, it happened. Annie, with hands over her face, lets out a gut-wrenching scream as she stumbles back from the window. She falls against Adam, her shoulders heaving against him. He leads her to a set of chairs along the far wall and just holds on to her. I am torn. Part of me wants to run to the people I love and do what I can to comfort them while another part wants to race out the door. If I did that, though, I would have to run right past them. That won't work. My emotions finally get the best of me as the tears begin to cascade down my face; tears of love, tears of loss, but mostly tears of guilt. I'm heartbroken and ashamed, deeply ashamed of what I have done. The one thing I didn't want to happen will happen anyway—being rejected by those that I love. Not by Adam and Annie's choice, but by mine. How can I ever face them, and not feel the shame I'm experiencing? I have truly ruined everything.

At that moment, still flooded by my own tears, a hand rests on my shoulder. I look up to find Adam inches away. "Will? Will, is that you? What are you doing here?" I try to form words, but none come. He takes me by the arm and leads me over to Annie. "Mom, look who's here. It's Will." She looks up at me through reddened eyes.

"Will, dear," is all she offers. I reach my hand out to her and she pulls me down onto the seat next to her. I match her tear for tear, sob for heart-wrenching sob. I notice the concept of time disappears as we hang onto each other for what seems like decades. She exchanges a few words with Adam but my ability to communicate is lost.

It is here that things go from incredibly bad to incredibly horrifying. Adam bends down and puts his hands on both of our shoulders and says, "Mom, I will be right back. Someone needs to talk to me." Annie straightens up and nods to her son as she glances up to the entrance. I sit up a bit too and follow her eyes. They lead me to a Buffalo police officer waiting at the door for Adam. My heart stops beating, and I'm sure all the blood drains from my face. They know. They must know. I have no idea what gave me away but it's over. Jail, a trial, and prison for the rest of my life. No one will understand and the people I love will hate me. I want to stand up and run out the door as fast as humanly possible and never see any of them again. I am doomed. Wait. What if they don't know it's me? Running for my life past the inquiring police would sure shine a klieg light on me. Stay put, Will. Wait this out.

After an eternity, Adam returns with a manila envelope in his hand. I look past him to the glass doors, but he is alone. No cop, no sirens, no posse, and no guns drawn. Air slowly creeps back into my lungs. As the terror subsides, the awkwardness soon follows. I lean in and kiss Annie on the forehead and then stand and give Adam a hug which quickly becomes a bear hug. I turn without a word and walk slowly out the sliding doors. I continue my pace as I walk down the sidewalk until I'm sure I'm out of range of the door cameras and sprint the rest of the way to my car. I pull onto Grider St., then move throughout the city from side street to side street, constantly checking my rear-view mirror until I'm sure no one is following me. The lights downtown remain bright. I find a place to park along a side street that will not get me noticed or ticketed. I stay in my car trying desperately to calm myself, dry my eyes, and try to look normal again. Once I have calmed down, I get out of my car and head for Main Street. I keep my head down and walk, constantly moving, trying not to bring any attention to myself. I say hello to no one, avoid eye contact and just keep moving.

I turn left on Main and just keep going, not in a hurry but not dragging either. I want…no, I need…to think…need to deal with the enormous lump that has formed in my gut. I want to blend in, not be noticed by anyone. Of course, at this hour on a weeknight, I won't be weaving through crowds. Empty shops and equally empty restaurants pass on both sides. A few teenagers are walking and laughing, and fewer homeless souls huddle up against buildings.

The surroundings begin to blur as my vision turns inward. First of all, I am a murderer. I never imagined that word applying to me but now that is all I can see about myself. How do I go back to my life as it was yesterday? Before I put this plan in motion, why didn't I take the time to see how all this would affect me and the people I love? I can't imagine my relationship with Adam ever being the same. How do I look him or Annie in the eye again? Is it possible to go back to being a landscaper and living a normal life? I don't know. I have employees, machinery and customers who depend on me. Why didn't I just focus on that and stay out of everyone else's business? It really wasn't my business. Even if I was the only person in the world who knew Jesse's secret it was stuff that he needed to work out with Adam, Annie, and Mary Beth. My business was starting to grow, my life was coming together. I let everything get out of hand.

Now, I'm a walking zombie overdosed on guilt. I have to unload this somehow, but who can I possibly talk to? I can't just find a shrink and say, "Hi, I'm Will and I'm a murderer." I don't think that falls under doctor/patient privilege. Tears begin to fall again as I think of watching my favorite people in the world discover that their husband and father is gone. I am a blind fool. I pull my hat down further over my eyes to cover my shame but to no avail. The front of my shirt is spotted with moisture and the back of my hands are damp from wiping my running nose. The knot in my stomach grows bigger, causing me to stop and double over. A couple of punks walk past me and find my condition funny, assuming I'm just another homeless drunk. Off to my left is a planter and I run to it as the contents of my stomach leave me. My hands hold me up against the planter, until the last wretch is over. I drop down onto the sidewalk and push my back up against the building. My body aches as my hands shake and the tears continue to fall.

Twenty minutes (or was it twenty hours?) later, I push myself back onto my feet and continue walking toward Harbor Center, struggling to bring my breathing back to normal. After another fifteen minutes of walking, I turn around and start to retrace my steps back up Main Street. As my physical symptoms subside, I try once again to weigh my options. The first thing I have to deal with is the weight of the guilt I'm feeling. I'm guessing that by the end of the night, both families will discover that Jesse was not quite the man they thought they knew. That will undoubtedly infuse the grieving process with megawatts of anger. There was one police officer at the emergency room, but he did not talk to the doctor and no more officers appeared, so I have to think that no one suspects foul play, at least for now. So maybe, just maybe, I might be clear on the legal side. I suppose that might be some consolation, except that my time at the emergency room tonight showed me that I'm still a prisoner of my own conscience.

My parents may not have spent much time with me growing up, but they did imbue me with a sense of right and wrong, as ironic as that may seem right now. I got the same lessons Adam received from his parents, also ironic, about doing the right thing, keeping your head up, and living with integrity. Yet, had there been any doubt regarding the love I felt for my second family, it was vanquished by the gut-wrenching pain I experienced in the emergency room. I love Annie as if she is my own mother and Adam as if he is my brother. Watching the agony, they experienced and knowing that it was caused by me, well, my prison will be the exile my guilt will sentence me to for not being there for them.

Keeping my mind focused on the issues at hand and not on my physical ailments has helped me cover more distance than I expected. I have passed the point where my car is parked and continue heading through the theater district and away from the city center. The number of pedestrians and homeless is thinning. I'm still lightheaded and probably in need of fluids since losing my dinner. The knot in my stomach remains, and I have no expectation that it will shrink anytime soon. I'm going to have to learn to deal with it. For now, walking and clearing my head appears to be the best solution.

I have made it all the way down to Bryant Street. I turn and look back down Main and figure it is time to head back to my car. I cross the road and head into the store at the car wash to get a bottle of water then cross back over Main to retrace my steps. So, now what? Where do I go and what do I do from here? I suppose I could turn myself in; throw myself on the court's mercy. Maybe I could work my way through the legal system and gain the sympathy of a jury, say it was an accident and that the contents of the needle weren't meant to kill Jesse. But even if I manipulated the system for a reduced charge or a not-guilty verdict, I'll still know the truth and the guilt will not just go away. Besides, if no one suspects foul play, I may never face charges.

The real issue is, how do I live with myself? I only see one option. I have to sit down with Adam and bare my soul, lay out what I had discovered, and how tortured I was, knowing that Jesse was leading a double life. I felt I needed to do something, not out of anger or revenge but out of my love for him and for Annie. Maybe, if I can find the right time and the right place, I can make him listen to me and understand why I killed (killed!) his father.

Gary Friedman

But when, really, is the right time to tell a man that you murdered his father?

If I can win Adam's support, maybe I can get back to my life again. With his blessing, I can get past the guilt that is sure to haunt me otherwise, and maybe even save my friendship with him and my relationship with his mother. Annie never has to know and neither does Mary Beth. Yes, Adam is the key. Do I approach him right away or should I wait until after the funeral when things settle down? I think for now I need to spend some time with him to see if the secret is out and how everyone handled it. I should also have a reason for being at the emergency room tonight. He is sure to ask, and I should be prepared.

I walk back through the theater district where the lights are a little brighter and the sidewalk a little more crowded as three couples leave a club and walk in front of me. It has been a long night, and I don't see myself sleeping anytime soon. I can't say I feel better, but I do have the sense that I may have settled on a plan to return to my normal life. I don't suppose I will ever be the same man I was last week, before Jesse's deceptions came to light. No matter what happens in the future, the events of this day have caused a change to my life, and I will never return to the way I was.

I climb back into my car and turn the key. With both hands on the wheel, I drop my head back onto the head rest. One question keeps running through my brain. If I could turn back the clock a couple of days with the knowledge of what today feels like, and I am faced with the same decision all over again, would I make the same choices, plunge the same needle? Maybe I need to let this all play out before I know the answer. I do know that if I could have predicted how I would feel afterward...the pain, the guilt, the potential loss of family, I probably would have taken another road. Lesson learned. I just hope not too late.

CHAPTER FOURTEEN
ADAM

———•———

When you work in emergency response in the city of Buffalo, you get accustomed to the highs and lows of the job. Of course, the highs are few and far between. The street accidents can be pretty brutal, but they are one-time events where you rarely see the same people twice. But then, there is the other side. Where, because of the turf war among the city gangs, it's not surprising to see the same people multiple times a month. We had one night when we had three calls on the same street. The bad guys tend to leave us alone since they never know when they might depend on us to save their own life.

The same is also true in domestic abuse cases. The dual emotions of "I need to stop this," and "I need to get out of here," never seem to result in the abuser stopping or the abused leaving. We have responded to calls at this one house on the east side four times. Each time a drunk husband answers the door and sweeps us into the home to see his bleeding wife who claims that she keeps walking into the same door. We keep our mouths closed (I had to coach Devon), because you don't want to get involved with the violence. That doesn't stop me from leaving the wife a card with the number of the family justice center on it. I have come to know many officers of the Buffalo Police who cruise the worst areas, so I call in domestic violence cases when it's warranted.

The other thing you get used to is the hospitals. The largest trauma center in this part of New York State is at the Erie County Medical Center. The locals call it ECMC. I think Devon's and my personal record for pulling into the ECMC Trauma Center is eight times in one shift. As frequent flyers, we got to know the hospital staff pretty well, and they know us on a first name basis. As a result, I have gotten to know Dr. Dylan fairly well. He is one of the good guys; down-to-earth, easy going and never condescending. I can't say that for some of the younger, less experienced physicians. He has a tendency to connect with the EMTs directly, avoiding second-hand stats from over-worked nurses. He is always highly attentive and appreciative of my thoroughness and ends each report with a "Thanks, I'm sure we'll see you later." I can honestly say I like the guy.

So, as he approaches Mom and me in the waiting room, I assume it will be more of the same. As he draws closer, however, I can tell this will be anything but. He looks drained, bordering on exhaustion, not at all the professional I have come to know. His eyes are red and there is an unsteadiness that is so unlike him. By the end of the shift, the front of his scrubs is usually stained with blood. Tonight, the front of his scrubs is soaked, maybe from the tears of the woman he just walked away from, or maybe even from his own.

As he nears, I reach my hand out to shake his. "Hello Doctor, this is my mother Ann."

"Hello, Ann." He says as he shakes her hand as well. "What can I do for you, Adam?"

"Can you fill us in on what happened with my dad?" I replied.

"The last patient you brought in?"

"Yes, Doctor."

"He was your father and your husband?" as he glances from me to mom.

The look on his face was puzzling. I know him to be incredibly compassionate, but he is giving off a sarcastic vibe that seems so odd. "Is there something wrong, Doctor?"

"Possibly," he says with some hesitation. "Well, first, you have my deepest sympathy. It appears as if the patient you brought in suffered a heart attack while jogging. I'm sorry to tell you, but he didn't survive. We did everything we could to save him." Maybe common doctor talk, but Dr. Dylan is hardly common. He's being almost mechanical, as if he is holding something back. I turn and look at Mom, her eyes riveted on him. I look back at the doctor, feeling confused, with anger escalating from I don't know where.

"Ann, you say this man is your husband?" he asks.

"Doctor!" I bark. My anger is in full bloom, fertilized with shock. I take a full step toward him. Mom places a hand on my arm to pull me back.

"Yes, Doctor. My husband for thirty years. Why do you ask, at a time like this?"

Mom seems to be fixated on every word the doctor is saying. She takes a step closer and slides in front of me just a bit, maybe to keep me from attacking him. My ears feel red and hot, my face flushed.

"Excuse me, Ann, for the questions but please tell me, did your husband travel a lot?"

Mom has a shocked look on her face, not understanding the point of such a question.

"Yes, he did, if you must know."

"I'm not asking to be disrespectful in any way, please believe me. This is exceedingly difficult for me and is only going to get

121

worse. One last question, did he travel so much that he was only able to come home every other weekend?"

That does it. What the hell is he doing to my mother at a time like this? I would expect questions like this from law enforcement, but not this man.

"Doctor! I demand to know, right now, why you are asking all these questions."

I push Mom aside slightly to give myself better access to the man I used to respect. She stumbles a bit from my mild shove, but then regains her footing and pushes back, not wanting this night to bring any more ugliness. Even with her resistance, I move a step closer to the doctor.

"Please answer my question first, every other weekend?"

"Yes, every other weekend," Mom says softly while grabbing a hold of my sleeve.

"Now my question," I demand.

"Because for *every other weekend*, the weekends when he wasn't your husband and your father," he glances pointedly between my mom and me, "The dead man on the table in there was my father and her husband." He turns and points back to the woman he had been holding moments before. "For the last thirty-one years. The last *thirty-one years*. That son of a bitch!"

Dylan's words strike me as I can only imagine a lightning bolt would feel, hitting the top of my skull and sending red hot heat waves throughout my body, leaving only numbness behind. The anger that had been directed at the doctor moments ago transferred immediately to my father. As bizarre as the accusation sounded, I had no doubt to its accuracy. There always seemed to be something left unspoken between us, something I could never quite put my finger on, like he wanted to tell me a deep dark secret but never knew how to start the conversation.

Looking over at Mom, I could tell she was having a similar reaction to mine, like a light switch flipping on in a long-forgotten room.

"Did you know?" I ask Dylan quietly.

"Honestly, Adam, I had no idea. It just all came together at this moment. I know it's shocking but suddenly everything in my life makes sense for the first time. Why he was never around when I needed him, why I knew so little about his business, why we would go days without hearing from him. The monster juggled two families and not for a short period of time, not a year or two but for over thirty-one freakin' years. It all makes sense now."

"You know what, Doctor?"

"Please call me Dylan."

"You know what, Dylan? I understand that his heart gave out, but I don't think it was his intention to live out the night under any circumstances."

"I don't understand," he replied.

I turn and look back at the bench I had just been sitting on. I go back and pick up the manila envelope and pull out the contents.

"He left these on the driver's seat of his car. There is a letter to me and there are four envelopes. There is one for my mom, one for you, Dylan, and I'm guessing this one is for you."

I turn to hand an envelope to the woman whom Dylan had been consoling moments before, who has quietly walked up and joined us. I'm assuming that she is Dylan's mother and my father's other wife.

"I believe he was planning on ending his life tonight and that I was to become his mailman. It looks like fate took away his choice. These are goodbye letters. Maybe he knew his heart was failing, maybe he wanted to say goodbye, maybe he was just nothing but a coward and couldn't face anybody with the truth. You are right, Dylan. We have all been making excuses for him for years. Now, all the trips, all the absences, all the excuses piled on top of excuses makes sense. I simply can't believe it. I don't want to have to believe it, yet I know it's true."

I remain locked in my place. Dylan reaches a hand out to me. We shake hands as if for the first time. He smiles at me as if I were a patient at an initial visit, cordial but unsure, wanting to present himself in the best possible light. I shake his hand again and return the same smile, as awkward as his.

Mom remains still. She holds her envelope with both hands, staring at her name. Despite being a dedicated mother, and despite her success in the corporate world, Mom always considered her most important role to be Jesse's wife. The initial shock appears to be wearing off as anger rushes in to fill the void. Her fingers show the first sign, closing to white-knuckled fists, first wrinkling then crushing the unopened envelope in her hands. She tips her head back slowly and lets loose a primal scream that I have no doubt filled the halls of the hospital, this floor and six stories above. I believe she would have choked Dad to death if he had been standing in this room and not lying dead in the next one. She is way past tears. She rips the letter apart, slaps the two pieces together and proceeds to tear them into the smallest pieces she can, throws them to the floor and stomps on them. The scream turns into growling as she dances on the litter. In seconds, she has gone from grieving wife to wounded animal.

To my surprise, her anguish is soothed briefly by Dylan's mother. She steps forward and offers her sympathy to Mom in a most peaceful, accepting way. Mom returns her sentiments as they settle into a hug that seems genuine for both women. The doctor and I can only watch in awe.

After a few moments, I go over and place my hand on my mother's trembling shoulder, not hoping to soothe her anger, but just to let her know that I'm here for her. The shaking has eased somewhat as she turns and rests her head on my shoulder. Finally, she finds her voice.

"I'm okay, Baby. I'm okay," she whispers in a hoarse voice, "but your father, your father is dead to me in every way imaginable." She pulls from my arms and sits back down on the bench, her elbows on her knees, her hands holding her head as she shakes it slowly back and forth.

I sit down on the seat next to her, my letter still in my hand. I turn it around, right-side-up, and try to focus on the words. This is the last conversation my father and I will ever have, as one sided as it may be.

Dear Adam,

I write this note in hopes that it will find you at the appropriate time. That you are reading it means it has. I'm truly sorry that I didn't have the ability or courage to say these words to you in person. The fact that I have to write this at all is further proof of the cowardly way I have lived my life.

I know I haven't spent nearly enough time being a good father to you. I tried, as you were growing up to make what little time I offered you quality time. In the end, it was not nearly enough. I have never really been particularly good at saying goodbye as I have no doubt you will discover over the next few hours and days. This weak attempt at that effort will just serve to prove my point.

I want you to know how proud I am of the man you have become. I know things haven't gone the way you would have predicted or wanted but you have always had a work ethic that will make you a success in life. Even though you may not see the ultimate path for your success right now, know that it will show up when you least expect it.

I am sorry to put this on you, but I'm asking you to fulfill one last task for me. With your letter, you will find four envelopes. One is for your mother and the recipients of the other three will become obvious to you at the appropriate time. I humbly ask that you serve as my messenger, to be sure that these letters reach the right hands. I know I can count on you here. Also, I know this will be terribly hard on your mother. She is a wonderful woman with a bottomless well of strength and courage. I know she will be fine but do all you can to support her during what I'm sure will be a difficult time of discovery for her.

Goodbye my son. Despite what you will surely figure out about me in the next few hours and days, please know that I have always loved you and will carry that love with me to my grave.

Dad

My eyes run off the bottom of the page and then turn the page over, expecting to see more—a much clearer explanation maybe—not regarding what I read, but why it was written. He certainly couldn't have suspected a heart attack during his jog, but he certainly knew that his end was imminent.

Was that why a gun was found in his car?

If I live to be a hundred, I will never understand any of this. How can any man live the life he chose to live? Was it all a game to him? When we were together as a family, it always felt so real, so honest. He loved my mother; I had no doubt of that. No one can pretend for thirty years and carry it off with that kind of believability. I know he cared deeply for me and was always concerned about how my actions reflected on my future. During my party days, he let his displeasure show. I wanted to please him and make him proud of me. To have to wait for his suicide note to discover that he was proud feels incredibly empty now.

126

I glance over at my mother. She still sits with her head buried in her hands, shaking it back and forth in disbelief. Dad was right when he called her strong, but how does any woman recover from thirty years of deceit? The tears are gone for now, but I have no doubt they will return in the privacy of the bedroom she shared with her cheating husband.

In all the years of their marriage, the only recurring fight that ever came up between them was over my mother's disappointment at his inability to attend the important events in my life. She could excuse his absence for herself, but she wanted more for her son. My big games, graduations, proms, awards, he missed them all. He always tried to make up for those times, but he never quite refilled the glass to even half-full. Should it really come as any surprise that when it came time to say goodbye that he should do so without being present? In truth, now more so than ever, who he was and what he had to offer me as his son was never going to measure up. Why would I expect the end to be any different?

I fold the letter and stuff it into my back pocket. I slide down the bench closer to my mother and place an arm around her shoulder, pulling her closer to me. She turns enough to place her head on my shoulder, takes my hand and holds it softly on her lap. We are alone with our thoughts and our grief.

The silence is broken as a siren crashes through the air. Nurses come running out of the examining area and race through the double doors, followed closely by Dr. Dylan, back in the saddle. He gives us a brief nod as he runs out the doors. Did he take the time to read his letter before running out to save another life? Dr. Dylan, my newly-found brother. Now it's my turn to shake my head. While it's nice to know I have a brother, it adds to my sadness at the thought of not having known he was my brother until a few minutes ago. I spent many a frustrating night wishing

I had a sibling. Maybe a part time replacement for the father who was never there. Will was a great substitute, but it's different from having a big brother to mentor me. My head drops down again.

Mom must have noticed. She pats my hand and sits up a little straighter, leans over and plants a soft kiss on my cheek. "Don't worry, Adam. We will get through this, you, and me, just like we always have. We never needed his help for that. In fact, imagine all the time we will have on our hands, not having to worry about when he might show up. We will be fine." She pats my hand and made an effort at a smile.

She is right, of course. We will get through it. It's not like he was a major part of either of our daily routines, even weekly ones. Eventually the anger and the hurt will subside, and we will move on. We'll do what we have always done without having to wait to share the moment with him. What I will miss is the image of a man doing what he needed to do to serve his family. That was always his excuse: "I'm doing this for you guys." Now, even that excuse is empty. In the end, as in all things in his life, it was always just for him.

CHAPTER FIFTEEN
ANNIE

———— • ————

I have never been a big music fan. I think I have been to one concert my whole life. I don't own any albums or CDs. I never play music in the background when I'm at work or at home. It's just not a part of my DNA. I can't hum a few bars or repeat a lyric. Jesse had quite a collection of music, but it was all his. So, all the more reason to be confused by this young doctor who was walking toward me, in a slow steady rhythm. Each step resounds like a bass beat, almost choreographed. When he started to speak, even his words had a familiar tone. They were set way too slow, as if Jesse had put on a 45 single at 33 speed. The sound of each step was deep, hollow, and echoing. Over his shoulder came his back-up singer, a woman who kept coming closer, hanging on his every word. I could hear him, but my eyes were fixed on her.

Adam is focused on this man's every word. He is becoming more flushed with anger by the moment. Of course, we are both hurting, and this is the doctor who can explain what happened to Jesse and offer his condolences. However, I can't get past the image of him hugging, and then kissing my now-dead husband. What was all that about? Does he kiss all his lost cases? If this is to be such a private, heart wrenching moment, why is this woman getting closer and closer, trying to listen in?

Clearly something is horribly wrong here. Adam is growing incensed. Maybe I should try to focus on what this doctor is saying.

"Yes, every other weekend," I mechanically answer.

"Because for *every other weekend*, the weekends when he wasn't your husband and your father, the dead man on the table in there was my father and her husband," pointing back to the woman he had been holding moments before, "for the last thirty-one years. The last *thirty-one years.* That son of a bitch!"

I have been on this earth for over fifty years, as a wife and mother, as an employee and eventually as a corporate executive. Yet nothing in all those experiences ever prepared me for being struck down by a sledgehammer of words. What is he saying? Is he trying to tell me that my beloved husband cheated on me with another woman, particularly that woman over there, for three decades? Not some brief fling, not some tawdry affair but a *marriage* of thirty-one years? Wait, thirty-one years? We were just about to celebrate our thirtieth anniversary. He wasn't cheating on me with her! He was cheating on her with me. *I* was the other woman, not her. Who does that? What kind of a man lives the kind of fraud he perpetrated?

I'm drained of emotion as my body grows silent, frozen in time. Suddenly, everything makes sense. The long absences, the distant stares, the uncomfortable silences, the missed holidays, and events. I never had more than a fraction of that man and not even a half of a marriage. He cheated, he lied and tried to cover his guilt by his extreme attempts at passion. Maybe he thought if the sex was good, he could ease his conscience about his abysmal behavior, and obscene choices. Every moment of it was faked, contrived. What kind of a man does that to a woman?

My eyes slowly rise up off the floor. Adam is clearly stunned. The doctor appears to be suffering from a combination of anger at my husband—*his father*—and embarrassment for losing control of his emotions. The woman? My dead husband's other wife of a year longer than me? She looks almost at peace, relieved to hear the truth. Her eyes are locked on mine as she seems to be trying to understand me as I evaluate her, neither of us having any words, not wanting to be the first to speak. Somehow, it is clear to me that she is as much a victim as I am, that she is as surprised as I am that our husband was a philanderer. I don't hate her. I sympathize with her.

My thoughts are interrupted by Adam as he lifts the manila envelope off the bench. He pulls out separate envelopes and distributes them among us. I don't reach for mine, so Adam lifts my arm and places the envelope in my hand. I hold it in both hands and look down at my name, written in his familiar scribble most likely created by his favorite Mont Blanc pen. As I hold it, I can feel the rage building inside of me, like a mountain full of lava waiting to erupt. The roiling starts in my stomach, rising full force into my lungs, up my throat and out my mouth in the form of a scream like I have never heard nor caused. I didn't care who heard me. A stew of anger and hatred spewed forth, my whole body shaking violently.

I can sense Adam's hands on me, but my body goes numb. I try to open my eyes, but everything in my sight is tinged with red, as if my eyes are bleeding. I can feel another eruption coming on, building from my toes, and racing higher. My knuckles are white as I grip the letter on each end. As my second scream ignites, head back and body stiff, I rip the envelope into two halves. As the scream subsides, I take the two halves and tear them into little pieces no larger than a postage stamp. I let them all rain onto the floor and when they land, I stomp on each piece as if the soles of my feet could erase all memory of him.

I remain frozen in place, staring at the pieces on the floor, lost in grief and shame. I was lost in the realization that I loved a man that I never really knew for thirty years. We shared a life and planned for what comes next...retirement, travel, family. I fight to bring myself back into the moment. As I open my eyes, I can see the other woman, the other wife, in front of me. She reaches her arms out to me as she steps closer.

"I am so sorry for all of this," she whispers.

"Me too," I manage.

She reaches out as we fall into each other's arms. Not a word is spoken, yet we clearly understand the mutual pain. The crying, the despair has stopped for both of us. In their place is a realization that the life we knew is over but not the living, not for either of us. The hug feels real and warm and deeply appreciated. Maybe someday we will be able to talk about our shared lives, but not today. This is simply for now. I feel a hand on my shoulder. I look up to see Adam waiting for his turn. I kiss Dylan's mother on the cheek and slowly turn to my son and into his arms. The anger is subsiding. Even the shaking has eased. I rest my head on Adam's shoulder and a sense of calm washes over me. I have never allowed myself to be a victim at home or at work. I'll be damned if I'm going to allow the dead man in the next room make me one now.

I pull back slowly from Adam while I offer him the best smile I can manage. "I'm okay, Baby. I'm okay," I force from my lips, "but your father, your father is dead to me in every way imaginable."

I take his hand as I sit back down on the bench. He sits next to me as we both seem to be pondering the next step in our lives. I watch Adam as he reads his letter. He shows no emotion that would betray its content. I watch as Dylan holds his mother, then walks with her to the door of the emergency room, where they hug one more time. He gently kisses his mother on her cheek and his hand stays on her lower back in support as she turns and walks confidently out through the emergency room doors and into the dark night. The doctor glances our way one more time, nods and smiles a deeply sad, resigned smile, then disappears back through the examination room door.

The waiting room is empty once more. We sit in silence. Adam has finished his letter and stuffed it into his back pocket. His right hand rests in mine while his left hand supports part of his weight on his knee. He is staring at the tiled floor, rarely blinking, head shaking occasionally, trying to absorb the events of the evening.

The silence is broken by a blaring siren, bright headlights, and flickering emergency lights. Adam barely responds; he is used to the scene. I am fascinated by it all. EMTs are racing around their vehicle, as nurses burst out the door of the ER to meet the gurney. This is what it must have been like when Adam brought in his father. The examining room door bursts open, and Dylan joins the responders. He has clearly returned to work and left the life-changing moments behind. I envy his ability to focus on the moment, to leave the dwelling on our situation for Adam and me.

Just as quickly as it began, it ends. Doctors and nurses begin performing their magic behind the blue curtains while the first responders load the gurney back into their ambulance, pull back onto the ramp, and leave, only the red glow of their taillights in their wake. Silence returns while Adam and I exhale as one. We turn and look at each other and hug one more time before getting to our feet.

I look back at the examining room one last time. The blue curtains now hold someone new. Where they have pushed Jesse off to, I don't know, and at this point don't care. I had heard mention of getting together tomorrow with the members of our newly-expanded family to discuss arrangements. I don't need a discussion. I have no interest in a wake or church service, no interest in any kind of social gathering. This situation will be embarrassing enough without hanging out our collective dirty laundry in a gathering place. I would tolerate a ceremony at the cemetery...brief enough to cover the bases. Then I want to start the hard work of putting our lives back together. I refuse to offer him any of the consideration in death that he refused all of us in life.

"Adam, do you have a car here?"

"No, Mom. All my gear is in my rig and my car is parked at my work lot."

"Can I take you to your car? Give you a lift somewhere? Or if it's easier, come home with me for tonight."

"Mom, are you okay to drive? You have been through a lot tonight."

"I'm okay, I really am. I need to get out of here though. So, what works best for you?"

"Unfortunately, my car keys are with my gear, so I have to hook up with my partner at some point. Let me try and reach him now."

He takes a few steps away from me and pulls out his cell phone. The call is brief.

"He isn't that far away. He is going to come, pick me up and take me to my car. When I get to my office, I have to let my dispatch know I will be off duty for a few days. Then, I will come home. Can you get home on your own?"

"I will be fine. I doubt I will still be up when you get home, but I'll see you in the morning."

"Don't forget we have arrangements to make in the morning."

"Too bad it's too late for a firing squad."

"Mom!"

I feel a resigned smile appear on my face, realizing that my attempt at gallows humor fell flat.

"See you in the morning, Adam."

One last hug and I pass through the emergency doors for the last time. The night is quiet and cooler than when I arrived. The security guard nods as I slowly walk to my car, the one I picked out with my husband. I will drive home to the house we built together, where we picked paint colors and carpeting, light fixtures, and cabinets, all by mutual consent. Where we (I!) raised my son. I thought I knew him so well. The truth is I hardly knew him at all.

My car drives up the entrance ramp to the 33 as I head home, to what used to be our home. All the windows in my car are open, letting the wind run through me while blocking out the sounds of the highway. For once, I'm actually traveling below the speed limit, being in no hurry to arrive anywhere. My emotions are electric, darting back and forth between moments of peace to raging anger. The longer I drive, the more peace wins the fight. As the anger over Jesse drifts away, the reality of what might happen next takes over. I have so many options to consider with really nothing holding me back. Despite being a miserable example of a human being, Jesse was a good provider. Combine that with my own job and income and the possibilities are truly endless. Of course, I have to consider how all this will affect Adam.

He seems to have inherited much of my toughness. There was a time when I worried about that, but no more. He has done well with WNY Response, and he appears to be respected at work. He certainly handled himself well tonight, ready to protect me from what he thought was the rudeness of the doctor. He is compassionate about all the people and things in his life. I always wondered why he gave his father so much of a benefit of the doubt. He never seemed hurt by Jesse's extended absences and accepted any excuse his father made for missing the big moments. Even tonight, at the end of his father's life and the end of his charade, Adam floated through it. He got quiet, pondered, read his letter, but managed to keep extreme emotions to himself, making me his first priority.

Traffic is light with the roadside brightened by a full moon that has taken over a totally cloudless sky. Normally, I wouldn't notice such things. I would be focused on work, my next tennis match, or when my husband would be coming home. My speed would be closer to eighty than fifty, as I thought about what else I could cross off on my to-do list before the day was over. Not tonight.

Tonight, it feels like my life down-shifted to a different gear. Could this all happen so quickly? Is it possible that I saw this coming, that I knew all along that everything wasn't right? That accepting Jesse's excuses was just easier and less painful than making each point of contention a hill to die on? Maybe this isn't that big of a shock, all things considered. Was my marriage really a marriage in any sense of the word? I maintained a home for his brief appearances but kept my own life organized by my needs when he was gone. I enjoyed our passionate weekends together, but it was more a physical release than an expression of love. With his bi-monthly visits to my bed, I could focus on the rest of my life without weighing it down with other men. "An affair of convenience..." I didn't want that or need it. The best thing about being married was my son, my Adam.

Oh yeah, Adam. Back to that thought. My thoughts feel like they're doing somersaults, but I kind of like these random moments. I should try it more often. So, Adam and his steady emotions. Maybe his balance was about me all along. Maybe he accepted his father and his schedule because I did, because I never made a big deal or complained about it. He has always been my steadying force in his father's absence, taking on the role of substitute spouse. Not in any way over the top, obsessive or inappropriate. He just knew, like tonight, when to step in and be there for me. Maybe Jesse's death has opened doors for Adam as well as for me.

The moon is high above the University of Buffalo campus. I'm kind of liking the slower speed. That may be the first of many changes being made. I have to slow down in my life, learn to appreciate things like the full moon. Maybe I can move. I don't need such a big house for just me. I've been thinking about downsizing for a while. Now is my chance, no longer burdened by one of those husband things. First, though, I have to set Adam free. As much as I adore him, I don't need or want him feeling like he is responsible for my well-being. He has his own life to live, and I don't want to hinder his growth. It's his time now.

Back in our driveway. No, my driveway, not ours. There is no more "ours" in anything. Jesse never appreciated it enough, never valued this home. It was just his personal hotel to check-in to every two weeks. No more. No more waiting or wondering when I will be important enough for him to change his life. Tonight, Adam and I got the answers. Never! I have never been that important to him. The realization hits me square in the chest as I exhale suddenly, letting my head fall back on the headrest for a short moment to ponder that thought before I meander into MY house. In reality, it was never really was anything but mine.

Gary Friedman

CHAPTER SIXTEEN
DYLAN

———◆·———

The door to the doctor's lounge eases closed behind me. The hydraulic mechanism at the top of the door squeaks as it seals against the frame. The room is dark for the most part with only the parking area's lights weaving in among the vinyl slats of the Venetian blinds. Headlights of the cars pulling in and out of the parking spaces cause the light to dance along the wall across from the blinds. Those lights try desperately to distract me from the events of the last hour yet fail miserably.

My head slowly settles into the too-soft pillow on the only cot in the room. My eyes couldn't be more-wide open if I tried. The screen for my brain's never-ending movie is projected on the ceiling above my bed, the events of the night playing over and over in a continuous loop. The gurney rolling in, the update from the EMT, the realization of the identity of the patient whose life I am supposed to save…it all floods back and plays on loop. Did I respond properly? Did I do all I could to save the poor-excuse-of-a-man's life? Should I have passed him on to another doctor rather than allow my actions to be second guessed by an outsider or a board of insiders? Did I act appropriately every step of the way?

I review the procedures over and over again across the ceiling screen. I roll over to pick up the chart where I let it fall on the floor and settle back down on the cot. I reach over and turn on the mostly-useless desk lamp attempting to illuminate the pages before me. I check every field of information captured, every note or observation recorded, and every quantity of every drug administered in an attempt to change the outcome. I review the final determination I signed off on; natural causes—heart failure. I recheck the printouts of the monitors that record the patient's vital signs. The result shows nothing inconsistent with the cause of death. When I reach the last page of the chart, I flip back to page one and start all over again, and then again. The conclusion is that the trauma staff did everything it could to avoid the ultimate outcome, that the son of a bitch died. I let my arm rest at my side, allowing the chart to drop back to the floor. Another case closed...but is it?

What about the human debris left behind by the patient, the emotional bodies spread out across the waiting room?

One of the biggest surprises of a night chock full of them, was Mom's response. She doesn't exactly have a long history of accepting life as it arrives. I would have expected her to crumble as reality set in. Instead, she showed a strength that I had never seen in her. Yes, she crumbled into my arms as she received the news of Dad's passing, but when confronted with the story of who the man was and how he lived, well, it was almost as if she stepped into a shower of peace and came out refreshed by the truth. To think that she could uncover a thirty-year-plus lie and be improved emotionally by its discovery is about as far-fetched a story as I could imagine. I love her to pieces, and grateful she has been my anchor in a dockless life, but I'm not unaware of her relationship with the bottle. Yet, she walked in here tonight stone-cold sober, and I didn't get the sense that she was about to rush home and pop a cork. Maybe my father's non-existence was as much responsible for her condition as she was.

Then there is Adam. I have seen him come and go from here over the last year and have always been impressed by him. As an EMT, his reports have always been concise, accurate and to the point. He doesn't go off on wild tangents like some do and doesn't make attempts to diagnose the patient. The facts and nothing but the facts. As a doctor, it has always been a relief to see Adam as the attendant on an arrival. I wish we had more like him. None of that, however, was as impressive as tonight when he protected his mother in her time of need. Maybe my approach was a bit heartless, as I have a tendency to be, but he was a bulldog on his mother's behalf. I'm looking forward to getting to know him better. It's possible the best thing to come out of this whole mess is a real chance to gain a brother.

Meeting Adam's mom was extremely weird. She is an impressive woman, even in a tennis outfit. Extremely attractive and fit and I can see why a man would have a hard time saying goodbye to her. She made no attempt to hide her emotions as the truth came out, which is far healthier than keeping her anguish buried. While no woman deserves to be treated as she has, being married to my (our!) father, she clearly has done a great job with Adam and will have him by her side throughout the ordeal yet to come...the funeral, the finances and the like.

I slowly start to roll over to ease the tension in my back when I feel something caught by the blanket beneath me. I reach back and pull out the wrinkled envelope that Adam had given me. I straighten it out as best I can. My name is scrawled across the front by a man clearly too busy to fret over penmanship. I stare at my name on the envelope for a few minutes, my mind flashing back to Mom, throwing her letter into a waste basket and Ann turning hers into confetti. The temptation to follow their lead is overpowering. Yet, something within forces me to slide my finger under the gummed flap. It pulls open neatly and without a tear. I pull out a handwritten note written on a legal pad in a handwriting more legible than the scrawl on the envelope. I roll back over to take full advantage of the limited desk lamp next to the cot. Fighting the intense temptation to crush it in my hands and throw the ball across the room, I move as close to the light as possible.

Dear Dylan,

Of all the letters I have chosen to write, this one is turning out to be the toughest. For you to have this in your hands means that who and what I am is clearer to you than at any other point in your life. It was never my intention to cause you such pain. In fact, I have never intended to hurt anyone. I love all the people in my life. I am, at best, a weak man, prone to shielding those I love from pain and making a mess of things in the process.

You, my son, have become an amazing man. Your intelligence, confidence, your social skills, your commitment to your profession have always impressed me. I wish I could be half the man you are and half the father you deserve. I need you to understand, it was never about you or for that matter, never about your mother. I love you both dearly. It has always been about my shortcomings as a father and a husband, never carving enough time out of my life to be either.

I wish I had the courage to say all these things to your face during the normal course of events, but I couldn't. That is my own weakness and a treatment neither you nor your mother deserved. When you try to fit fourteen days of loving into two days twice a month, you are setting yourself up for failure on all fronts. If any of this even matters to you at this point, please know that I'm immensely proud of the man you have become and love you dearly. It wouldn't surprise me in the least if you set fire to this note the

142

minute you finish or even before you start. I would understand completely. I deserve it. I know you have closed me out of your life out of necessity. I just hope it hasn't evolved to hate, even though I would understand that as well.

Please be there for you mother. I know I have no right to saddle you with that responsibility, but I can't help but worry about her. She has not handled the life I have forced upon her well, and she may need a shoulder to lean on during the crisis I have created. I'm not blaming her for anything as I take full blame for any and all pain I have caused. Just be there for her and guide her in the right direction should she need such guidance. Of course, knowing who you are, I have no doubt you will be there for her even without my asking.

Goodbye, Dylan. I wish you all the happiness a father can wish on his son. I hope everything you seek in life gathers around your feet. Know that wherever I am, I will be cheering for your success.

Love,

Dad

My arms drop down to my chest, the letter still clutched in both hands. To my surprise, tears are streaming down my face and onto the pillow. My right hand falls to the cot while my left hangs off the edge, dropping the note to the floor. My eyes are fixed, once again, to the ceiling where video snippets play, showing rare memories of times I spent with my father. It's not movie length, more like a commercial. My tears are not a sign of sadness for times lost, more a loss for what never was and what will never be. He made the choice to make my life a second priority behind my mother or maybe even third choice behind his career, whatever that was. Now I learn that there was another wife and another son and that could have moved me further down his list of priorities. Then he writes me this sappy letter in hopes that I will love him in my memories and forgive him for his faults. Well, the hell with him.

I crumple up the note and fling it across the room toward the waste basket. It bounces off the rim and falls meekly to the floor. I sit up, swing my legs over the side of the cot, pull my sneakers back on and lace them tightly. Who the hell does he think he is? Did he really believe that one note would give him a pass on being a horrible father, a horrible husband (times two) and an equally horrible human being? All the tears, the pain, the wondering why I wasn't good enough to be his son; the bottles consumed, and the pills ingested by my mother. Did he think all of that would all go away with a simple "oops, my bad" letter? What is wrong with him? There must be a defective gene, a missing synapse, a lobe of his brain absent if he thinks that's what it takes to have a soul.

I get up and cross the room, pick up the crumpled paper and throw it, as hard as I can, to the bottom of the basket. Then I jam my foot down on top of it, so it never again sees the light of day. I look back down into the basket at the letter.

"To say you are dead to me would be wrong because that would infer you ever existed. You never existed as a father or a husband or a man and if you never existed, you can never be mourned. I can't even hate you for the same reasons. You just never were."

I tip my head back, looking at the blank wall, letting the anger flush through me, willing it away. I take a deep breath and let it out slowly, trying to return to the same sense of peace in which I resided before that gurney ever entered my trauma room. In that moment, I take back a sense of control I allowed him to steal away from me for just a moment.

The silence is broken by the wail of a siren cutting through the night. I open my eyes to find the lights breaking through the blinds and reflecting off the wall. Time to go back to work. I kick the basket one last time and reach for the door handle. The light from the trauma center explodes into the room as two nurses run past and out toward the emergency ramp. I turn and follow their lead.

As I run through the waiting area, I can see Adam and Ann still sitting on the bench along the wall. Ann is silent with her head in her hands. Adam is still holding his letter. Despite my anger at my dead father, I have nothing but compassion for the families that he left behind. Adam looks up at me and our eyes connect. He is taking all this much better than I am, at least more thoughtfully. I had a sour taste in my mouth for dear old Dad before tonight, so there wasn't all that much of an adjustment. For him, it looks like he has lost his puppy. I was struck by the sadness on his face when I broke the news to him. Whether that anguish was for him or for his mother, I don't know.

What I do know is that I want to get to know him better, spend some time with him. We could be good for each other and it would be nice to have a brother. As for Ann, I'm not sure how that would work. I would like to think that I know what she is going through, and I wish there could be some way I can help her. It's not like I need to be some agent to mend the tear that my father's choices rendered in her life, but I would like to help her as one human being to another.

The EMT and one of the nurses are pulling the stretcher out of the ambulance. The EMT calls out "Double GSW, chest and abdomen. Vitals currently steady." That makes the second gunshot wound of the night. Like the last one, my goal will be to stabilize her and get her up to an operating room alive, then let the surgeons take over.

I'm at the lead end of the stretcher as the wheels touch the ground, my hands on the metal tubing at the feet of the patient. I'm back-pedaling as the stretcher moves away from the ambulance. I look up and to my right and catch the sight of my mother sitting in her car watching me in her side view mirror. To my surprise she is smiling. She sends a small wave. I smile and nod at her, my mind far away from the gurney in front of me. I'm not doing my part to help move the patient to the examining area.

"We got this, Doctor," Lisa yells, almost pulling the metal bar out of my hands. She and the EMT take off with the gurney, leaving me standing by the curb. Embarrassed by my lack of focus, I shake my head to try and clear out the mental debris gathered between my ears. One more look to the parking lot, and I can see my mother's taillights moving slowly down the ramp.

What an incredible woman. I couldn't have been prouder of the way she conducted herself in this awful situation. Under no circumstances, in any area of my memory, could I remember any time when she took command of a situation, but she did tonight. She was the most controlled person in the room. The way she calmly joined our conversation, and the way she comforted Ann. I was so touched. It is difficult to imagine how the death of a spouse, or the death of any person for that matter, could have such a positive impact on another, but I watched it happen.

For so many years, as many as I can remember, she acted like the loyal house pet, waiting for her master to return home. If it felt demeaning to me, I can only imagine how it felt to her. I have no doubt that the weight of her choices led to her decision to make a home in the bottom of a bottle. I don't know how tonight's events could change all that, but if the woman I saw tonight is any indication of the future for her, then she will be the silver lining to the band of grey clouds that moved across all of our lives over the last hour.

"Doctor!" Lisa calls out from the doorway of the examining room. Her yell shakes me out of my daydream and back to the reality of a busy emergency room. I turn and run back across the waiting area and through the curtains holding the waiting patient. Clothes cut off, tubes and wires connected, nurses cleaning up the wounds. For a brief moment, the young woman in distress becomes my father, as he slowly faded from my life. The vision makes me take a step back, hesitating just a moment. "Doctor, should I call Dr. Riley?" Lisa asks.

"No, Lisa, I got this." I move quickly to the sink to wash my hands. I slide into a gown and have two gloves waiting for me. They snap on one at a time. I turn back to the ring of blue curtains and slide into the opening. I look down at the woman in need of my skills.

Back to the work I was always meant to do. Yes, my father provided for my mother and me financially, providing money that helped with my education. That, however, is where my appreciation ends. I am a doctor, a trauma care professional. I am, today, the man I am because of the love, care and attention provided by my mother, doing the best she could, virtually alone in the world. From now on, she is my life.

James? James is dead to me. Any positive he provided in my life was wiped out by the deceit he lived by and forced on others. Life goes on; my memory of him will not.

Gary Friedman

CHAPTER SEVENTEEN
MARY BETH

———•———

It's another peaceful, quiet night in Orchard Park. My garage door went up ten minutes ago, but I don't want to pull inside. It is far too nice a night to have a roof over my head. The convertible's top is down as are all the windows. The full moon is high in the sky keeping the stars from full display. The outside lights have been switched on by their timer, but the rest of the house is dark. The timed lights attached to the garage door opener have also blinked off. My seat is tilted back as I take in all the sights around me.

We own a beautiful home, four bedrooms with two and a half baths, beautifully landscaped, swimming pool in the back yard. Well, I guess it isn't "we" anymore. I own a beautiful home. I never imagined myself being a widow, divorced maybe, but never a widow. Jay was in such wonderful shape, looking at least ten years younger than his age of fifty-five. I always figured he would live longer than me, considering the damage I have done to my health over the years with drinking and the rare addition of drugs. What a fool I have been, in so many ways.

I climb slowly out of my car and walk back to the foot of my driveway, looking up and down the street of my perfect little neighborhood. Not a car in sight, no noise, no people on their front porch or walking about. I really don't know many of the people who live in my neighborhood. Everyone pretty much keeps to themselves except for some occasional social events. I didn't generally attend because I felt awkward without my husband joining me. It got tiresome having to explain why my man was away again.

I must admit, as a newly-crowned widow, other than being suddenly single, I don't have a lot to complain about. I paid all the bills, so I know our...umm...*my* financial position. Assuming there are no more secrets out there waiting for me, I'm debt free, living in a house that is almost paid for. I have seen a copy of Jay's will, and I know how much life insurance he carried. Say what you want about the deceptive way he led his life; he has departed this world leaving behind a financially-comfortable widow. Had he lived long enough to kill himself, as his goodbye letters to everyone indicated, his policy wouldn't have paid out. So, three cheers for natural causes.

I walk back up the driveway and lean gently on the front hood of my car, feeling a little guilty for being so flippant about his passing. He has taken good care of me financially and was always kind and considerate to me. He was just really busy, taking care of his business while considering the needs of a whole other family. I should be angry—no *furious*—about that. He lied to me daily, cheated on me bi-monthly, ignored *my* son to raise another, gave half of his income and assets to another woman, missed birthdays, missed anniversaries and more than half of all holidays. All while I waited patiently for his return, like the wife of a ship's captain, waiting and watching from the widow's walk for a sighting of a ship's mast on the horizon, a hint that her husband survived another tour at sea. Yes, I should be furious at all of that, but in truth, I'm really not.

My mind rolls softly back to the moment in the emergency waiting room when I discovered the truth about my marriage. The sudden realization of who and what my husband and my marriage was washed over me like a bucket of ice water dumped on my head. I felt a brief surge of anger, but it was immediately replaced by an image in my life's mirror. I have spent thirty years staring at that mirror, seeing the image of a failure of a woman, not good enough to keep the interest of her husband. I felt that if I were more attractive, more interesting, less needy, Jay would want to spend more time with me, take me out in public and be proud to have me on his arm. I have felt emotionally impoverished all these years, not good enough in any aspect of my life. It was a painful, painful image. One I tried to ignore, trying to pretend it didn't exist, and wanting it to just go away. When it wouldn't, I filled a glass with any liquid that would make me forget the image in that mirror.

I attended enough AA meetings to know that alcoholism is a "feelings" disease. We nameless souls get drunk to stop feeling. I viewed myself as so weak that I couldn't even blame my absent husband for my pain. After all, who could blame him for not wanting to be around such an emotional failure, with circles under her eyes and alcohol on her breath? When he was home, I wanted so desperately to be the sober women he married, but I would still sneak to my secret bottle in the garage to down a quick one when he wasn't looking. I was angry. Not at him, but at the mess I had become.

That moment in the waiting room was the revelation of a lifetime, a cleansing of my soul, like Windex to my life's mirror. It felt like a HazMat team was hosing me down to get all the deadly debris of my life off of me. I came out cleansed at the other end. The puddles of my trashed self-image dripping slowly down a drain in the middle of the room. I couldn't be angry. I couldn't even mourn. I was too thankful for the reprieve. I had been through hell, and hell had won. Now I have a second chance at life and I'm feeling thankful for that opportunity. "Hi, my name is Mary Beth, and I'm an alcoholic."

At that moment, the back wall of the garage lights up and my shadow is projected on that wall, larger than life. What perfect timing. I turn to see Dylan's car pulling into the driveway. The driver's side opens slowly as my son steps out, displaying an exhaustion he rarely reveals. He walks slowly toward me and pulls me into a hug. No words are spoken. Just the physical connection we both need. He takes me by the hand and leads me through the garage and into the mud room. He walks into the kitchen, opens the refrigerator, pulls out a bottle of sparkling water and drains half of the bottle without even looking up.

"I told them at the hospital that I would not be in tomorrow or possibly the next few days, so you and I are going to have a lot of time to talk. How about we call it a night and start that talk in the morning, Mom? I'm beat and might just fall asleep in the middle of a sentence if we try tonight. I know it's been an impossible day for both of us, but I think it best we sleep on it. You okay with that?"

"I am, Dylan. I really am. Why don't you go to bed, and we will definitely talk tomorrow. I've got some things to do before heading upstairs. We should have time before our meeting tomorrow morning to talk, so we're good." I walk over to him and give him another hug.

"Okay, Mom. See you in the morning." He turns and heads for the staircase. I can hear each step creak, as he slowly drags himself to bed. His old room is just at the top of the stairs, so he should make it without collapsing in the hallway. After the events of the day, it's comforting to know I'm not alone, just in case my positive reaction doesn't last through the night. It's not that I can't be alone. My marriage managed to leave me in that state most of the time.

"Hey, Mom!" Dylan calls to me from the top of the stairs. I walk quickly into the foyer and look up where he waits, a beatific smile across his face. "I just wanted you to know how proud I was of you tonight. You know, the way you handled everything. I saw a strength in you tonight that I didn't know you had, but I always suspected existed. Good night, Mom." He turns back to his room and closes the door, not waiting for a response. It's just as well since I'm not sure I could have answered without breaking into tears, not out of grief, but from my son saying the nicest thing he ever could have said to me at a time when I needed it the most.

I walk back through the foyer and into the family room, to the bar my late husband designed and had custom built. I swing open the double doors to reveal nearly two dozen bottles of a wide variety of alcohol. I take four bottles off of the shelf and bring them to the kitchen counter. I go back and get four more —and then four more—until the shelves are empty. With the last bottles on the counter, I methodically take one bottle at a time and pour the contents down the kitchen sink. I take each empty bottle and place it on the kitchen table. One by one, bottle after bottle, I watch the liquids of various colors and scents circle the drain. When the last drop of each bottle disappears, I say a simple goodbye and move onto the next one. When all the bottles are on the kitchen table, I walk the empties out to the garage and into the recycling bin as quietly as possible so as to not wake Dylan, whose bedroom is directly above the garage. Once the bar is empty, I repeat the process with the sixteen bottles that fill the wine rack next to the bar. I pull the corkscrew from the kitchen drawer and start to line up the corks on the countertop. No screw top bottles for my husband. He kept his wife inebriated with the best quality of grape. The fragrance of the wine fills the room as the liquid drains into the sewer lines far below.

Now the real detective work begins. I start with each kitchen cabinet to seek out my prey. First, I find the three-quarter empty bottle of white vinegar that isn't really vinegar at all but disguised vodka. Then the bottle of extra virgin olive oil that is really

153

bourbon. Not far away the tightly-capped bottle of red vinegar that is really red wine. The true alcoholic is also a master of disguise, able to hide booze in any available bottle so as to never leave behind evidence of their own weakness. The final recovery of the evening is the bottle of Listerine in the linen closet upstairs that really isn't Listerine at all.

Satisfied that the search is complete, I move the last of the bottles to the recycling bin, wipe down the entire kitchen counter, run hot water down the drain to remove any scent, then run cold water and turn on the disposal to leave no drops behind. I then spray Glade throughout the kitchen to remove any odor still lingering. Convinced finally that the cleansing is complete, I walk out through the family room, pull open the sliding door and step into the cool night air, onto the deck, and into my favorite lounge chair. I drop down exhausted from the emotional upheaval of Jay's death and from my physical labors of this evening. I have laid out here on many a night, glass in hand, wondering where my husband was, where my son was and if I was going to make it through another lonely day. Those thoughts were always followed by wondering, "What is wrong with me? Why do I chase people away from me? My son is brilliant, hard-working, and dedicated to his career, but he never comes around. My husband is successful, outgoing, handsome and I am the farthest thing from his mind." And I sit alone, night after night, knowing, without the shadow of a doubt that it's all my fault.

But not tonight. Tonight, I'm experiencing a sense of peace and accomplishment that I have not known since my twenties. Not that I have done great things, but more that I have survived a very subtle form of domestic abuse. No, he never hit me, never emotionally attacked me or raised his voice, but his silence, his keeping a second family, his refusal to make me an integral part of his life, leaving me dangling hour after hour, was abuse just the same. Some might say I encouraged his deception by not asking him what was going on and demanding to be a larger part of his world. As a result, they might also say that I have a responsibility for my lot in life, but I wouldn't agree. That's like saying the woman being physically abused is at fault for not ducking sooner.

In reality, despite my hidden bottles all over the house, he had to know I was drinking and drinking a lot. He knew the reason that I was drinking, but he let it go on, year after year, bottle after bottle. That made me easier to manage. It was more convenient to let me stay pickled all the time, making it easier to maintain two families. The truth is, his other wife probably doesn't see it the same way because she is so accomplished, so busy, so confident. She might even argue that I'm at fault for not forcing him to be more of a husband. I didn't, but neither did she. We were both abused, plain and simple.

The breeze picks up, pushing a cooler air across my deck. It's time to go in and go to bed. I walk slowly across the deck, back inside and up the stairs. I turn on the light on my nightstand and look at my king-size bed. It looks bigger than it ever did before. Moving forward, I probably won't need a bed this huge or a house this spacious. I stagger at the thoughts of the changes I'm about to exact in my life. So much to consider in the months ahead, but I'm too exhausted to even think about it tonight. I throw my shorts and top over the chair and walk into the master bathroom, flipping on the overhead light. Double sinks on one side with a jacuzzi bath and glass shower stall on the opposite wall. The area above the sinks is all mirror and an additional full-length mirror hangs on the back of the closed door. I let my bra and panties drop to floor and stare at my naked body in the assorted reflections that surround me.

For a woman in my mid-fifties, even for one rarely sober during the last twenty of those years, I still look surprisingly good. I might not have said that yesterday. There are plenty of men my age who would be attracted to me, if that were at all important to me. For now, though, I need to get to know me, build a new self-image. I need to accept the reality of my situation and start stepping out to live my own life. Money won't be a problem in the foreseeable future, so I will have some choices. Maybe I could travel a bit or volunteer and do some good around the community. I could concentrate on rebuilding my relationship with Dylan, spend time together, laugh a little or a lot. I'm so touched by his comment tonight. He is really proud of me. I'm kind of proud of me too.

I haven't touched the dimmer switches but suddenly the room feels brighter, almost glowing. Yes, I am proud of me. Proud of the image looking back at me. I guess you could say I am a woman of great potential. You're never too old to have potential, are you? I have an awful lot to offer this world. Better late than never. I run a brush through my hair, wash up and brush my teeth. I look once more into the mirror and smile back at my reflection as I leave the bathroom, switching off the light.

I pull back the sheets and slide into bed, getting my pillow just right before reaching over and turning off the light. I usually feel weighted down when I come to bed, like I might sink into the box springs below the mattress. Tonight, I feel light as a feather, like I'm floating above the sheets. Tomorrow will be another tough day, but I'm actually looking forward to it. The worst is over. Enough of the dead, now, on to living. Thank you, Jay.

CHAPTER EIGHTEEN
WILL

———•·•———

This has easily become the longest day of my life. Planning was the easy part. Once the plan was in place, all I had to do was follow it. Now I have to live with myself.

I have spent the last hour driving around the city streets of Buffalo and then working my way from suburb to suburb. From busy thoroughfares to quiet neighborhoods, I'm in no hurry to get anywhere. It feels like a penny hike, where you come to an intersection and flip a coin, heads you go left and tails you go right, never knowing where you might end up. It's great for killing time but horrible for accomplishing even the smallest of things. I have a destination in mind, but I manage to fill my head with every reason not to get there. I finally cross the southern-most border of the town of Amherst. My target is here but in the northern part of town. Considering Amherst is the largest town in the state of New York, I still have lots of pennies to flip.

I finally turn onto the street where Annie and Jesse live. Annie and Jesse? I don't even know if that is the right way to say it anymore. Most of the neighborhood is dark as I pass in front of what I considered my second home. I even have a key to the house on my keychain. I quietly drift past the house and stop at the curb two driveways past the lawn I have mowed so many times. I turn off my car and slowly look back at the house. It is completely dark with no cars in the driveway. I consider going inside the house to wait but decide I can't handle that. I choose instead to add a few more miles to my night's walk. Strolling through a neighborhood late at night tends to bring unwanted attention, but since it is cooler than most summer nights, most of the front porches are empty. That, plus wearing a black shirt and shorts, helps me to blend in.

The truth is I'm in no hurry to knock on Adam's door. Confessing to your best friend that you just murdered his father is tough to casually sneak into a conversation. I know I have no choice. I can't hold onto this forever. The guilt will eat me alive. Is there any chance he will understand? For him to appreciate my motivation, I have to tell him his father had another life, another wife, and another son. I also have to tell him I may have accidently killed him.

What am I saying? How do you accidently kill someone by plunging a hypodermic needle into their neck? What if I told him I was just patting him on the back for being in such great shape and I forgot I had the needle in my hand? He probably wouldn't buy that. I know I wouldn't. No! No lame excuses. Be honest with him. Explain what was going on in your head. Tell him how confused and hurt you were; how you wanted to tell him but didn't know how...not wanting to be the whistleblower. I didn't want them to "shoot the messenger," and push me away from the only family I knew. So, I did the only thing that made sense in my distraught mind. Maybe he will be so upset about the existence of another family that he will forget about the murder part and let it slide.

I get to the end of a cul-de-sac and turn back toward the entrance of the development, keeping my eyes open for oncoming headlights. The more I walk, the more I think, and the more I think the less anything makes sense. If my entire body is wracked with guilt, the last thing I can do is lie to Adam and in the process, create more guilt. I have to be honest. I have no choice but to tell the truth. I walk past my car and lean against the trunk, facing Annie's house. I take a deep breath and look up to the stars, hoping to find a new answer but there is none to be found. I have to tell Adam the truth. There is no other choice to make.

Just then, a car turns the corner toward me. I step around to the passenger side of the car so as not to be too obvious. As it drives under the streetlight, I can see Annie alone behind the wheel. She pulls into the driveway as the garage door slowly climbs upward. The car stops to give the door time to open then pulls into the middle of the two-car garage. I move back around to the trunk to get a better view. Annie sits in the car and doesn't seem to be in a hurry to get out. Maybe she is still crying or maybe she is on the phone. Whatever the reason, she sits for almost fifteen minutes before slowly opening the door and getting out. She looks exhausted. She reaches back inside the car and pushes the garage door button on her visor, disappearing behind the dropping gate. I see a dim light come on in the foyer when she flicks on the kitchen lights.

I start to walk slowly toward the house. I cut across the lawn toward the front porch. I take one step up and reach for the doorbell. Even though I have a key, I wouldn't feel right walking in at a time like this. If I ring the bell and she isn't up for company she will either tell me so or simply not come to the door. Do I want her to have to make that choice? What if she is really upset, crying? Then what do I do? My finger hovers an inch from the doorbell and freezes. This doesn't feel right. Maybe I can go around to the back and see what she is doing, see if it's a good time for company. I walk slowly around the garage side of the house, along the hedges I trimmed just yesterday. I lean around the corner and look at the back patio. Thankfully, it's empty. I walk around to the family room window and step lightly between the perennials I planted three years ago. I can see Annie through the window. She is walking slowly around the room, her arms crossed in front of her and her head down. She walks along the bar, a custom one that Jesse had built, running her fingers along the countertop. She strolls along the fireplace, touching some of the memorabilia on the mantle as she moves. Every once in a while, I can see her head shake.

I glance back over my shoulder to be sure I'm not being watched. I wouldn't want Peeping Tom added to the charge of murder.

Annie crosses the living room to come to the heavy, high-backed chair that was well known as Jesse's chair. For the many hours I have spent in this room, I have never seen anyone sit in that chair but him, which is part of the reason it still looks brand new. Annie turns and sits down in the chair, putting her head back as she looks up to the ceiling. Running her hands along the arm rests, she slowly folds her hands into fists, tightening until her knuckles turn white. She raises her hands up and slams them back down on the chair's arms. Then again, even harder. She pounds the chair three more times before jumping to her feet.

Stepping back from the chair she spins around, eyes locked on the back of the chair as if Jesse was still sitting there. Moving quickly, she walks into the kitchen and then returns with a long knife in her hand. Standing in front of the chair, she starts talking at it, then she gets loud enough that I can almost make out her words. Annie lets out a startling scream that runs right though me, forcing me to take a quick step back from the window. In the middle of the shriek, she drives the kitchen knife down through the seat back again and again. Her last swing brings the knife down through the middle of the seat. She falls back onto the ottoman, leaving the knife sticking straight up from the chair. Her screams have finally stopped. She falls silent, surveying the damage she has done. She gets back up and moves quickly to the fireplace and picks up the two-family pictures that include Jesse, Adam and her and smashes them against the hearth before returning to the ottoman. Annie takes in the scene and looks at the knife sticking out of the cushion and starts to laugh, a little snicker at first and then a full-throated roar.

I need to get in there but how do I do it? I can't let on that I have been watching and yet I can't just let myself in on a night like this. Will she answer the door if I ring the bell? I take a step back from the window trying to remain as quiet as possible while still visualizing Annie's attack. One more step and I hear another noise coming from the family room. I step back toward the window to see Annie still laughing and Adam standing in the doorway of the room. I can see the shock on his face and the hesitancy in his body, not knowing how to react to the scene before him. He stands with his legs spread and his arms slightly raised, with his hands open and his palms up. It doesn't appear as if Annie knows yet that he is there. One doesn't have to be a lip reader to see the word "Mom" form on his lips as he calls out to her. Still sitting on the ottoman, Annie's head snaps toward the sound. Seeing Adam standing there, she starts to laugh even harder, doubling over, holding her sides while staring at the floor. Adam crosses the room and sits down on the ottoman while he puts his arm on her back. She sits back up, looks at him, tries to hold back her next laugh but fails miserably. They are close enough to the window now that I can make out some of the words.

They're walking to the patio! I have to get out of here. I jump out of the garden and race around the corner of the house. I sprint across the front yard as quickly as possible, looking around to make sure no one is running after me. The combination of the sprint, the fear and the adrenaline have me panting heavily by the time I reach my car. I place my hand on the trunk as I bend over to try and catch my breath.

"You okay, boy?"

I jump up to see an elderly man wearing a light sweater and shorts walking his dog. He stares at me, perplexed, as he watches me try to recover my breathing.

"Yes, sir, I'm alright."

"What are you doing out here at this hour?" he asks.

"Oh, I got home late from work and still wanted to squeeze my evening run in before bed. You know, gotta stay in shape at my age," I reply while patting my stomach.

"Gotcha, well good luck with that." He starts to walk again slowly along the sidewalk while his dog sniffs every blade of grass he passes before finally lifting his leg on a small bush.

"One suggestion though," he calls back from half a yard away. "You might want to stick to the streets or sidewalk to run on instead of cutting through people's yards. Someone might get the wrong idea about you."

"Yes, sir," is all I can find to say as he turns and walks away, but he isn't done.

"Oh, and those boots you wear aren't great for running long distance. You might want to think about running shoes."

"Are you some sort of detective, Mister?"

"Used to be," he responded.

"Good night, sir."

"Night, boy."

Exasperated, I sit down on the curb behind my car and drop my head into my hands. Since starting my business a few years ago, I cannot remember being so wrong so many times in one day.

After what I just witnessed, I can't go back and knock on that door tonight. Adam will not have his usual patience with me although Annie might consider throwing me a parade.

Everyone's emotions are at an extreme and somehow, I need to have a calm, unemotional conversation with Adam. I'm not sure I can do that right now and he probably couldn't either. I slowly get to my feet and pull open the door to my car. I look back over my shoulder one last time only to see a shadow in Adam's bedroom window. Is he looking back at me? I hesitate for a second, thinking maybe I should go back, then jump behind the wheel and drive away as quickly as possible with two hands on the steering wheel and one eye on the rear-view mirror. My cell phone starts to buzz but I ignore it, knowing full well who would be calling me at this hour, I can't go back to that house.

I need sleep but I know that won't happen. My eyes are heavy, and my hands continue to shake. The rumblings have returned to my stomach and I can't decide whether to feed it or look for another potted plant to invade. I turn on to Transit Road and look for an open restaurant with an available booth in which I can collapse. I can see a sign alive in a strip plaza on my left and decide to give it a chance. I pull in and have my choice of hundreds of parking places as the plaza looks deserted. I pull on the door to the diner and to my surprise it opens. There is a cook in the kitchen, and a waitress at the register...and me with twenty empty booths to choose from.

"Does it matter where I sit?" I ask the waitress.

"Sit anywhere you like, honey. You want some coffee?"

"That would be great." She brings over a mug and what looks like a fresh pot of coffee. She tosses some creamer cups on the table from a pocket on her apron. She returns the pot to its holder and comes back with a one-page laminated menu with pictures on both sides.

"You know what you want, or should I come back in a bit?" she asks.

"I'm not quite sure yet. Could you come back?"

"Well, I do have a lot of other tables to attend to, but I'll see if I can squeeze you in."

"Seems like everyone is a comedian tonight," I mumble.

"You okay, Honey?" she asks

"Don't I look okay?"

"To be honest, not so much. Looks like you been in an argument and the other person won. I'm sorry, I'll leave you be."

"No, I'm sorry. I'm not being very polite and that's not me. Yeah, it's been a very long day, and it doesn't appear as if it's going to end any time soon, no matter what the clock says. Is the coffee good enough for now?

"Sure, Hon. Take all the time you need. You know where to find me."

That may have been the first sign of compassion I've heard all day. My head continues to pound although my stomach seems to be settling down. I have no interest in going home. I look at my phone and see the missed call from Adam. I don't know how to make things right when you murder your best friend's father, but I have to find a way. I already know I can't live with myself constantly holding this in and worrying that I will be discovered. Even if I was convinced that I was doing the right thing when I did it. I will never be able to look Adam or Annie in the eye if I don't bare my soul to them. I look at the neon clock on the wall above the register and see that it's too late to go back tonight. I'll go first thing in the morning then. That's what I have to do, without fail.

I pour the creamer into my cup and look down into the swirls it creates. For a moment it mesmerizes me, takes me back to a time at Annie and Jesse's kitchen table when, after playing in the snow with Adam for what seemed like all day, we came inside and Annie made us hot chocolate. My hair was still wet from the shovel full of snow that Adam had dumped on my head. Neither one of us could stop laughing. My childhood is stocked with memories of the happiest moments in my life and all of them were in that house, in their company. In the weakest moment of my existence on this earth, I did what I thought would right a wrong brought by and against two people that I love so much. The swirls in my cup disappear but the vision stays with me.

I have messed up, big time. I have to make it right. When the sun comes up, when I see the first sign of life come from that house, I will be ringing that doorbell. Another cup of coffee, maybe breakfast of some sort, then I will take my car right back there and park until morning. I owe them that and so much more. I can't take back the plunge of the needle. I can't bring Jesse back to life, but I can be honest with the people I love even if it costs me the freedom I can't imagine living without. The truth is, I will never be free from this, never. Any hope I have of living again begins at that doorbell. I have no choice.

Gary Friedman

CHAPTER NINETEEN
ADAM

———•———

It feels like it has been a week since my daydream near the art gallery. Floating along in my own world, ignoring Devon, listening to the music from the park-like lawn, with hardly a care in the world. In reality, it's been a measly four hours or so since the radio blasted the "runner down" alert. Standing here, just outside the double sliding doors of the emergency room at ECMC, I watch the taillights of my mother's car disappear around the curve of the entry ramp to the trauma unit. I wish I felt more comfortable about her driving home on her own. Despite my hesitancy, she insisted and when Mom insists, she almost always gets her way. Even though Dad got his way occasionally, I always thought it was because Mom was winning, and he didn't want to ruin their short weekend together.

I had a front-row seat tonight to Mom's extreme mood swings. She went from grieving widow to screaming victim and back to controlled bulldog mom. It was like a ride on a roller coaster. Just like at the end of the ride, it took me a few minutes to catch my breath. Add that to the revelation that my father was not the most honorable man, dead or alive, and I was left wondering if I'd ever breathe again.

I pull my cell phone off my belt and call the dispatcher at WNY Response to see if there is some way they could help me connect with Devon or get me a ride back to the garage. Sarah, the dispatcher, told me to stand by at my location while they work something out. She added, "Hey Adam, sorry to hear about your dad." Clearly, word travels fast. Following a quick thank you, I hang my phone back on my belt and wait for a reply. My wait is relatively short. The sound of tires squealing breaks the silence, followed by the sound of the same tires thumping over the curb, accompanied by headlights bouncing violently up and down. The rig screeches to a halt directly in front of me.

"Hey Bro, let's go," calls Devon through the open passenger window.

"What? Were you waiting in the hospital parking lot for me?"

"Of course," he replied.

"And what if I ended up getting another ride home? Would you have sat there all night?"

"It's not like I could take a call all by myself, you know."

"No, but you could have gone back to the garage. They might have been able to scrape up another partner for you."

"I never thought of that. You mean me work with someone besides you? Bro, that would feel like sacrilege, practically illegal."

"Gee, Devon, I almost feel honored by your loyalty."

"So, how are you doing, man? I am really sorry about your old man. I'm not too good about sentiments and all, but I know you must be hurting."

"Thanks. How about a lift back to the garage?"

"No problemo."

"You know, Devon, this may be the longest two-way conversation of our partnership."

"How about that? I guess I'm better at sentiments than I thought."

And there it ended. We rode quietly through the streets of Buffalo until we got back to the garage. Devon backs the rig into our assigned spot. I gather up my gear and throw it into the trunk of my car. We both walk into the small dispatch office where only Sarah is on duty.

"Hey guys," she calls out. "Adam, you doing okay?"

"I am, Sarah. Thanks for asking. I'm probably going to need the next three days off though. Actually, I think I'm already off one of those days, so I just need the two days of leave."

"I will put you in for bereavement leave. What about you, Devon? I'll see if I can set you up for a couple of days with someone else."

"Oh, heck no, Sarah. I gotta be there for my partner. You know, the funeral and all that. He's gonna need me. Besides, Robin doesn't save lives without Batman."

Sarah stares blankly at him for a few moments, a response to which Devon is more than accustomed.

"Devon, I can't put you in for bereavement leave too. It's gotta be a relative."

"But he is my Bro. I would be sick working without him."

"Alright, I will put you in for sick leave. How's your family doing, Adam?"

"It's only me and my mom. I'm going home to be with her now, so I'll have to let you know how she's doing. Thanks for everything, Sarah. G'night." We turn and head out into the cooling night air. I walk to my car and look back to see Devon right behind me.

"Where to now?" he asks.

"Me? I'm going to my mom's to be there for her."

"Okay," says Devon as he walks around to the passenger side door.

"No, Devon. I'm going to my mom's; you're going to wherever it is that you sleep. You do sleep, right?"

"Oh, right. Sorry man," he says as he walks back around my car. "I just wanted to be there for you." He gives me an unexpected hug.

"I will keep you posted on the arrangements when we make them. You will be there at the funeral?"

"I'll be there. And yes."

"Yes, what?"

"I do sleep." And with that he silently walks to his pick-up truck and pulls away into the moonlight. This night keeps getting stranger. I never expected that kind of a response from Devon. I never felt we had connected in that way, because clearly, he sees things differently than I do. Maybe I should work a little harder at being a better partner when we ride together again. Through all his babbling, he has a pretty big heart hidden in there somewhere.

I can feel a wave of exhaustion coming over me as I slide into the driver's seat of my SUV. A large part of me wants to make this all go away, simply dial the clock back to this afternoon when life seemed so much simpler. It has gotten complicated real fast. Even though my father and I did not have the closest of relationships, he was still my father. I wasn't happy about his long absences but if my mother was okay with it, then who was I to complain? Sure, he missed a good deal of the important events in my life, but I guess he was just a busy man. He was attentive when he was around and took great care of Mom and me. I knew guys who had it much worse. All you need to do is look at Will to see a guy who has had no father figure his whole life; no family for that matter, other than us. The bottom line is, I will miss my father; an exercise I have had a lot of practice in.

And then suddenly I not only have to deal with his unexpected death, but also, I discover he was hiding another wife and son on the other side of town and had been doing it for long time. I'm not sure about all the emotions that exploded in me at that moment. I started out angry; angry at what he did to my mother and how he had been lying to me about why he was so busy and unavailable. I felt betrayed, cheated out of a real family.

The anger gave way to confusion. I tried to understand why he would do this, why he didn't just choose one family or the other. Whatever reason he had; he didn't do either side any favors. Instead of committing to one wife or the other, making at least one family fulfilled, he gave a half measure to both families, leaving them both neglected. Dad wasn't a stupid man; he surely knew this, but he just kept it up. Maybe he was a coward, afraid of making a decision...or maybe he didn't want to deal with a divorce. Confronting one wife would surely have drawn the other family into the legal proceedings. Financial disclosures would have been a quagmire.

Confusion then gave way to sadness. I actually felt sorry for him, trying to imagine what his day-to-day life had to be like. In seeking happiness, he placed himself in a never-ending conflict, a misery he could never avoid. No wonder he was planning to take his own life. You think you know someone as well as one person can ever know another only to discover you really never had a clue. My sadness then becomes frustration, and I am right back where I started.

What the heck was Will doing at the hospital tonight? How did he find out about my dad being there? Why didn't he just walk over to us instead of hiding in the corner of the waiting room? I have never seen him like that before. He has always been so sure of himself, so confident in everything he does. He seemed like a little lost dog tonight. I need to reach out to him in the morning, first thing. I'm more than a bit worried about him. I guess Dad was the closest thing he ever had to a father. Whatever arrangements we make tomorrow, I need to be sure to include him.

I close my car windows as the night continues to cool off. I head to my family's home in Amherst. I want to be there for my mother, but I'm in no hurry to get there. I don't know which of Mom's moods would have won out once she got home. I'll find out soon enough. With any luck, she will be asleep in bed when I get there, although I highly doubt it.

I slowly pull into the double driveway. The second floor of the house is dark, but the first floor is well lit, so most likely, Mom is still awake. I decide to go in through the front door rather than through the garage, making my entrance more obvious and not spooking her. I enter and walk through the foyer, past the spiral staircase and toward the family room. When I reach the threshold of the family room, I'm frozen in shock by the sight before me.

My eyes start with the debris on the floor near the fireplace where at least two pictures and a couple of my father's awards have been smashed on the hearth. It looked like someone had dragged their hand along the mantle and knocked off anything in their way. In the other corner is my father's chair, the one only he was allowed to sit in. I tried once and got pulled out by my collar. It was a tall back leather chair. The back cushion was sliced apart with stuffing hanging down. The seat cushion had one wound that still had the weapon imbedded in it. Had Dad been sitting there at the time and had he survived the first few slices, he would have watched that kitchen knife separate himself from his manhood.

Between the fireplace mess and the chair, my mother sat on the ottoman, laughing like I had never seen her laugh before. I stood staring at her with my arms raised and my palms up, not knowing what to do or say. I took one more step into the room, wondering if doing so would catch my mother's attention.

"Mom?" was the best I could do.

She snapped her head toward me, shocked by my presence. She looked at the chair and then back at me and broke out in another round of hysterical laughter. I slowly move toward the fireplace and sit down on the ottoman next to her and put my arm around her shoulder.

"Mom, what is it? What's going on? Are you okay?"

"Yes, honey, I'm fine. It's just...well, I'm afraid I killed your father again." The laughing resumes in earnest, but this time, because of that last line, combined with the innocent look on her face, I burst into laughter right along with her.

"I guess so, Mom. That last shot must have really hurt." I wipe the tears of laughter from my cheek. "Look, let's go out on the patio and get some air and try to come back down to earth a bit."

She nods her head and quietly rises from the ottoman. She takes my hand and as I open the French doors, I hear a rustling coming from the bushes at the corner of the house. I step down to the lawn and move toward the noise. As I get to the corner, I can see a man running across the lawn to the street. My first inclination is to run after him, and I take two steps toward the sprinting shadow. I stop short, not knowing whether it is better to charge after the departing figure or return to the patio to protect my mother. I watch him run to the street and stop for a moment just as I turn back to the patio. Mom had pulled another chaise lounge next to the one she always sits in and sat down. I walk back to her and put a hand on her shoulder.

Gary Friedman

"You alright? I ask.

"Like I said, Adam, I'm fine. Just a momentary loss of control."

"Okay, Mom, just checking. I'll be right back."

I walk back into the house so as not to alarm Mom, then sprint into the foyer and up the spiral stairs to my old bedroom. I look out the window, down to the street. The stranger I had seen moments ago is getting into his car. As he pulls open the driver side door, he turns and looks up at me.

"Will! What the heck?" I exclaim to the closed window. He jumps into his car and pulls away, heading down the street and out of the development. I pull my cell phone off my belt and hit the speed dial button to connect with him. No answer. I try again with the same result. It's too late now to keep trying. I will reach out again in the morning before Mom and I head out to breakfast.

I return to the patio and settle in the chair next to my mother. She is reclined in her chair with her head back, looking up at the stars, deep in thought. We sit in silence with Mom still looking up and me scanning everything in view, taking in the patio, the yard, and the whole back of the house, finally settling my eyes back on her. Despite all the tears and anguish of the night, she looks at peace. She is every bit the beautiful woman she has been my whole life. I honestly can't think of one major disagreement or cross word we have shared in the last fifteen years. We have always been more like best friends than mother and son, except for the weekends when Dad was around. Then I became a distant relative, an old acquaintance.

"Did you ever know, even suspect?" she asked quietly.

"I really didn't, Mom. Never had a clue he was anything other than what we saw. You?"

"There were times, Adam, that I wondered what occupied his mind. Times in bed at night when he seemed miles and miles away. Turns out he was only twenty miles away. Other than those fleeting moments, I never really doubted him. That's part of what angers me; he was so good at this manipulation, so good at fooling me that I never considered any alternative."

"I know. That's why when Dylan…"

"Dylan?"

"Dylan, the doctor."

"Oh, right. Your half-brother."

"Yeah, that guy. When he started telling us the truth for the first time, it felt like a two-by-four across my face. I was absolutely stunned. I thought I knew Dad so well, and yet I didn't know him at all. All I could keep thinking was what kind of a man does that? I am still at a loss."

She nods her head and falls silent, going back to her study of the stars above. The silence continues to grow between us. I consider telling her about Will but decide to wait until I know more. Now that he knows I saw him I don't think he will come back. No need to upset Mom right now.

I continue to watch her. Nothing moves but her eyelids, occasionally blinking away the night. Every once in a while, a blink will last a bit longer than the rest, making me think that sleep isn't far away. Somehow, I wish I could make all this disappear for her, ease her pain in some way. She didn't deserve this, not like anybody does, but least of all her. She works so hard at being an executive, a mother, and a wife, and this is not a fair way for her marriage to end. It would have been hard enough just being a widow but being the widow of a world-class bigamist must be even more agonizing. Along with the grief of loss, Mom has to be filled with questions that can no longer be answered, while realizing that in the coming days and weeks, others will discover the truth about her marriage.

Funny how I'm feeling blank about all this. I don't even know what to think, how to classify the man I thought I knew. I just feel so bad for Mom right now that there doesn't seem to be a place to consider what I'm going through. I'm sure the time will come for my own emotions; there will be no escaping the reality of what happened. Just not now. I have to be there for Mom, and maybe even for Will. I worry about him as well.

I look back at Mom as my own eyes close. I think back to a basketball game I played in high school, maybe ten years ago. There was a time out and I was looking up into the stands. Mom was in a row with what looked like four couples and her...four cheering mothers with their husbands at their sides and in the middle was my mother, alone again. I remember feeling so bad for her. I remember thinking that I needed to talk to Dad about this, about being there more for her, not for me but for her. I even remember practicing my speech in my room, what I would say and how I would say it. The moment passed and by the next weekend when he re-entered our lives for his typical forty-eight hours, it was all forgotten. Now, I wish I had followed through, told him what I thought. Maybe it would have made a difference. Maybe not. In my mind I could see my father standing in front of me while I read him the riot act, tears falling down my face. He puts his hand on my shoulder.

"Adam."

"Yes, Dad."

"Adam!"

My eyes open, and I look up at my mother as she tries to stir me from my dreams.

"Yeah, Mom."

"Let's go to bed. It's going to be another long day tomorrow."

If I said Dad out loud, she didn't seem to hear it or react. I rise slowly, and we lock arms and walk silently together into the house, turning off the lights in the family room and with that one gesture, life as we knew it. After today, nothing will ever be the same again. I miss the past already.

Gary Friedman

CHAPTER TWENTY
ANNIE

———•———

The garage door seems to open slower than usual as I wait patiently in the driveway. As I do, I can feel a wave of exhaustion flow over my body, feeling like I had played ten sets of tennis instead of just sitting around all night. I pull slowly into the garage and shut down my car. I recline the seat just a bit as I try and catch my breath. My eyes close, and the memories of all this house has meant to me come rushing back. I take some deep breaths before feeling ready to go inside. If a cluttered, messy garage is bringing back memories, what is the interior going to do to me? I grab my purse and swing my legs out, settling my feet on the concrete floor. I take two steps toward the door before spinning back around and closing the garage door from my visor button. The three steps leading into the laundry room feel like a mountain to climb as I drag myself into the house.

I flip on the kitchen light then walk across the family room and drop my purse and keys onto the kitchen table. My hand rests on the back of a kitchen chair where I bend over, letting my head rest on my hands as my eyes close again. Every sense engages in its own favorite memory. The rough feel of the chair where Jesse usually sat, the aroma of meals shared, the distant sound of music that always played in the background during his visits, even the memory of the crazy Saturday night when we made love on the kitchen floor. I should be sad, tears should be flowing, but they are not. I stand straight up and spin around the kitchen one more time, trying to shake off every memory that comes rushing at me like a stampede. I walk away from the memories and back into the family room, where another stampede begins.

I walk around the perimeter of the room, one painful step after another. I run my hand along the bar that Jesse had custom made, just the way he liked it, perfect for us and perfect for anyone we chose to entertain. Not that we entertained much, with his schedule and our mutual desire to catch up from our lost time together. The bar just suited him. I wonder if he had one in his other house as well. I walk in front of the sofa and gaze at the pictures along the wall, some artwork but mostly family pictures of the two or three of us. I turn the corner toward the fireplace. That was my design. It took up the entire wall with a woodburning opening and a built-in box to hold the extra logs. The mantle also runs the full length of the room, filled with memories from end to end. A couple of plants, some Christmas gifts, a few tennis trophies, plaques and many, many pictures. Three or four of the happy couple, one of Adam and his father, one of Adam and me and one of all of us. One big happy family, weren't we?

I reach the next corner of the room and come to the high back leather chair we'd come to know as his majesty's throne. Whenever he was home, rare as it was, it was his place of rest. No one ever sat in that chair but him. Even when we had a dog, he was banned from the throne as well. Unimaginable as it seemed, even I had never sat in it before. It was a rule. It was a symbol. It was tradition. I look around the room as if somebody might be watching. With no one in sight, I turn slowly and settle into Jesse's cherished throne for the first time ever. I ease down slowly, feeling the air escape from the black seat. I lean my head back. My hands settle on the arm rests, running my fingers back and forth from end to end, finally staying at rest. My eyes close as I can almost catch a hint of his cologne. Silence, dead silence. Then it happened.

With my head against the leather, I breathe deeply, letting every bit of air flow back out slowly. The smell of the cologne grows stronger, so familiar, so real. I can feel the arm rests soften and become warm flesh. The arms move, slowly at first, until they hold my hands as his arms wrap around me, holding me close, two bodies breathing instead of one. The hands cup my breasts and hold me close against him. I can begin to feel his breath against my neck, then his lips against my skin, nibbling at my ear. My body can't help responding to his every caress, like it always has. I can hear myself let go of a slow, quiet moan, feeling my body coming alive, becoming aroused, like it always was in his arms. I begin to squirm against him. I can feel that part of him grow, pushing against me. I crave his touch, his lips against mine. I want to give myself to him one last time. My hands close into fists. My head drops hard against the leather as my eyes open.

Son of a bitch. "SON OF A BITCH!"

I jump from the chair and spin around. Its emptiness stares back at me. My hands are still clenched fists, shaking at my side. I storm off into the kitchen and cross to my work area. I draw the longest knife from its block, wrapping my fingers around the black handle. Turning, I stride back into the family room and march directly to his throne. I raise the knife above my head and with both hands gripping the handle I slam it down into the back of the chair, exactly where his eyes would have been. I charge a second time and drive the blade a little lower, where his lips would have been. I plunge it again, still lower, where his black heart used to be. I raise it above my head one last time and grind it into the seat cushion, right between where his legs would have been and then drop back onto the ottoman directly in front of the chair, with the knife still stuck in the seat, handle sticking straight up.

I leap from the ottoman and grab a picture of us off the mantle and smash it on the hearth. I take another and throw it against the family portrait hanging above the sofa. I take the last picture and heave it across the room into his precious bar, breaking half a dozen glasses and a carafe. I drop back onto the ottoman, looking at the broken glass around the room and the damage I have done. My eyes finally come to rest on the knife, erect and rising from the torn cushion. As if all that wasn't enough, while staring at the knife handle, I start to smile, then a giggle escapes, then the giggle evolves into a full-throated laugh, one that shows no sign of letting up.

As the laughing subsides, I get a sense that I am no longer alone. I look up quickly and see Adam standing in the doorway, arms raised in a "Ma? What the heck?" gesture. He walks slowly across the room to the sound of crunching glass under his feet. He sits down next to me on the ottoman, putting his arm around me.

"Mom, what is it? What's going on? Are you okay?"

"Yes, honey, I'm fine. It's just...well, I'm afraid I killed your father again." The laughing begins again but this time I am not alone.

"I guess so, Mom. That last shot must have really hurt." Now we are both laughing, his arm around me and my head on his shoulder.

"Look, Mom, let's go out on the patio and get some air and try to come back down to earth a bit." I look at my beautiful boy and wipe the tears from his face. I smile and nod. We stand as if choreographed and walk through the doors to a cooling night breeze. Adam rushes to the edge of the patio for a moment as I pull another chaise lounge out for Adam then settle in mine.

Adam comes back to me for a moment to check on me then heads back into the house. I sit back and look out at the yard, illuminated in the beautiful moonlight, waiting for Adam to return.

I do love my home and this patio has always been my getaway, at least in those few months in Buffalo where you can go outside and really enjoy it. Will has maintained our property for years and it is lovely; simply and elegantly landscaped. It is tempting to want to stay in this house forever, but it makes no sense. This house is way too big for me alone and obviously contains too many memories. Adam has his own life to lead, and I have to make some major decisions about my own life.

I know I have been left a fairly well-funded life insurance policy, and I have a great deal of equity in this house. Add to that my 401K and a savings account I have set aside for myself for a rainy day, and I can say that I will be...comfortable. Never did I imagine that the rainy day would pour so heavy and so soon. Yet all this leaves me with options and there may be no better time than now. I'm going to be the subject of some "oh, you poor woman" stares from quite a few people for a while and I hate the idea of it. Maybe it's time to move on, start a new career, maybe even in a new part of the country. Yes, lots of options. I don't have to make any moves tomorrow, but it's all something I can consider.

Adam comes back out the door and settles down next to me.

"Did you ever know, even suspect?" I ask.

"I really didn't, Mom. Never had a clue he was anything other than what we saw. You?"

"There were times, Adam, that I wondered what occupied his mind. Times in bed at night when he seemed miles and miles away. Turns out he was only twenty miles away. Other than those fleeting moments, I never really doubted him. That's part of what

183

angers me is that he was so good at this manipulation, so good at fooling me that I never considered any alternative."

"I know. That's why when Dylan…"

"Dylan?"

"Dylan, the doctor."

"Oh, right. Your half-brother." I cringe at the thought of adding to my family like this but I suppose in time, I will get used to it. His other wife really touched me. She seems like a lovely woman despite the fact that she slept with my husband once or twice over the past three decades. I did appreciate the hug at the emergency room, and I need to tell her so tomorrow.

"Yeah, that guy. When he started telling us the truth for the first time, it felt like a two-by-four across the face. I was absolutely stunned. I thought I knew Dad so well and yet I didn't know him at all. All I could keep thinking was what kind of a man does that? Why did he do that to us? I am still at a loss."

All I can manage is a nod, having no way to describe that moment for myself. No words even come close. I have gone numb, as if every system in my body has shut down. There is no sadness, no remorse for a wasted life; just anger, a seething red-hot boiling anger. I can feel the heat rising again through my body as I relive the moment. No, I don't want to do this. I have lived the last thirty years of my life with one man. He never forced me to do anything, and I never begged him to change his ways. I lived my life, and he lived his. I thought it was an agreement, a pact. The anger? That comes from the knowledge that I was the only one that honored that pact. He abused it, lied to me, took advantage of my nature not to probe. He honored nothing, least of all me.

I close my eyes and think about the world as it appears tonight. I want the funeral over with, like right now. I need to start writing down my thoughts, maybe keep a journal, weigh all my options. Apply everything I have used in business to my personal life and create a well-thought-out plan. Maybe I will create a spreadsheet or two, make it seem official. I should sit down with Adam and see what we can come up with together. It really does hurt that Adam had to go through what he went through tonight. He is hiding his distress well. I have to include him in this adjustment.

I open my eyes and look over at my son. He is sound asleep in the chair next to me. His body is twitching like a puppy as he works through whatever dream occupies his mind tonight. I get up and walk over to his chair, reach down to his shoulder, and give him a little shake.

"Adam."

"Yes, Dad." His reply unnerves me.

"Adam!" as I shake him again.

His eyes open in shock.

"Yeah, Mom."

"Let's go to bed. It's going to be another long day tomorrow."

He shakes off the sleep and climbs to his feet. We lock arms and walk back into the house. I look around at the mess I will have to clean up tomorrow and shake my head in disgust. We tip-toe across the broken glass and into the foyer, heading for the stairs. I let Adam go up before me. Sticking out of his back pocket is an envelope similar to the one I tore apart a few hours earlier.

"Adam, what's that sticking out of your pocket?"

He reaches back and pulls it out. "It's a letter for Will."

"From your father?"

"Yeah, it was in the envelope with the others. I'll give it to him next time I see him, whenever that may be. He is behaving weirdly."

185

"Did you read yours?"

"I did."

"Do you want to talk about it?"

"Maybe at some point, Mom, but not tonight. I gotta get some sleep."

He turns and finishes the stairs two at a time and ducks behind his bedroom door.

"Good night, Adam."

No reply from the closed door. For all I have to deal with, Adam has twice as much. Yes, we both lost a loved one, but he was the one who tried to save his father. Knowing Adam, the responsibility for that will weigh heavily on his conscience. I'm sure he is questioning his every action, wondering if he did everything he could to save his father.

I close my bedroom door behind me, feeling the exhaustion return. I toss my tennis outfit over the chair and head for the bathroom for my nightly ritual. I turn on the water and load my toothbrush, before looking up at the mirror that had held my gaze only a few hours earlier. At first glance, I look like I have aged twenty years in a night. New bags under my eyes and wrinkles where there had been none. My shoulders droop as my posture sags. I look like I'm carrying the weight of the world.

Since my last view of myself in this mirror, my whole world has changed. My beloved husband, the love of my life, died, taking with him the seemingly unreal image of a man who could do no wrong. That image was quickly replaced by one of a man with no honor, no integrity...without a truthful bone in his body. I'm glad Adam read his letter, but there was no point in my reading mine, and I have no remorse for destroying it before I had the chance. After all, there is no explanation, no apology, no justification that would ease the pain caused by his deception. There are no retrievable facts or loving memories that will supplant the words spoken by that doctor.

In one sentence, he reconstructed history and ruined the life I have known for the last thirty years. *Thirty years*. I keep repeating the same words over and over again in my head. Thirty years. How can someone be that deceitful for that long a period of time? My biggest regret in his death is that I will never get the chance to ask him how he managed it all this time. *Thirty years*. I will never know what any of this ever meant to him and if he truly valued me at all, how he could think his deceit showed me that he valued me in any way. Did he lie in bed with her and think of me? Did he lie in bed with me and think of her? Was he ever truly mine by any definition? Thirty years. Questions with no answers, now or ever.

Routine finished; I look one last time in the mirror at my naked body. I throw back my shoulders and lift my head up. I smile back at what I see. This isn't on me. I never failed him as a wife or a lover. What I offered as his wife would have been treasured by most men, would have been enough to fulfill their needs. A beautiful wife, a lovely home, a fine son, and all the passion that any one man would ever crave. I was great for him. That this wasn't enough for Jesse is not a reflection on me. No sir, not on me at all. Not now. Not ever.

Gary Friedman

CHAPTER TWENTY-ONE
DYLAN

— · —

I know it's time to open my eyes. Maybe, if I just lie here for a while, ignoring reality, maybe last night will never have happened. I could pretend it's just another day, relax with a morning cup of coffee, cruise the internet, have a bowl of cereal, start getting ready to spend another night in the trauma center. I could, if yesterday hadn't happened, but it did. It would take a night like last night to find me waking up in my mother's house. The last time that happened was about five years ago after a long night at a stag party for a med school buddy. I am not normally a big drinker, but that party just got out of hand. I can't even recall how I ended up here, but apparently, somebody dumped my body on Mom's front porch.

My right eye cracks open to a blast of bright morning sunshine sneaking through the open shades. A lesser man would have pulled the covers over his head or rolled over to make the sunlight disappear. Instead, my left eye also opens to the new day. I reach for my cell phone for a time check and to see if anyone is wondering where I am. I push myself up to a sitting position while trying to stretch the kinks out of my aching body.

The clinking of dishes tells me I'm not the first one up. It's hard to imagine Mom being up early, straightening up the kitchen just twelve hours after the death of her husband, given that for years her ability to cope with any distress was found in the bottom of a bottle. The memory of my father dying on the examination table in the ER comes rushing back. The only part that haunts me is my decision not to step out of the case as soon as I realized it was my father on the table before me. I balanced proper procedures against the need to act quickly and was convinced that any delay would have been detrimental to the survival of the patient, relative or not. I was thinking rationally and not emotionally. The bottom line is I can justify all of my actions last night as well as those of my team.

I swing my legs over the side of the bed and slowly make my way to the bathroom.

"Dylan, you want some coffee?" comes Mom's voice from the bottom of the stairs.

"No, Mom, I'm good for now." I'm kind of surprised by the lightness in her voice but by now I probably shouldn't be. From the moment Dad's secrets came to light, she has been a new woman, surer of herself, more at peace, behaving like someone more concerned about the people around her than obsessing over her own issues. It's refreshing to be sure. It doesn't appear as if a night back in her own house has caused my mother to backslide into her old habits.

I trudge down the stairs to find my mother sitting at the kitchen table, a mug of coffee in her hand while she peruses the morning paper. She looks up and smiles as I enter the kitchen. I pour some orange juice and take the chair next to her. I marvel over the change in her appearance in less than one day. She is like a medical miracle. That tired listless look so common among someone who previously spent too much time in a bottle seems to have disappeared overnight. Her brown hair, lightly flecked with grey strands, is pulled back neatly, and is held in place with a hair tie. Her lovely green eyes actually glitter. She was never one to wear much make-up and this morning is no exception, and she looks lovely. Is it possible that twenty-four hours can turn back ten years of aging?

"How are you doing this morning, Mom?"

She looks up over her reading glasses and offers a soft smile. "I'm doing okay, Honey. How are you?"

"It's way too early to tell." I reply. "Are you ready for this big meeting?"

"Tell me, how do you get ready for a meeting like this? It's hard enough planning a funeral for someone you love, but under circumstances like these, well, I just don't know what to expect. They seem like nice people, Annie, and Adam. I feel sorry for them. Don't you?"

"Sure, I do," I reply. "Yeah, they seem like good people, considering we met them at a time like this. Of course, I've known Adam from WNY Response, but not like this, you know? I guess I am still amazed Dad could pull this off. The two families were so close these last thirty years. We were what, twenty miles apart? What are the odds that this situation never blew up in his face before this? Of course, it all hits the fan after he dies so he never has to face the music. Do you think that when this story gets out, anyone will believe we weren't aware of the other wife? You know, guilty by association?"

"Dylan, I can't worry about what other people think. They are going to believe what they want. We know what the truth is. We just have to get through this. I don't think we will have any problems dealing with these arrangements."

"It's not like we have to be concerned with the wishes of the deceased," I commented.

"Be nice."

"Seriously, Mom. How can you give a damn about what he wants after what he has done to all of us? I say we bury him Viking

191

style. Put him on a raft, push it out onto Lake Erie and set it on fire with flaming arrows. He can sleep with the fishes."

"Dylan, stop it. He was still your father."

"Genetically, maybe. He was never much of a father to me and quite frankly, I think you'd not rate him very highly as a husband either."

"Honey, he is dead and gone. It serves no purpose to harbor any ill will against him. We need to move on."

"You are unbelievable. He cheated on you for thirty years and you are okay with just moving on. I don't know how you can forgive him that easily."

"It's not a matter of forgiving or not. It's getting on with my life. Yes, he cheated on me, and yes, I have wasted much of my life waiting for your father to come home. I have no plans to waste one more minute of what I have left of my life mourning him. I have to think about me, and what's in my best interest is to get on with my life. That's what I am going to do.

"Listen to yourself, Mom, you sound like a self-help book. Tell me something, what happened to you last night? I left Lisa with you because you were crying so hard, I didn't want to leave you alone. The next thing I know, there you are, all Mother Teresa, calming everybody else. So, what gives?"

"It's really difficult to explain, Dylan. Yes, I was pretty upset at the news of your father's passing, and I'm sure that you know about my drinking problem."

"It hasn't really been much of a secret, Mom."

"I'm sure. It has been a constant struggle for years. I had made a promise to myself just yesterday morning to get my life in order and stop drinking. To try and be a better wife and mother. I have not felt good about who I am; how I have behaved and how I have let everybody down, especially myself. I have considered myself a failure for a long time. I felt that if I had been a better wife, your father would have tried to spend more time with me, that somehow, I wasn't worth it. And that starting yesterday, I was going to be better for my family.

"Then, Honey, when I heard you tell Annie and Adam about your father, well, it was like every bad image I had of myself drained away. My troubled marriage, my husband's lack of interest in being home…they weren't my fault. Not now, not ever. I looked at Annie and saw the kind of woman I shared your father with, how beautiful and confident she is. It occurred to me that if she couldn't keep him home and committed, then no one could, least of all me. Suddenly, in the midst of finding out my husband was dead, I felt free, and I felt forgiven for every negative thought I ever had about myself. Isn't that strange? I suddenly realized that the reason my husband wasn't happy with me was that he was a lousy husband and a lousy human being. I could have been a queen, and he would still have been the same man. Do you understand what I'm trying to say?"

"I think I do, Mom. I think I do. He was quite a piece of work, wasn't he?"

"Without a doubt. But I don't want the two of us spending the rest of our days on this earth tearing him down. It has no point."

"So, what now? What are you going to now?"

"I don't feel like I have to make any quick decisions. Maybe it was your father's guilty conscience, assuming he had one, but he didn't leave me destitute. I have money in the bank, equity in this house, and he left me a very nice insurance policy. On top of that, I never touched the money I received from my parent's estate. I was looking over our stuff this morning …"

"Could you stop saying 'our'?"

"I was looking over MY stuff this morning, and I don't think I'll even have to move."

"Much better."

"What about you, Dylan? What are you going to do?"

"To be honest, Mom, Dad hasn't been a part of my life for a long time. Nothing much is going to change for me. I'm going to continue being a doctor at ECMC and if I'm lucky, stay in trauma medicine. I'm single with no prospects for that changing anytime soon. Outside of my undergraduate and medical school loans, I'm mostly debt free."

"Then you don't know, do you?"

"Know what?"

"I saw a notice last month that your father paid off your undergraduate loan."

"He did what?"

"You heard me."

"I had no idea at all. Why would he do that all of a sudden?"

"Best I can figure, knowing what I know now, he was trying to tie up loose ends. He didn't want to leave anything undone behind. The man was a puzzle, that's for sure."

"I'll say. I can't believe he did that, but to be honest, it doesn't change my opinion of him one whit."

"Not even his arrangements?"

"I still vote for a Viking send off. What about you?"

"I honestly don't know. Small and quiet are the words that keep slipping into my head. Just us, no publicity, no obituary, no marching band. I just want it over."

With that, our conversation ends. Mom gets up and refills her coffee mug and empties the rest of the pot into a cup for me. I take it without argument. I stand up from the table and take my half-filled cup out onto the deck. It is as beautiful a summer morning as you will find in this part of the world. A trio of birds are bathing in the garden fountain while a couple of rabbits look surprised at my presence. I pace slowly back and forth across the wood slats of the deck. I can still hear the very few conversations my father and I had about life. They were usually late in the evening with the tiki lamps scaring off the mosquitos. He would go on about the unexpected moments in life, the surprises that tend to take our breath away.

Boy, he wasn't kidding about unexpected moments. First his death, then his secret life...and then, in the middle of that, he pays off my under-grad college loans. The memories sadden me. Not enough to call off the Vikings but a reminder of the man he could have been, the family we could have had. I ache for the years my mother lost while drowning her misery. I never really considered that in my desire to make a life without a father, I also distanced myself from her, which in all likelihood drove her further into her addiction. That saddens me most of all. I feel a sudden urge to tell her so.

I walk back into the house and find the kitchen empty. Her mug is drying in the sink and the table has been wiped down. I walk into the kitchen and see a white garbage bag sitting on the floor waiting to be hauled out to the garbage cans. I can hear some water running upstairs. I'm sure Mom is getting ready for the big meeting. I grab the bag and carry it out to the garage. I reach for the lid, realizing after I open it that I'd actually opened the recyclable bin and not the regular garbage. What I see takes my breath away. The container is filled, almost to the top, with empty bottles of wine and alcohol. Curious, I reach over to the other garbage container and toss the bag in where it belongs. With the top of the recycle bin still open, I try to do a mental count of the bottles stacked inside. Probably a four-foot-high container,

195

it is filled almost to the rim with the top three-feet nothing but empty containers. I reach in to look at a few. They all seem to have moisture inside, telling me that they were just recently tossed on the pile. No human being could have drunk this much alcohol since last week's garbage pick-up and lived to talk about it, so she hasn't been draining these bottles one at a time. My best guess is that Mom did this last night after I went to bed. This is her commitment to sobriety, front and center. Her determination touches me deeply and opens my eyes to the battle she has fought. I go back to the other container and lift up the bag I had just deposited. I undo the black plastic tie and open the bag. There on the top of the pile is about two dozen screw tops and maybe another couple of dozen corks from the wine bottles. So, I was right. She spent a long-time taking care of all of this last night. It's like the period at the end of a sentence…a closing statement.

I close the bag back up and peer one more time into the pile of bottles. Before I realize it's happening, a single tear rolls down my face, soon followed by another and then another. My hands rest on either side of the container as my tears rain down upon the bottles. I'm engulfed in shame. How many of these bottles have my name on them? In my mother's period of utter need, where was I? The dynamic of my family has been Dad comes, Dad goes, Mom dotes on him and whatever he needs when he is here, and then she desperately misses him when he is gone. And me? I learned to believe that I was a second-class citizen in my own home, that I wasn't missed by my own father when he was gone and wasn't good enough to be loved by my mother in his absence. Instead of trying to understand, instead of easing my mother's burden by being there for her, I buried myself in my books. I closed her out of my life, wrongfully blaming her for my father's disappearance, serving only to add to her self-loathing. What was wrong with me?

I have become a doctor and a damn good one at that. I have worked my way through college and med school and done what I needed to do for myself without one thought about what Mom needed from me. As a doctor, I am supposed to care about people, help them to feel better about their health and their future. I'm supposed to give a damn. Nothing riles me more than a doctor who just sees the patient whose name is printed on the chart in front of them and not as a human being. I have done the same thing to my own mother. What does that make me?

I slowly lower the lid on the recycling bin and sit on the stairs leading from the garage to the laundry room. The tears continue to fall. I think I have cried more in the last twelve hours than I have in the last twelve years. I rest my head in my hands with no effort to dry my face. A very small part of me mourns my father, yet a very large part of me mourns for the woman that waited night after long night for him to come home. The remainder of my tears water a growing shame for the son I have been. He didn't deserve much better from me, but she did.

One thing is for sure, I am damn proud of the woman that she has become in the last twelve hours. The way she stood up at the hospital, the commitment she showed last night in flushing away every ounce of weakness in her life. The way she defended her vision of the future this morning over coffee. The least, the very least I can do is be there for her and lift her up every chance I get. Spend more time with her, hang with her, have dinner, celebrate the holidays, and be a son. She deserves all of that and so much more. I'm a good doctor; it's time for me to be a good human being.

I can hear Mom puttering around in the kitchen. I do what I can to dry my tears and head back into the house. She is turning off the water in the sink and placing my coffee mug into the dishwasher. I walk into the kitchen and just as she turns around to face me, I take her into my arms and silently hold her for the first time in a very long time. Neither of us is in a hurry for the moment to end. Finally, I lead her back to the kitchen table and sit her down. I join her and take her hand in mine. "I have so much to say to you and I don't know where to begin."

"Just say what's on your heart, Honey."

"Mom, first I want to apologize. I have been one lousy son."

"Oh, you have…"

"Mom, please let me finish. Yes, I have. I have not been here for you at any level. I now recognize that I took what happened in this family personally, just like you did, and I ran from it. I'm not running any more. I want you to know how much I love you and how proud I am of you. You have handled all this mess better than any of us and from now on I'm here to support you. Whatever you want to do about arrangements, I'm on your side. You decide."

"No more Viking funeral references?" she asks through a smile, with a small tear running down her face.

"Well, I might vote for it if it was on the table, but I won't bring it up again. Besides, none of us are that good with a bow and arrow and someone has to shoot the flame to set it on fire. I just want to be here for you, now and in the future. That being said, I want you to know, I just saw the bottle pyramid you built in the recyclables. I'm there for you with all that represents too. I think it's important for you to get to some AA meetings, work the twelve-steps, find yourself a sponsor, and really work at your sobriety. You might be strong and determined right now, but you will have low points. You will need support to get through them. I mean, besides me."

Mom pulls a small slip of paper from her robe, lays it on the table and pushes it over to me. On it are three locations, dates, and times of meetings less than fifteen minutes from her house. "I know, Baby, see? I'm going to tackle this head on, and you are welcome to join in the battle. I know I will need it. And Dylan, thank you for your love; and I love you too. Now let's not be late for this meeting. Go get ready."

She gets up from the table and briefly rests her hand on my shoulder as she passes by and kisses the top of my head like she did when I was a kid. I pat her hand as she slips away and up the stairs to change her clothes. She is an amazing woman. I wish I had come to that conclusion on my own and much sooner. I will never underestimate her again. Never.

Gary Friedman

CHAPTER TWENTY-TWO
WILL

———◆———

There is no such thing as all-night restaurants anymore. Extended hours maybe but not the choice to come in on Tuesday and leave Wednesday morning. It's approaching 2:00 am and I could tell the walls in the restaurant would be closing in around me soon. I'm the only customer left and after three hours of drinking coffee, eating a full breakfast, and taking at least three trips to the men's room, it is time for me to leave. The grills have been cleaned and my waitress has long since hung up her apron. The way she and the cook are looking at me tells me I'm ruining their plans for an early escape. I leave her a nice tip, so her night isn't a total loss.

I walk slowly to my car and hunt down the first Tim Horton's coffee shop I can find. They are open all night but only for drive-through. I order two extra-large cups of coffee and a box of ten assorted Timbits doughnut holes and head back toward Adam's house. I park in the same spot I had earlier in the evening with my rear-view mirror pointed where I would go first thing in the morning. I lower the driver's seat in my car to avoid being too obvious and having a concerned neighbor call the Amherst Police to investigate. A late-night thunderstorm helps keep me relatively invisible. My plan is to wait and watch. As soon as I see some movement at the house, a light on or a window opening, I'll immediately head for the front door and throw myself at Adam and Annie's feet.

My next problem is thinking about how I even begin to tell my tale. How do you tell your best friends in the world that their husband and father is a liar and a cheat? Do I take a slow and quiet approach or a hurt and angry one? I suppose I should be prepared for the worst and just let the events unfold naturally. Maybe they will understand, put their arms around me and forgive me, promise to keep my involvement a secret. Or maybe Adam will take me down, tie me up and call the police. I suppose, in the end, it just won't matter. Unloading my guilty conscience will be a relief all by itself. Clearly, I would be a lousy criminal; the guilt would wear me out.

By 5:00 a.m. I'm well into my second cup of coffee and the Timbits box is lying empty on the floor of the back seat. The sky is beginning to lighten. I close my eyes and lay my head back on the headrest, trying to focus on my confession and how best to approach it. The problem is the more I think about telling the truth, the more my mind goes back to yesterday evening and squatting down in the bushes, waiting for Jesse to stroll by. I waited there, prepared to drive the syringe deep into his neck. I remember when I first discovered his crimes, I kept coming back to the same thought: how does a man do what he has done? How does he juggle two families for three decades, lie to his wives, his sons, to me? What kind of a man learns to live with such deceit? Unfortunately, that thought has begun to fade into another one: how does a man take the life of another? Not just another human being, but a man I genuinely loved, a man who was more a father to me than my birth or adopted father ever could be? Does my discovery of his secret justify my actions? Will Adam and Annie understand and forgive me?

The sun is brightening the horizon as I accept the fact that my bladder will not wait until daylight. I raise my seat, get out of the car, and stand on the curb, stretching to awaken my body. I find what looks like a shielded bush where I can avoid getting arrested for indecent exposure before I try to deal with being a murderer. I look around quickly and take care of my business. I walk back across the grass and pull open my car door.

"You sure do your running at strange times." It was the same old man walking his dog again.

"Umm...No sir, I realized I lost my wallet last night while I was running so I came back early to look for it," I replied.

"Let me see if I got this right. While you were running on the street last night, you thought you lost your wallet in those bushes over there, thirty feet from the road. That about right?"

"Something like that."

"Look, son, I don't see you as a bad type, but you really are a lousy liar. You need to work on that. It rained last night and the rain on your car is undisturbed, so you have been sitting here for a while, explaining why you felt a need to water my neighbor's bushes."

"Sort of like what your dog is doing right now," I reply, glancing at the dog and avoiding the stranger's gaze. "Mister, you're right, I'm not a trouble maker, but I have to deliver some really bad news to my friends who live in that house over there, and I don't want to wake them up to tell them. So, I'm waiting here until I see some movement and then I will go break that news. I'm guessing after tonight you will never see me again. You okay with that?"

"See, I knew you had the truth in you. Hope it all works out for you, Son."

The old man gives a quick tug on the leash and his dog prances off down the sidewalk without a care in the world. Oh, if only I was that dog! I drop back into my car and take another draw of cold coffee. I readjust my rear-view mirror for the one-hundredth time and get my focus back on Adam's house. With the sun rising, its rays reflect off the windows on the east side of the house, making it almost impossible to judge if any lights are on. My hopes rest on shades moving or the front door opening to give me the clue that it's time to move forward, leaving me afraid to blink in fear of missing a sign. Ironic how I'm watching a house I was always welcome in, where I never needed to knock or announce myself. It was almost as much my home as Adam's. Now I sit shaking over the possibilities of what could happen there this morning. Walking in that door could end up being the last free decision I'll make in my lifetime, or at least the next twenty years of it. I let the last drop of coffee drip onto my tongue and survey the neighborhood to see if I have drawn any other attention to myself, but everything is quiet around me and stays that way for another couple of hours or so.

With my patience just about worn out, I glance back into my rear-view mirror and see the garage door half-way up and moving. I open my door and start to stand, focusing my eyes on my target. No sooner do I take a step than the brake lights blink. Are they both leaving? If not, who's still in the house? Do I make my confession to whomever is left behind? The car starts to back down the driveway. I'm frozen in place being too far from the car to catch the driver and too late to jump back into my car to avoid being seen. The back end of the car reaches the street and turns toward me. Adam is driving and Annie is in the passenger seat. The gears shift and they begin to pull away from me. Now what?

I jump back into my car and pull into a neighbor's driveway, back out and head in the same direction as Adam and Annie. I try and stay far enough back that I won't be noticed. I want this to happen on my terms, not because I'm caught following someone. I want to tell my story my way and not be on the defensive. Adam is waiting for traffic to clear so he can pull out onto Transit Road. I stay about half a block back along the curb. Once he pulls out, I race to the corner. I only have to wait for two cars to pass before I can join the traffic flow. Adam is only five or six cars ahead. This tailing people thing looks a lot easier on television. As we pass Maple Road, the traffic increases, pushing me another three or four cars back. Passing Sheridan Drive only adds to the mass of cars, leaving me struggling to keep Adam in my sights. I move over to the far-left lane to get a better view, except when I find them again, they are making a right turn on Main Street. I panic as I have to cross two lanes of steady traffic to get from my lane to the turning lane. I turn hard into the middle lane, cutting off an SUV, whose driver feverishly works his horn to express how he feels about my crazy driving. I make the same move into the right lane and now have two horns screaming in harmony. I manage to make the turn at the light with at least two different middle fingers wishing me well on my journey.

I close the gap again to maybe five car lengths and manage to remain there through the Village of Williamsville. The hardest part is not getting left behind at a streetlight along the way, and there are plenty. Adam hits his turn signal as he makes a left into a small plaza. I'm forced to go by and turn right into another plaza across the street. I watch as Adam and Annie get out and walk into a Panera restaurant. Maybe I could join them for breakfast and open my soul there. I park my car, grab a pair of sunglasses from the visor and a Bills hat from the back seat and wait for traffic to clear enough so I can trot across Main Street.

Just as my foot hits the curb, I see another couple getting out of a car. It's the doctor from the emergency room and a woman who I immediately recognize as Mary Beth, my customer, and the other woman in this triangle. This can't be a coincidence. What are the odds that both of these families show up at the same place and the same time? Unless...the secret I'm holding is no longer a secret. Something must have hit the fan at the emergency room last night.

I hold back a bit and let them go inside. I recall being in this Panera before and remember that there is a back entrance. I walk around the side of the building and pull open the door. To my surprise, Adam and his mom are sitting at the same table as the doctor and Mary Beth. There is a table just to the right of the door, and I sit down quickly. Adam and Annie have their backs to me, so I feel somewhat safe. Being only two tables away, I'm able to pick up most of the conversation.

I immediately feel uncomfortable. What has happened to me? Two days ago, I was a hard-working business owner with employees who counted on me. I have totally lost control. In the last twenty-four hours, I have become a conspirator, a murderer, a peeping tom, a stalker and now an eavesdropper. I really should just leave and try to do this later, but of course I don't.

It doesn't take long to discover that the doctor is Mary Beth's son. The circle continues to tighten. It's obvious that that they all know Jesse's secret, or why else would they all be here together? That takes away at least half of my confession. Surprisingly, there doesn't seem to be any anger, nor any tears at the table. They are conversing with each other, like any other group at any other table in the restaurant. They just discovered this life-altering secret and now they are chatting like old friends. How does that happen? My main motive in attacking Jesse was to seek revenge for the devastation these families would experience and now look at them. They are talking quietly, smiling, even chuckling a little at times. What have I done? How could I have gotten this so wrong?

I drop my head into my hands in disbelief, knocking my hat to the floor. I bend over to pick it up and when I straighten back up, I notice that Mary Beth is staring right at me. She smiles at the recognition.

"Hi, Will!" she calls out. She says to the rest of the table, "He's my landscaper."

Adam straightens up immediately and spins around. Our eyes lock. I jump up quickly and run for the door, pushing it open into the face of a customer about to enter the restaurant. As she recovers her balance, Adam bursts through the same door. I sprint across the parking lot toward Main Street. Adam was always faster than me and I can feel him gaining on me. I dodge through the heavy morning traffic, trying to get across the street to my car. Drivers are slamming on their brakes, yelling out their windows. Each stopped car avoids hitting me and this clears the path for Adam to cut the distance between us. I get across the five-lane highway and reach my car. I grab the door handle and pull it open just as Adam places his hand on the window and slams the door shut again. His angry face is inches from my own.

"What is going on with you?" he screams.

"Nothing," is the best I can come up with.

"Nothing my ass! First you show up at the hospital even before my mother does and you hide in the corner. How did you even know we were there? Then I catch you looking in our windows last night and I see you run away to your car. Then you refuse to answer your phone when I try to call you, and now you follow us to this restaurant and sit down, listening in on our conversation. Don't insult my intelligence and tell me nothing is going on!"

I look up into Adam's blazing eyes and tears begin to fall from my own. All I've wanted since last night is the chance to confess my sins and now that I have the opportunity, my mind freezes up.

I try to speak but nothing happens. I put my arms around Adam and bury my face in his shoulder, tears soaking his shirt. He puts his arms around me and pats me on the back.

"Will, it's okay. Everything will be okay."

"I'm so sorry," my words muffled in his shoulder.

"Sorry? Sorry for what? Talk to me."

"I can't. Not right here. We do need to talk, but it can't be in the middle of a parking lot. I've really messed up, Adam. I am so sorry."

"All right, man, listen. I've got to get back in there. We are making arrangements for the funeral, and I have to go. I will call you later and we can set something up. Are you okay for now?"

"Yeah, I'm fine," I sniffled.

"Don't worry about anything. We can fix this. I love you, Brother."

His words open up the flood gates again and tears roll down my face. "Thanks."

Adam turns to walk away, takes two steps and stops suddenly. He turns back around. "Oh, I almost forgot," he says while reaching around to his back pocket. "This is for you."

He hands me an envelope that has my name written on it, still sealed by its author. I look up and smile but say nothing. Adam turns again and takes on the traffic of Main Street. I watch him until he disappears into the front door of Panera. I reach again for the door handle and slide in behind the steering wheel. I hold the envelope in both hands, afraid to find out what may be inside. I slowly turn it over and slide my finger under the flap, tearing it open with one pull. I toss the envelope on the passenger seat while I unfold the paper that was inside and hold it against the steering wheel.

Dear Will,

First, let me tell you that I have always considered you to be a part of our family and loved you like a father loves a son. You have been a welcomed addition at every level. I know how much your friendship has meant to Adam and I can't tell you how many times Annie has told me how glad she is to have you around. Please don't doubt the value you have added to all of us.

Secondly, I know. I know you saw me at Mary Beth's house, and I recognized you immediately. I had no idea what to do or say either at that moment or as that day wore on. I was so upset that I blew off my golf match. I can't begin to explain how awful I feel about this whole situation and that you had to be the one to fall in the middle of it. It is nothing I'm proud of nor do I have an adequate explanation for my behavior. Needless to say, I am a very weak man.

I want you to know that whatever you decide to do with the information you have acquired is okay with me. It is totally your call. I have no doubt, knowing the kind of man that you are, that you will do the right thing. I will never hold it against you nor, I am sure, will Annie or Adam. You are a good man and I trust your judgment. Please do what is in the best interest of them as I don't deserve an ounce of consideration. Just know, Will, that I will continue to love you, no matter what path you chose to take.

I am so sorry.

Jesse

I stare at the paper in my hands, expecting it to lift itself and drift out the window, like in some sort of dream. I'm absolutely speechless. I wander my whole life searching for a man I could honor with the name Dad and what do I do when I find him? I kill him. I deserve whatever punishment I receive for my crime. It's funny how time alters your perspective. When I first discovered Jesse's crimes, I judged him as a man who deserved the ultimate punishment. If that is the case, then how could I think for an instant that dealing with that sin by committing another sin, equally evil, could be a good choice? Looking back, if I were faced with the same decision again, I know now that I would seek another option. Now, my life will be altered by the choice that I made. If there is anything fair about life, and I'm not sure fairness comes into play, I will get what I have coming to me. It may not be fair, but it is just. I have been such a fool.

CHAPTER TWENTY-THREE
MARY BETH

———— • ————

I draw back the curtains in my bedroom and open them to a perfect morning, already in the mid-seventies. A cloudless blue sky greets me. The windows are wide open, and I feel a soft breeze. A dog barks in a distance, the next-door neighbors are already bouncing their basketball in the driveway and a couple of lawn mowers are finishing their work. I can't begin to count the number of hours and days I have spent looking out this same window, awaiting Jay's arrival, listening for the sound of his car door closing. Thank goodness I will never have to do that again.

I have frequently thought of this as the perfect suburban neighborhood where everyone watched out for everyone else. I wonder if any of those protective neighbors ever saw my husband out with another woman and if they would have told me if they had. In truth, few of my neighbors have ever laid eyes on him. With his visits being so short, we tended to focus on each other when he was home and when I did suggest a neighborhood event, he would politely turn it down. Now I understand why.

I look at the driveway and see Dylan's car parked behind mine. I was so touched by his words this morning. It was like watching a self-absorbed doctor become a man right before my eyes. There was a softness in his face and around his eyes that I have not seen in years. His brown eyes have an intensity that can bore a hole in your soul. His brown hair combed straight back is beginning to recede, just like his father's. Dylan is so handsome and yet his apparent ignorance to that fact makes him even more so. His promise to be more attentive to me, as well as his encouragement for me to pursue Alcoholics Anonymous is what I was hoping to hear from him someday. I just didn't expect to hear them so soon. I don't think anyone wants to tackle a twelve-step program by themselves, but I would have if necessary. I do know that if I'm going to make it, I have to do it for me and not for Dylan. I have to be the one who seeks sobriety. I want him to be proud of me and twice now, last night and this morning, he has used those exact words.

I pick up my purse and check for keys, phone, make up, tissues and a pen and paper for taking notes. I think I'm ready for whatever happens during this meeting and however it might affect me physically and emotionally. I hang the bag from my shoulder and turn for the door. After three steps, I come into full view of the mirror above my dresser. It's been barely half a day since the death of Jay and with it the revelation of the life he had been leading, yet I already see differences in my appearance. It looks like I'm standing straighter, the sagging shoulders gone, as if a weight has been lifted off them. I'm comfortable with the image before me, not something I would have said yesterday morning. My eyes seem softer to me, less tired, less pleading. That softness dulls the sharp edges of the wrinkles that have crept onto my face. I am so used to being my harshest critic. It's nice to be able to look in a mirror and be pleased by the person looking back at me. Being pleased adds to the peace I have felt since the scene in the emergency room. I'm actually smiling back at myself, a shock all by itself.

I move off down the stairs and find Dylan waiting and ready to go. He offers to drive, and I easily accept. We walk out through the garage as the kitchen door closes behind us. Dylan moves around and opens my door. I offer a slight smile at his chivalry and walk around him to the passenger seat.

"Who are you?" I ask with a grin.

"I am the son you raised all by yourself, manners and all," he replies, causing us both to laugh. I take my seat and watch him as he closes my door and walks around to his own side.

"I didn't even realize you had been listening all these years."

"Every word, Mom, every word."

He slowly backs down the driveway and then out of my development. We drive in silence as he deals with the moderate traffic heading toward Williamsville. Dylan purposely set the meeting for 10:00 a.m. so the worst of the rush hour traffic should be gone. We are on the 90, heading north, but a shade behind schedule. Long looks in the mirror tend to have that effect. The Panera we are searching for is just off the Main Street exit so it should be easy to find. Due to his normally excessive speed, a speed that leaves me clutching the door handle as if that will save me, Dylan almost misses the Main Street east exit but swerves hard to his right at just the last second, cutting off at least two other, less-than-happy motorists.

"It's supposed to be just past Union Road," Dylan remarks.

"There it is," I offer, pointing at a small plaza at the corner. He slows down and turns in as one of the drivers he cut off waves a single finger at us. We walk slowly across the parking lot; neither of us looking forward to the meeting that is about to begin. Once inside, we both g et coffee and begin to look for a table, one that gives us as much privacy as we can hope for. To my surprise, Adam and Annie are already seated side by side, facing the front of the restaurant, at a table near the back door. They stand at our arrival and we greet each other with hugs and handshakes.

Awkward doesn't begin to describe the moment. Two wives of the same man for thirty years sit across from each other the morning after our husband's death. We are accompanied by the two sons of different mothers, although somewhat acquainted before this whole mess came to light, torn between supporting their mother, avenging their father's behavior, and simply doing the right thing. Where do we even begin?

"Well," I stutter, trying to get things going. "I see we all made it through the first night. I'm not even sure where we start. Maybe we should go around the table and sort of introduce ourselves?"

"Just like the first day of school?" Adam asks.

"Something like that. I mean, we certainly have to make some decisions here, and we are all going to have our own perspective on things. We should at least know where we are all coming from. You know, understanding each other's point of view can't hurt."

"Mom, I think you're right." Dylan offered, clearly having my back. "I'll start. My name is Dylan. I'm a resident physician at ECMC with a focus on trauma care. I'm hoping to stay on at ECMC after my residency ends. They have a great trauma unit, and I want to be a part of it. I'm not sure how much we want to get into personal things but here goes anyway. I'm single, live alone in a two-bedroom apartment downtown. Sadly, I have kind of been estranged from my family the last few years. As we all know, my father wasn't around very much; when he did show up, I didn't feel like much of a priority, so I kind of drifted off. I can't say I had a lot of warm feelings toward my father, and although I love my mother dearly, her priorities were elsewhere. I'm here to support the majority say-so; I don't really have any opinions regarding the final arrangements."

I'm proud of my son and all he has accomplished, but I must admit that I'm fighting back tears as he describes our family. Tears not for my lost husband, but for the way my son had to grow up, suffering the absence of both parents, with his father's travels and my addictions. We will fix this. I know we can, and I know we both want to. It feels like I get a second chance with my own son, one I am looking forward to.

"I suppose I can go next. My name is Adam. I'm twenty-five and have been an EMT with WNY Response for the last few years."

"And a very good one, I might add," interrupts Dylan.

"Thank you, Doc...Dylan. I try to be involved. Maybe too much from time to time, but it's hard for me to just dump and run like a lot of guys."

"I can tell you that as doctors we don't mind one bit. We talk in the lounge, and your name has come up more than once. You really are respected and appreciated by the nurses and doctors, so don't change a thing."

"Wow! Thank you for sharing; that is very flattering. I had no idea." replied a flustered Adam. "I just take each shift as it comes and try to contribute where I can. Anyway, I can't say I had much of a relationship with my father, especially the last five or six years. I had my own stuff going on, so I left my parents to be together. I do have a great relationship with my mother and will do anything I can to support her. We do have another sort of member of the family. My friend Will is almost like a brother, and he spends a lot of time with us all. He's adopted and not awfully close to his adoptive parents at all, so we have kind of taken him in. He really has taken this hard. He is a landscaper by trade and a particularly good one. I wish he were here with us."

"Will? I have a landscaper named Will. What are the odds he's the same guy?" Just then, Annie's eyes appear locked across the room. She is staring at a young man bending over to pick up his baseball cap. "Hey! There he is now. Hi Will!" Adam spins around in his seat and sees Will sitting two tables away. Will jumps up and runs for the back door of the restaurant. Adam jumps up and runs after him as they both disappear through the door.

"What the hell was that all about?" Dylan asks.

"Will has not been himself since last night," Annie replies. "He showed up at the hospital and we don't even know how he knew to be there. He has been kind of stalking us, following us ever since. Adam has been trying to call him, but he hasn't picked up. It's all been very strange."

"I think I know what happened," I offered quietly. "The last time Jay came home from a trip, Will was cutting the grass. I know Will saw him because he asked me about him, you know, like who he was. I told him he was my husband. Will knew and Jay knew he knew. Maybe that is why all this talk is about suicide. Jay must have known he was trapped and that the truth would come out."

We all sat in silence, waiting for Adam to return. Annie was sort of fidgety, turning around every thirty seconds watching for his return. A couple of minutes pass before he walks back through the door, looking somewhat flustered.

"Is he okay?" Annie asked.

"I'm not sure. He seems somewhat messed up. He said he wants to talk but not here. I didn't even ask him to come back inside. I'm not sure he is even in any condition to add to the discussion."

"We may have just discovered his concern," Annie offered. "Mary Beth just told us that Will is her landscaper, and he was there the last time Jesse showed up. They saw each other so Will knows everything."

"Well, doesn't that explain it all? He must have been shocked to see all of us sitting here together this morning. I definitely have to get together with him before he implodes," Adam answered. "So, did I miss anything?"

"No, Honey. We waited for you to come back," replied Annie. "I guess I will go next. Jesse and I would have been married thirty years next month. I have worked most of our marriage, staying home for a while when Adam was born. I have been an employee of Libracon Health Services most of that time, and now I'm the CEO of the company. I have done my best to live a full life in my husband's extended absences. I'm active in a couple of charities, play tennis way too much, keep up my home, and spend as much time with my son as humanly possible under the circumstances. I never thought my husband was seeing other women, but I guess I knew something wasn't right. Even when he was home, he seemed like he was a thousand miles away, like there was a part of him he kept to himself, a part he couldn't share with me."

All the while Annie spoke, it seemed like she was talking only to me. Maybe she felt this was the part of the story that was just for us, between us. Her eyes were locked on mine the whole time, except when she got to strictly personal stuff about her marriage, then she looked down at the table. Then she would look back up at me, kind of squinting, trying to focus on something about my face. I have to admit it was making me squirm in my seat.

"When I heard the news last night," she continued, "I was angry, but I wasn't shocked. I was angry at him for playing me like a fool and angry at myself for not seeing through his cracks sooner."

She stopped talking, but she continued to stare at me. Part of me wanted to run out the door.

"You know, Mary Beth, when you walked into the emergency room last night, I got a feeling like I had seen you before, that you were familiar in some way. I just can't put my finger on it."

Gary Friedman

"I can't imagine why that would be. I guess you could call me a homebody. I don't go out very much."

"The airport," Annie blurted out.

"The Buffalo airport?" Mary Beth replied.

"Yes, the Buffalo airport. It was something like five years ago. I walked in and, in the distance, I saw you hug my husband. Then you walked away from him and right past me. I thought that strange enough but what struck me was that when you walked by, I thought I saw tears on your face. I was there to pick him up and saw you there."

"His wallet."

"What about his wallet?"

"He left home without his wallet. He said he didn't have time to make it home and back. Would I mind rushing it to him? So, I did. I don't remember seeing you there."

"Of course not, my being there had no connection to you or our husband in your mind."

"That's true. Did you ask him who I was?"

"I did," Annie replied. "He told me you were an old college friend he hadn't seen for twenty or so years and probably wouldn't see again for another twenty. He was very convincing. Or maybe I just wanted to be convinced. I knew I had seen you before."

"What is really amazing is that that was the only close call. There had to be times where we were on the verge of discovery and just misconnected. It would be hard to believe there weren't more near misses like that. And yes, there probably were tears on my face. It was one of those times when he was impersonal, like I was an employee. The hug came from me and he was almost resistant to it. That's why the tears."

"I know that side of him very well. He was great at home but when we were out in public, he was very stand-offish, almost distant again."

"I suppose it's my turn. Hi, I'm Mary Beth. Almost feels like an AA meeting. Jesse—I always called him Jay. Jay and I were married thirty-one years ago. About a year later we had Dylan. I worked a lot before we got married, but after our son was born, I settled in as a stay-at-home mom. I think that was the worst decision of my life. If I had stayed active and involved in something outside of my home, I probably would have been better adjusted. Since I didn't, I stayed at home, raised my son, and watched the clock and the calendar, waiting for Jay to come home. Dylan turned out to be an easy child to raise, so I got bored very easily."

I take a deep breath to prepare myself for the rest of the story. Dylan must have picked up on this as he put his hand on my back to show his support. "I'm not very proud of the fact that over time, I filled many of my days with drinking. A glass or two a day at first but my drinking only got worse from there. I blamed myself for Jay's long absences, like if I was a better wife or more attractive, he would have stayed home more often and for longer stretches. I beat myself up pretty badly. Ironically, it was only yesterday that I committed myself to recovery. When I got the call to come to the hospital, I almost took another drink before I left, but I didn't. Annie, meeting you, seeing you for the first time, lifted a huge weight off of my shoulders. Seeing how beautiful you are, how fit and how strong and accomplished you are, I realized it wasn't me all this time. It had nothing to do with you or me. Neither one of us are lacking. It was all him and his weaknesses. I'm going to make it this time. I know it."

Annie gets up and walks around the table and draws me into a long hug while our children watch. It isn't a hug because of the moment or an obligation. It is a deep, meaningful hug where words aren't necessary. It tells me that she understands my battle, and that means the world to me. I peek over and see the looks on both of our sons' faces who appreciate the moment too. Annie holds onto both of my arms as she pulls back and kisses me on the cheek.

She then extends her arms and looks me directly in the eye. "You know, Mary Beth," she begins, "there is a lot of talk out there about sisterhood. Well, I don't think there has ever been two women who have shared an event quite like this one. I was very skeptical of you at first but not anymore. There will be difficult times for both of us moving forward, and I want you to know I will be here for you whenever you need me. I don't qualify to be a sponsor but if you can't reach yours at a time of need, I hope I will be your second call. I mean that." She pulls me into another hug, and I can feel her sincerity in every bone of my body. A tear forms and slides down my cheek. I kiss her cheek as we separate, and she moves back around the table.

Just as Annie reaches her seat, Dylan slams his fist down on the table. "Will you listen to us. We are like the most politically correct, Sunday-go-to-churchers ever."

"Dylan!" I cry out in shock.

"I'm sorry, Mom, I have to say this. I have nothing nice to say about this man and what he has done to us. I hate the son of a bitch," he exclaims as he stands up. "And if he were alive right now, I would feel compelled to pummel him until he wasn't. He doesn't deserve a funeral. He deserves to be burned at the stake. Look at us! Listen to what we are saying. He married you, Mom, thirty-one years ago, and I was born a year later. He married you thirty years ago, Annie. Do you know, Mom, why he wasn't there when I was born like most fathers are? Because he was marrying her at the same time. What kind of a snake was this man!"

He pounds the table again. "Here is the hardest admission at all; if I knew about his lifestyle when they rolled him into my emergency room, I wouldn't have worked so hard to save him. I would have just let him die. In fact, I might have sped the process up. That's utter blasphemy for a doctor! There, I said it!"

He drops back into his chair and drops his head to the tabletop. People throughout the restaurant had stopped their own conversation to watch Dylan's outrage. I put my arm around him and my head on his shoulder. I can feel his body shaking.

Silence descends over the table and nobody makes eye contact. Dylan finally gets up and takes his and my cup for a refill. Adam does the same for his mother. We finally settle back down in our seats as Adam takes the floor.

"You know, we could probably sit around this table for days sharing stories and emotions and still not be done. Maybe we should consider sitting down again when this is over and do just that. Unfortunately, we are under the gun, so we need to figure out what we are going to do about his arrangements. Anybody have any thoughts?"

Annie jumps in first. "Personally, I don't want to see any family spectacle, people gathered around mourning his death. No preacher saying wonderful things about the deceased, saying what a fine and upstanding gentleman he was. I think the best way to bring reality to the event is to be honest. Ironic, huh? Honesty for the man who didn't know the meaning of the word? I don't want to be harsh; I just want to be honest. Does that make sense?

Dylan takes her cue. "I think it does. I don't want to be fake one more time on his last day above ground. I want it to be real for his survivors, for us. It's what we all deserve, including him."

"Dylan, be nice."

"I am being nice. I didn't mention the Vikings, did I?" he snickers.

"Vikings?" Adam asks.

"Dylan wants to bury his father Viking style. Put him on a raft and push him out into Lake Erie and then set the raft on fire with a flaming arrow," I explain.

"I like it!" Adam adds to the laughter.

"With our collective luck, the Lake Erie winds would blow him back to shore while he's still burning and wash up onto Sunset Bay," Dylan adds.

"Okay boys, can we get back to task here?" Annie counters.

"I don't know, Mom. Can you still call us boys at this age?"

"I think I speak for Annie when I say you two will always be our boys. I do agree that we should get back on the subject here."

"You're right, Mary Beth," Adam steps in. "Let's figure this out. We know what we don't want. What do we want?"

"I made up a list," Annie states.

"Of course, you did, Mom."

"Adam, get serious please. Anyway, I have a list of things we need to consider. Maybe we should go at them one at a time and take a vote."

"Sounds good to me," I add, letting Annie take the lead.

"Okay, first is it an announcement or an obituary?"

"None!" says Dylan. All heads nod in agreement as Annie writes down the results.

"Second, burial or cremation?"

"I vote for burial in the most basic casket available," Adam says. "Which one of us would want to take home his ashes? Yeah,

I didn't think so. This way, if we want the memory, we come to the cemetery. It's voluntary and not forced on us."

"Any debate?" Annie asks. "Good, it's settled. Adam, you want to handle that?"

"I got it." he replied.

"Next then. How about a church service?"

It's my turn to jump in. "I think that according to my faith, I would like to have a small church service. Just a simple ceremony with no homily. Just family and anyone the four of us want to include. I think I need that for me, not for him. I want to be right with my God and it gives me a sense of closure."

"I think that was well said, Mary Beth," Annie adds with a gentle smile. "That works for me in every way. Gentleman, do you agree?"

"Sounds better than putting out a fire at Sunset Beach," Dylan remarks with a smirk. Adam just smiles and nods his head in agreement.

"Then it's unanimous," Annie declares as she adds to her notes. "Do we follow through with a service at the grave site?"

"I would say so," Dylan replies. "Invite anyone who is at the church to come to the cemetery. Have the priest follow through with a graveside prayer with no fond farewell. Like Mom said, just enough to give us all closure."

I smile at Dylan, and just nod my head in agreement. Adam signals his acceptance as well.

Annie steps back in. "It sounds like we are all in agreement. How about after the cemetery, we all go back to my house for a meal, and we can invite anyone at the grave to join us? It won't be a sit-down thing, just finger foods and snacks."

"Can I help you with that?" I ask.

"Of course, you can. We can talk later and figure out who will bring what. That's all I have on my list. I think we did this pretty well. Anything else?"

"I have something we should talk about," Adam states.

"Go," Dylan says.

"I think we should agree to hire an independent attorney to go over all of Jesse's records. Here's why I think that. I have no doubt that he did everything he could to protect both of you. I'm sure you have life insurance and money in the bank, and I'm guessing you both have homes with some equity in them. He might have been clever, but he was no magician. We need to clarify whether his insurance policies have named beneficiaries, or say surviving spouse? Which one of you does he have listed as a spouse for the purpose of his Social Security? He had to file taxes for both of you. How did he pull that off? Did he have a retirement fund at work and who gets that? It's possible he left a real mess behind. If we got a forensic attorney to dig into all his records, we would be safer. I have no doubt he left you both okay, but there could be more and there could be debt no one knows anything about. Does he have an attorney who has his will? How could he have possibly set that up unless the attorney knew about both of you? Wouldn't that make the attorney complicit in a crime?"

"What crime?" Annie asked.

"Bigamy. Having two wives is illegal in New York State."

"I looked it up last night, Adam" Dylan added. "It carries like a five-year sentence."

"Even more of a reason to be sure. We don't want the IRS or the state coming after his estate. We really need help with this stuff."

"Oh, and by the way," Dylan continued, "my mother told me this morning that my father paid off my student loans last week. That tells me two things. One, he had a slush fund somewhere and two, he must have known the end was near, one way or another. Why else would he suddenly do that?"

I look at Annie and find her looking at me. We both started shaking our heads at the myriad possibilities. "I guess you're right, Adam," I added. "Would you mind checking out some attorneys?"

"No problem. I'll start working on it this afternoon. We also haven't discussed a schedule for all this. Any ideas?"

"As soon as possible," Dylan came back. "I shouldn't have any problem getting the body released to a funeral home today. I'm assuming no open casket. No autopsy has been requested. Day after tomorrow for the funeral if the church is available. Honestly, I think our goal should be as soon as possible, just for the sake of the closure we all want."

Again, all heads nod.

Annie looks like she is ready to close the meeting and maybe even run out the door. "Everything on my list is covered. Are we all set?"

"There is something I would like to say." They all turn to look at me which I take as a green light. "I was really apprehensive about coming here this morning. I'm sure we all were to some extent. You have all put me very much at ease. Annie, I can see why Jay fell in love with you. You are an amazing woman, and I'm sort of proud to be in your class."

Annie, her eyes welling up, replied. "I can see why he fell in love with you, too."

"And it's to our credit, yours, and mine, to be sitting her with two such fine young men. Let's face it, we are the ones who raised

225

them and with little help from Jay. So, hats off to us." I raise my coffee mug as a toast to all of us.

"And," Adam adds, "to two great mothers, not only for the way you raised us but for the example you are setting for me and Dylan, by the way you are handling this ridiculous situation. I know you are both hurting, but other than Viking boy over here, I don't see any hate around this table at all."

"Hey," Dylan cried out, "That's not hate. A Viking burial is a noble way to say goodbye…okay, maybe just a little hate."

"Right. I'm sure that's how you meant it. My point is that there are a lot of names we could call my…*our*…father and all of them would be deserved, but the best thing that we can say is that he had amazing taste. To our mothers!"

We all laugh and raise our mugs one more time. We stand and hug our way around the table, with quick hugs for Adam and Dylan and a much longer one for Annie. "You make sure you call me if you need anything, okay?"

"The same goes for you," she offers. Dylan clears all the mugs, and we head for the door, mothers, and sons with their arms around each other. We wave our goodbyes as we cross the parking lot. Dylan unlocks and opens my door for me. Still acting like a gentleman. We leave the plaza with much less urgency than when we drove in. We are silent for the first few miles, but we both sigh heavily more than once. Dylan finally breaks the ice.

"Considering the circumstances, that was pretty painless."

"I would agree."

"Once again, Mom, I gotta say, you are one impressive woman."

"Oh, Dylan, stop!"

"I'm serious. The way you held it all together. The way you told your story. I was and I am…very proud of you."

"That's the third time in two days that you told me you were proud of me. You are going to spoil me if you keep this up."

"Don't you think it's about time you were spoiled?"

I couldn't reply, at least not verbally. I reach over and take his hand. Dylan's last remark touches me deeply. The tears come back and drift down my face. I try to hide them as best I can, but I doubt they were invisible to a trained physician. My mind drifts back to my last weekend with Jay. The way he made me feel, his total focus on everything I had to say, the way he made love to me for what would be the last time. For two days every other week, maybe forty or fitty days a year, I was spoiled. How many wives married for over thirty years could say that? The deep conflict for me was how I felt the other three-hundred days: alone, empty, and unfulfilled. Was the trade-off worth it in the end?

I look over at Dylan as he focuses on the Thruway traffic. Handsome, intelligent, and hard-working, a dedicated doctor. He has so much to look forward to in life. I am truly proud of him. I know he has stayed away from anything to do with family over the past five years or so but knowing how he felt about his father and what he must have seen in me, I understand completely. I honestly don't blame him. We all have our ways of dealing with difficulties. His was to stay away while mine was to drink my way through them. Isn't it ironic that the death of my husband would open the door to a new relationship with my son? Talk about trade-offs. Considering what I know now about my marriage, it's a surprisingly good one.

I turn and look out the passenger window at the cars Dylan passes at an alarming rate. Each car traveling down this road in the same direction, each with their own destination in mind. I look at the driver in each of these cars and wonder what their path is like. Are they happy? Do they have a clear vision of what their future holds? Have they ever been blind-sided like we have?

I catch a view of myself in the side-view mirror and end up locking eyes with my reflection. When word leaks out about the demise of my marriage, when my husband's life becomes public knowledge, as I am sure it will, how will people look at me? Will they call me gullible or a fool? Will those who knew me better just call me a drunk who lost control of her husband?

In the end, it doesn't matter. As I sit here this morning, I'm strangely at peace. I know that whatever judgment they apply to me they will have to apply to Annie as well and she is no fool, not the least bit gullible and to my knowledge never a drunk. More irony. The woman who married my husband and supplied him a half-time home is also my alibi.

It has certainly been an interesting morning. Waking up in the same house with my son was an unexpected pleasure. It has been a while since that last happened. To have sat across a table, for an hour and a half, with my dead husband's other family and to have gotten along like long-time friends was a major surprise. Annie and Adam are good people and they mean well. We all have no reason to blame anyone for our dilemma other than our common husband and father. We managed to solve all the issues of Jesse's final arrangements without disagreement. The only major question left unanswered is Adam's concerns about the legal and financial end of things. That should worry us all.

My thoughts are interrupted by the bump of Dylan's car turning up my driveway. He pushes the button to turn off his car and sits for a moment. He turns and looks at me. "You doing okay?"

"I'm doing just fine, child of mine."

"You haven't called me that in a long time."

"I haven't had the chance to call you anything in a long time."

"*Touché.*"

"I really am fine, and I think you and I are going to be fine for a long time to come. Our relationship has been given a second chance and I, for one, don't intend to waste it."

"Neither do I, Mom, neither do I. Every time I look at you, I have a real desire to apologize for being such a lousy son. You deserved so much better. And I'm sorry for my explosion back there. I'm just furious with the position he has put us all in."

"Look, Dylan, you have to let the past go. It doesn't do either of us any good to hang on to it, and we can't change a bit of it. We both have been given a chance to pull the curtain closed on the past and start off fresh. Your father was who he was and who he was does not in any way reflect on who we are. Let's take advantage of this and just be mother and son again. Can we do that?"

"Absolutely but I have to say one more time how proud I am of you. The way you handled the meeting this morning and, by the way, where did all this wisdom come from?"

"Thank you, Honey. It's always been there; I've just never had the chance to use it much."

Dylan leans over and gives me another hug before we walk slowly into the house. I drop my purse on the kitchen counter and head upstairs to change my clothes. I walk past the mirror again and take another long look at the new me. I really am at peace and proud of having my son be proud of *me*. It's a new feeling for sure, one I could get used to. I'm going to spend the rest of the morning cleansing my house of any remnants of my dead mate. His clothes, his pictures and any other memorabilia left behind; it's all going to be thrown out or donated. A new house and a new me, and a new beginning. I plan to make the most of it.

Gary Friedman

CHAPTER TWENTY-FOUR
WILL

— • —

Today is one of those rare rainy days in Buffalo. If one were to walk around the lake, one would be wise to take an umbrella or at the very least, a hooded raincoat. I have not done well with wise choices lately. I'm on my seventh lap of the lake, and I'm soaked from my red hair to the exposed toes of my sandals. No raincoat, just a t-shirt and shorts. My cell phone is turned off and shoved away in my pocket, being blown up by the calls from my best friend Adam. I'm not ready to talk to him or anyone else for that matter.

I thought I had this all figured out. I thought I would sit down with Adam and tell him everything I did and why I did it. Then two things happened to rock my boat one more time. The first was finding both of Jesse's families sitting together at a table talking. That means the "why" of my confession is now public knowledge: they would have been able to figure out that I was the common denominator between Jesse and his families. While you would think that would make my confession easier, it definitely hasn't. It's not so much that they know that I figured out Jesse's deceit, it's that they all seem okay with it, and that it seems that they are dealing with it just fine. That means that they will think my decision to kill their husband and father was, at best, an over-reach. I doubt they will ever accept my decision as rational or

231

understandable. That alone is enough to put me back at square one.

Add to that the letter I received from Jesse, where he admitted to his bad choices and that he knew that I had discovered his deceit. Then he reaffirmed his love for me and asked for my forgiveness. If I hadn't already been inundated by guilt, that letter would have put me over the top. If only I had waited a day, just one day, Jesse might have ended his own life, and I would be free from the oppressive cloud that has engulfed me.

End of lap eight and the rain continues to fall, even more so than during lap seven. My sandals are squishing loudly with each step.

I have made such a mess of things. My adoptive parents have pretty much disappeared from my life. I have alienated myself from Adam and Annie, the only people on this earth I could call family. I have also let my business slide this past week. No one knows what to do, and they can't reach me to figure it out. I'm letting down all my customers and even worse than that, my employees, who count on me to provide their income. I wouldn't be surprised if there isn't already a missing person report being circulated as I walk this path. I haven't gone to my apartment or any place my friends would associate as a hang-out for me. As far as anyone knows, I have fallen off the face of the earth.

It was a text message from Adam that finally motivated me to turn off my phone. He left a text message for me that the funeral is tomorrow. He gave me the time and location of the church and the cemetery just in case I wanted to attend. He also said that both he and his mother hope I will decide to join them and go back to the house afterward for a get-together. How can I possibly do that? How do I look anyone in the eye after what I have done? Killers have one thing in common, don't they? A lack of a conscience, and no understanding or appreciation of the anguish they leave behind. I'm clearly a lousy killer.

I'm becoming more and more paranoid by the last lap. What if they determined Jesse's death was not natural causes? What if they found drugs in his system? Worse yet, what if they are out looking for me right now? I can't go home, and I'm afraid to use my credit card. I have to get some sleep before I pass out, but where? Sleeping in my car will surely draw attention, but I'm not carrying enough cash for a hotel.

Lap nine is done and the rain has lightened somewhat. Each step, however, still involves stepping into a puddle in some stage of development. Darkness settles on the path, forcing me to find another pastime. I start to walk down Elmwood, heading toward downtown. I cross over to Main Street to a small alcove I have discovered. It offers a place to rest that is out of the rain; I might even sleep a little. There are shelters available that would offer me a warm bed, but I'm not ready to be around people. I find my familiar doorway empty and awaiting my arrival. No check-in required.

The sun begins to present itself as a new day around 5:30 am. I have slept the night in soaked clothing and, not surprisingly, I wake up with a chill. I had left my car parked just off of Main Street, so I head there for a change of clothes and a couple of Tylenols, in hopes of forestalling any creeping illness. I walk a few more blocks to a shelter where I know they will allow me a hot shower and a place to change. Being a landscaper means always carrying a change of clothes...just in case you go out after work. I walk back to my car and toss my wet clothes in the trunk and pull out a pair of socks and some dry shoes.

As I settle into the driver's seat, I turn on my phone, which lights up with seventeen new messages, nine from Adam and the rest from my employees demanding to know what is going on. I answer none. I plug in my phone in hopes of getting a bit of a charge before I arrive at the church. I want to get there early to give myself a chance to scope out the building to see if there is a place where I can attend the service and still remain out of sight. Fortunately, this church has a balcony, so I climb the stairs, find a seat against the far wall, and wait for the services to begin.

The funeral home wheels in the casket; there aren't enough mourners to have pall bearers. Annie and Adam follow the casket; they take seats to the right of the aisle. Not far behind is Mary Beth and her son, the doctor. They slide into the same pew next to Annie. Adam keeps looking back over his shoulder as if he is looking for someone. I want to stand and wave but fight the urge. A priest is sitting in a chair on the altar and stands to present what I can only assume is the fastest funeral service in the history of the Catholic Church. No homily is provided. The priest and the two altar boys move rapidly through the service.

Besides the families, a small group of their closest friends is in attendance, along with a few parishioners here for the mass. Communion is offered and Mary Beth takes part along with some of the family friends and some of the regulars. Jesse's name is only mentioned twice, but the priest does manage to say a few words in support of the families. The casket is rolled back out followed by the family. When the church has emptied, I walk slowly down the stairs. At the bottom stands a different priest from the one who had conducted the service, he is arranging some pamphlets on a table and as I near, he straightens up and turns toward me.

"Good morning. I am Father Dominic."

"Hello, my name is Will."

"It's nice to meet you Will. I couldn't help but notice you stuffed away in a corner of the balcony. Are you hiding from someone?"

"No, Father, I wanted to attend the funeral, but didn't want to interact with anyone so I attended from up there."

"I see. I know we just met, but to be honest, you seem deeply troubled. Is there anything I can do to help?"

"You mean like confession? Well, Father, I'm not a member of this church. I'm not even Catholic, so I don't think confession is meant for me."

"In a formal sense you are probably right, but in a human sense, there is no reason that two people can't sit down and talk. I'm a pretty good listener."

"I really appreciate your help, but I do want to make it to the cemetery for the service there. What if I come back later? Maybe we could talk then. Would that be okay?"

"Perfectly fine, son. I will be here no matter what time you are ready. Oh, and Will, peace be with you."

"Yeah, Father. Not much hope of that." I turn quickly, walk down the stairs of the church, and the block to my car. I pull away from the curb and race through the streets not wanting to miss the graveside service.

When I arrive at the cemetery, I can see the small gathering from a distance. As I get closer, I can see the pile of dirt covered by a canvas on one side of the casket and five chairs side by side on the other. The priest is standing at the head of the casket. He is sprinkling holy water across the grave site. I park behind the group and walk up slowly. I take my place close enough to hear the ceremony but hidden from the family by a large oak tree. I settle in for the remainder of the event, unsure if I should leave early or approach Adam when it's all over. I suppose time will tell.

CHAPTER TWENTY-FIVE
ADAM

---·---

For all my ten-thousand days on this Earth, this is developing into one of the hardest. It is difficult enough to bury my father but add to it all the strife added to the day by Dad's life choices. Thankfully, the weather is going to cooperate. A rainy day would make this even worse. I spent last night helping Mom get ready for the gathering at the house after the funeral. I think she is slowly getting back to normal. She even complained last night about losing her first-place tennis ranking due to having to forfeit her last two matches.

I'm waiting in Mom's car for her to join me for the ride to the funeral home. She stated she had to put a couple of finishing touches on her make up. She is probably doing what she can to assure that her eye makeup is tear-proof. All the car windows are open and the radio is turned off. It will be a short drive, and I don't want to let the car get too heated up.

I pull out my cell phone and leave another message for Will. For a guy who wanted to talk he sure isn't making much of an effort at it. I must have left ten messages for him. I have driven by his shop and his apartment and no one has seen any sign of him. It's like he dropped off the face of the Earth. I wish there were something I could do to help him. Seeing Dad and Mary Beth together must have been devastating for him, believing that the only family he had ever considered himself a member of may be on the brink of destruction. I know how he felt about my dad and he even told me once that he wanted to spend more time with him to get to know him better. Will respected him so much. I honestly hope he shows up today. I want him next to me, for his friendship and support.

Mom walks out the front door dressed in all black. It's such an unusual look for her. Even for her semi-advanced years she still dresses, in what I can best describe, as somewhat perky clothes. Lots of color, almost breezy. Not like your typical business executive. She genuinely earned her promotions through hard work, intelligence, and the ability to make everyone around her feel better about themselves and their role in the company. She told me once that she is not the hard-driven woman executive who is afraid to display her femininity. Whatever works for her is fine with me. She climbs in next to me and immediately closes her window, protecting her hair and all the effort she put into it.

I back out of the driveway and start the less than five-minute drive to the funeral home. We are both quiet. The parking lot is almost empty since we decided that this part of the morning would be for family only. I had told the funeral home that we would be unable to provide pall bearers for the day and asked if their staff could fill in. They were more than happy to oblige, for the right fee. The room is darkened and holds the plain wooden casket and five chairs. I insisted on the fifth just in case Will showed up. There was no service, no prayers, and no one said a word. I had suggested that each of us be given a few minutes alone with the casket to say some final words or tell him off, whatever served the purpose. I got out-voted as neither wife had any desire to address the dead. After a few minutes, the pall bearers came in and escorted the casket to the hearse. We followed in two separate cars. No limos, escorts or flags stuck on for the sake of the procession. Just another five-minute drive to the church. Mom and I walked in behind the casket and slid into the front pew on the right. Mary Beth and Dylan slid into the same pew to join us. I made sure I was on the end, just in case Will decided to show up. I probably looked over my shoulder twenty times throughout the service in hopes of seeing him, but to no avail.

In attendance are a few people from Mom's company, a few of Mary Beth's neighbors, Lisa, and Kathy, the two nurses on duty in the emergency room the night of Dad's death, and of course, Devon, my partner from work. There were a few others I didn't recognize and a few members of the church congregation. The service was your basic Catholic mass. The priest and the altar boys went through their paces, including offering communion to the attendees. The priest, to whom I had revealed the story behind Dad's death and the existence of two wives and two sons, agreed to pass on the standard homily. At first, he was hesitant to be involved in the service at all, considering the sinner to be buried, but he agreed to honor the living in general and Mary Beth in particular, who was a devout Catholic. Instead of saying any prayers for the dead, he instead prayed over the family in hopes of bringing us peace in difficult times. It was appreciated.

On cue, the pall bearers took the casket and rolled it silently back down the aisle. We had requested no organist, so you could hear a pin drop. We followed the casket out the church in reverse order of how we arrived. The drive to the cemetery was the longest leg of our morning's travel. Most of the church attendees followed us to the grave site. We slowly went through the gates of White Chapel Memorial Park and followed along the winding roads until we could see a mounded pile of dirt covered by a green canvas. Once again, the pall bearers did their thing and set the casket down on the green straps that will gently lower the casket to its final resting place. It occurred to me, as we got out of our cars, that the term, "Here Lies" was never more appropriate than when applied to my father. At the grave site, just like in the church, five chairs awaited us. We took our seats and the rest of the small gathering stood across from us. The dutiful priest stood at the head of the casket.

As he went through his service, my eyes fell upon a woman across from us. I had never seen her before today. I asked Dylan if he knew her and he shook his head no. She was well-dressed in a black outfit and a wide-rimmed stylish hat on her flaming red hair. What struck me about her as odd wasn't necessarily her appearance. It was the fact that she never looked at the casket or the priest or anyone else in the small crowd. Instead, her eyes seemed to be glued to the four of us. We were being observed, almost studied. Her attention made me extremely uneasy.

The service continued but I am afraid I wasn't paying much attention. Besides the woman in the crowd distracting me, I also kept looking over my shoulder in hopes that Will would fill the fifth chair. That he has chosen to stay away from the ceremonies entirely is deeply disappointing.

I also find my mind floating back to somewhat happier times. I try to bring back memories of good times with my father but find them to be evasive and rare. There are no father and son moments to revisit because he was never around enough to carve out exclusive time with just the two of us. We never played catch or went to sporting events. He never saw me participate in my own brief athletic career. Try as I might to say goodbye to him in a positive way, I couldn't muster up one memory that would bring about an honest "gee, I'm gonna miss ya, Dad," moment. I did all the missing of him in my youth and there was no more left to revisit.

With the service concluded, the cemetery workers slowly lowered the casket on its final journey. There were no tears shed this morning, no flowers for us to place on the casket and no memorabilia to evoke memories of happier times. Had I been an unwitting observer, I would have found the whole day a bit off, to say the least. As a family member, it wasn't about him. It was about being able to neatly close one door to our past and open up new windows to our future. The energy the four of us have expended in missed family moments over the last thirty years was enough to fill ten lifetimes. I can speak for the group when I say we were all ready to get on with our lives.

The priest came over to shake all of our hands and stopped while he said a prayer over our families. He announced to those present that there would be a gathering at our house after the services, and all were invited to attend. He then turned to Mom and apologized that he would, unfortunately, be unable to join us. As he departed, others came by to wish us well. Mom had printed up some sheets that had our address and quick directions to our house for those who wanted to come by. Hugs and handshakes were shared by all. When it appeared as if the line had ended, we hugged each other and congratulated ourselves on making it through the toughest part of the day. We thought we were the last to leave and were surprised to hear a new voice. It would not be the last surprise of the morning.

"Excuse me." We all turn to the new voice. It belonged to the red-headed woman who had caught my attention earlier.

"Yes?" Mom answers.

"I'm sorry to bother you all on a day like this."

"It's no bother at all," Mary Beth replies.

"My name is Emily Williams. I was Jesse's secretary for the last twenty-nine years."

"It's nice to meet you, Emily. My name is Ann, and this is..."

"I know who you all are."

"So, you knew my father's lifestyle," Dylan asks.

241

"I'm probably the only person on the planet who was aware of the choices he made."

"What an honor for you," Dylan snaps.

"I didn't say I approved of what he did because I certainly didn't. He was a difficult man to understand."

"At least you had a chance to understand him, since you were the only person who knew all his lies. Too bad his wives were never offered that opportunity," Dylan replied angrily.

"Calm down, Honey," Mary Beth urges Dylan, as she puts a hand on his arm.

"No, Mom, I won't calm down. We are all here at this man's funeral, in mourning, if you call it that, and this woman waltzes in here as a conspirator to his crimes. Make no mistake about it, he was a criminal." Dylan yells directly at our visitor, "Did you expect some sort of warm welcome?"

"No, I really didn't. I actually expected no less than your last statement. I came here in hopes of filling in some gaps for you all. A perspective only I can offer."

"Go ahead," Mom replies curtly, her arms crossed tightly around her body.

"Sure, why not," Dylan adds.

"Thank you. As I said, I was Jesse's personal secretary for a long time. After I had been with him a few years, I walked into his office and found him very distraught. He had his back to the door and was facing out his window, a box of tissues on his desk with a small pile of used tissues on the floor next to him. I asked him what was wrong."

"Emily, I have made a total mess of my life."

"What's wrong, Jesse? What did you do?"

"You have to promise me that you will keep this between us. Will you?"

"You have my word."

"You know I'm married to Mary Beth and have been for eleven years and that we have a son, Dylan."

"Of course."

"Well...I also married a woman named Annie ten years ago and we have a son, Adam."

"You mean you divorced Mary Beth?"

"No. Actually I'm happily married to both women."

"And they are both okay with this?"

"They have no idea each other exists."

"How in God's name have you kept this a secret? They know nothing?"

"Not a clue. I've managed to juggle both marriages for ten years and in all honesty, it's killing me. It's like having a twelve-inch hunting knife stuck in my gut and having it spin constantly. I feel like I am about to explode.

"So, he bared his soul to me for the next four hours. How it happened and that he was deeply in love with both of you and couldn't bear bringing either of you any pain."

I could see she was fighting back tears. I assumed she felt guilty for keeping the secret all these years and guiltier still in confessing what she knew to his two wives. Mom and Mary Beth are still hanging on, not showing any emotion to this newcomer. The only one fuming at this point was Dylan.

"You must understand that he was deeply in love with both of you and loved both of his sons equally. He took no joy in the situation he was in."

"Em, I really need your help."

243

"*Find you a good attorney, you mean?*

"*No, not that. I know sooner or later I have to fix this, but I don't want to hurt either of them. Maybe when the boys are older.*"

"*Jesse! You're telling me that you want to wait until Adam, who is only six years old and you want to wait until he's what, eighteen to break the news to your wives? That's twelve years from now! How do you expect to pull this off for all that time?*"

"*With your help.*"

"*What?!*"

"*I need you to help me keep my life in order. I can't do it alone anymore.*"

"*What can I possibly do to help you out of this mess?*"

"*I don't want you to help me out of a mess. I want you to help me keep this crazy life organized. My appointments, my meetings, my travel, important dates. Help me maintain some sanity in my dual lives.*"

"*You're not asking me to make excuses to your bevy of spouses because that is out of the question. I won't do that!*"

"*No, just help me stay organized and keep me from screwing up.*"

"So, you were a co-conspirator?" Dylan jumps in.

"And you sound more like a lawyer than a doctor," Emily spat back.

"What else would you call it?" Dylan continues.

"Why would you agree to such a thing?" I ask.

"Loyalty," she replies.

"Bullshit!" Annie cries out. "It was more than loyalty. This goes beyond being a good employee. And as a woman, for you, it was more than pity, more than empathy," Annie goes on, circling her prey. "You didn't just feel sorry for him."

"No."

"You loved him," Mary Beth offers quietly.

"Yes, I loved him," Emily cries, looking down at her clenched fists.

She turns quickly to hide her tears. She takes two steps away from us and looks down into the open grave as if she is about to jump in. Mom and Mary Beth look at each other in disbelief as Dylan throws his hands into the air in disgust.

"For how long?" I ask.

"How long what?" Emily replies.

"How long did you love him?"

"I think I have always loved him in one way or another. The intense love flamed out many years ago, and we have just been remarkably close friends ever since. I wish I could explain it all. My support for him was out of loyalty but that loyalty grew from the love we shared. As time went on, I felt a distance between us. I know he was struggling over his marriages and how he was ever going to reconcile it all."

"You said 'our love.' Are you saying he loved you too?" Mary Beth queried.

"He did, but that was many years ago, probably over twenty years ago."

"Did you sleep with him too? Mary Beth continues.

"Yes, but I am not proud of that. Our affair lasted only a year."

Dylan jumps up onto one of the chairs, flailing his arms as they stretched to the heavens. "You have got to be kidding!" He exclaims. "Let me see if I've got this straight. You came to this funeral today with some sort of plan to bare your soul."

245

"Not exactly a plan."

"Oh, not a plan. A desire then, maybe a deep need. So, you approach these two women, who you know, better than anyone, just discovered that their husband, who just died, was having an affair and was secretly married to them both and you somehow thought that you would bring them comfort by explaining their dead husband's motives and the pain his situation caused him. That he loved them both equally, you thought, was a message that would soothe their grieving." He jumps down from the chair and moves closer to Emily. "And in the process of all this soothing, you oh, so helplessly need to disclose that you had an affair with their husband as well. Does that just about cover it?"

The tears are now pouring down Emily's face, her eyes reddened. She backs up another step, placing the heels of her shoes close to the edge of the grave. She looks like she wants to run but with the grave behind her and the four of us surrounding her, there is no easy avenue of escape. She is trapped.

"I didn't exactly have a plan to do this," she sobbed. "I have wanted to approach you both for years but never knew how or even if you would believe me. I've been fighting with him for what seemed like forever, telling him he needed to tell the truth. He just wouldn't do it. I really am sorry."

"You're sorry?" Dylan begins again, frantically pulling his arm away from Mary Beth who was trying desperately to calm him down. "Being sorry makes it all better, does it? Being sorry absolves you from having an affair with a man who you knew was already married to two other women? Did you just want to join the team? Maybe if you had a son with him, we could form a fraternity."

"Dylan!" Mary Beth yelled.

"Please stop, Dylan," Annie pleads.

"Not another word!" Mary Beth yells with a finger pointed in Dylan's face. He seems taken aback by his mother's sudden strength.

In the meantime, Emily whips around and covers her face with her hands as her sobs grow. She bends over and screams at the top of her lungs into the grave. Mary Beth, who is holding both of Dylan's forearms, trying to rein him in, looks over her shoulder as Emily's wails fill the air.

"You did, didn't you?" Mary Beth asks quietly.

Emily keeps her back to the others as she tries to catch her breath. She straightens and looks up to the sky. "Did what?" she whispers in a raspy voice, clearly exhausted by the moment.

"You got pregnant," she answers.

Emily slowly turns and faces Mary Beth. Her eye makeup is streaked along her cheeks. She tries several times to form the words. Finally, she simply nods her head...yes.

"A boy or girl?" Annie asks.

"A boy."

"When was he born?" I ask.

"About a month after you were," Emily whispers, looking at me.

"Did you and Jesse raise him?" Mom demands.

"No. I chose to give him up for adoption. I have not been in contact with him since I sent him away. I wanted to but I couldn't."

"But Jesse was, wasn't he?" Mom asks as she takes another step closer.

"Yes."

"More than once?"

"Yes."

"Way more than once."

"Please stop," Emily yells, looking up at the gathering clouds.

"Answer me!" Mom yells like I have never heard before.

The moment has us all frozen, mentally, and emotionally, with the four of us staring intently, waiting for the next word, the next admission. We are so focused, so drawn to the scene before us, that none of us heard. The rustle of a leaf; the snap of a twig. The approach of someone coming upon us from behind. He walks past us and moves in front of us before any of us realize he is even there. I am the first to notice.

"Will!"

He ignores me. Instead he walks cautiously toward Emily, examining her from all angles, walking in a semi-circle around her. For her part, Emily's eyes have widened as the color starts to drain from her face. The silent dance continues; no one dares speak. Will finally stops, moving directly in front of her.

"Mom?" he utters. Emily's lips move, but nothing comes out. Their eyes are locked on each other. The comparison leaves little doubt. The exact same shade of flaming red hair, the same fair skin, the same pattern of freckles spread across their cheeks. She raises her hand and runs it along his unshaven face. He asks again, "Are you my mother?"

"Yes, Will. I am." She drops her hand back to her side.

Will's body starts to shake, slowly at first but increasing in intensity. He spins around and moves directly in front of me. I have never seen him look so frightened, so upset. His eyes are staring into my soul, reaching out to me for help. He looks like a volcano that is about to erupt.

"Oh, Adam," he finally murmurs.

"Yeah, buddy. What is it?"

"Adam, what have I done? What have I done? What have I done?"

"Will. Get a grip man. Calm down."

"Adam, I can't. There is no coming back from this."

"Why? What did you do?" I ask as I put my hands on his shoulders. "Tell me!"

"I..."

"What?"

"I killed my own father," he screamed. Will pulls himself away from my hands and sprints for the trees where he had been hidden. He keeps going until he passes the pickup truck and backhoe and their operators who are waiting for us to leave so they can fill in the grave. Across the road and into his car, he races out of the cemetery.

I turn to chase after him, but Mom grabs my sleeve and pulls me back. "Adam, let him go."

"I can't, Mom. He needs my support now!"

"No, Adam, he doesn't. Let him deal with all this and he will come to you when he settles down. He will be okay. Please stay."

I spin quickly to Dylan. "What did he mean he killed him?"

"I have no idea. I signed off on the death certificate with a cause of death being a heart attack. I stand by that. I saw no signs whatsoever of foul play. If I had, I would have referred it to the coroner for an autopsy."

Mom has her arm interlocked with mine and pulls me closer. Mary Beth has taken the same pose with Dylan. Emily remains alone next to the grave, looking down into the darkness below. No one talks, no one moves as the shock of the moment settles around us. One of the workers climbs aboard the backhoe and starts it up, sending us the signal that he has work to do before the rain clouds in the west move in on us.

Annie breaks the silence. "Emily, we are having a gathering at my house for some friends if you would like to join us."

"Thank you, Ann, but I think I have done enough damage to your day. I have already overstayed my welcome."

Mary Beth walks up to Emily and, despite the newcomer's mild resistance, pulls her into a hug. "What are your plans now?"

"I'm sure I will help the company through the transition. After that, I'm not sure. I have a sister in Florida who has been bugging me for a while to move down there. Maybe this is a good time for a change."

"You know, Emily," Mom adds, "Will is a close part of our family and once all the dust settles, he will be again. You are welcome to reach out to him. I think it would mean the world to him to finally have a parent in his life, no matter what the circumstances. You should at least try. Let me know if I can help."

"I will and thank you. I'm willing to try and build something, but I think the first step must come from Will. I will send you my contact information in case he ever wants to reach out."

Mom takes my arm again as we turn and head for the cars. Dylan and Mary Beth are right behind us. Emily turns back to the grave. I stop abruptly, so suddenly that Dylan almost runs into me from behind. I turn back to the grave.

"Emily, I do have one more question."

"Yes?"

"Did you know about the suicide?"

"What suicide?"

"My dad's suicide, the one he was planning."

"He wasn't planning...Oh...you mean the notes?"

"You know about the notes?"

"Yes, he showed them to me before he sealed them up."

"Did you try to talk him out of it?"

"Adam, he wasn't going to commit suicide, never in a million years. He was way too much of a coward for that," she snickers.

"Then what about the notes?"

"I told him you would think that. No, he was planning on leaving, more like running away."

"WHAT?" we all call out in unison.

"Did he tell you why?" I ask.

"He said he wanted to start over, begin a new life, that he couldn't live like this another day."

"Were you going with him?" Mary Beth inquires.

She snickered again. "No, I was part of what he was running from. He was leaving us all behind with a letter for a goodbye. I got one too. Like I said, a coward."

"Unbelievable," Dylan cries out.

We all turn and head for our cars. Emily turns and walks in the other direction. The backhoe driver puts his machine in gear as we near and takes a wide path around us to the gravesite. The other worker in the pickup follows close behind.

As Mom and I drive slowly home, not a word is spoken. When we arrive, there are a few cars waiting in the street for our arrival. We pull into the driveway and Dylan pulls in right behind us. The others in the street give us a few minutes to get settled before knocking on the door. Annie hustles to get the plates out with Mary Beth working alongside her. Dylan and I take direction to help out as best we can. No one took a count but I'm guessing a couple of dozen people came through over the next few hours. The last two women there pitched in to assist in the clean-up, leaving Dylan and me free to roam. I look at Dylan and then motion toward the bar, silently offering a drink. He didn't hesitate to accept.

He follows me out to the deck and as we settle in at the table. "Did you see any of this coming?" I ask.

"I can't say I was really close to my father or that I even paid him much attention at all over the last four or five years but no, not a bit of it. From the distant observations I made, my parents seemed deeply in love. Obviously, he was exceptionally talented in hiding who he was and compartmentalizing his worlds. He was clearly an incredibly talented man, to be able to juggle two wives, three sons and a mistress with only one person knowing the three-ring circus was even in town. He never confused names, never had a slip of the tongue, never was in the wrong place at wrong time. He was the master juggler."

"You have to admit he was quite a performer," I add. "I never saw any sign that he was anything other than what he wanted us to see. Maybe magician is a better description than juggler. Trust me, though, these are not words of admiration. It sounds like I have more pleasant memories of him than you do, but those memories have all been supplanted by the new reality."

"Maybe con-man is better than magician or juggler," Dylan adds.

"You may be right." The sliding door opens, and Mom and Mary Beth join us at the table. "Can I get you ladies a drink too?" I ask.

"No, thank you," Mary Beth responds immediately, causing me to blush at the awkward moment. Mom looks at her new friend and declines as well. We all settle into a conversation about ourselves, with moms telling uncomfortable son stories and sons spinning crazy mom tales. At no time, not once, did anyone reference the dearly departed.

Where this weekend takes us from here, none of us sitting around this table on this cloud-covered evening could even begin to guess. We have all undergone drastic changes in a matter of a few days, and more changes will surely follow. For now, for this evening, we have created new bonds, new friends who have shared an experience that none of us could have predicted. It is a bond that will unite us, based on common pain and as such, common understanding in our shared experience. We will each become the other's lifeline, a bottomless well of support.

This is our new reality, where the events of one weekend alter our present and, most assuredly, our future. It is not easy to remove the existence of a man who was at least a part of our collective lives the better part of three decades. The man in those memories was not a true picture of the man that he was, and the man that he was is no longer welcome at our table.

Gary Friedman

CHAPTER TWENTY-SIX
HUMANITY

———•———

It has been neither my goal nor my purpose to create a narrative for you. The story you have read has been a description of the events as they happened through the eyes of the participants. Nothing has been altered to make a case or put forth a point of view. Having observed these events, I can attest to their validity. As I stated from the beginning, it was my intent to share with you a story of a collection of people tied up in the life of one man, a man so obsessed with not hurting another soul that he became immobilized in his search for right and wrong. So, confused by his options, he gave up the search for what was right for the ones he loved, and instead, focused on what was right for him. He would tell you that he meant well, that he loved all the people in his life and only had their best interests at heart. Unfortunately, this man was so self-focused that he couldn't imagine that anyone who loved him would be able to get through life without him. He believed, in his own distorted way, that for their benefit, a little bit of him was much better than none of him at all.

Jesse saw himself as a man who provided for his loved ones. He was not, however, blind to the reality he had created. He knew that someday his secrets would come out. It was that day he dreaded. The premise I set forth early on in this story was that all behaviors of Humans are followed by the consequences of those behaviors. It is a steadfast, unequivocal law of Humanity. The premise also says that the consequences do not necessarily follow a specific timeline. It could be immediate, such as touching your finger to a flame brings an immediate burn, or it can be delayed, like the thirty years between Jesse's second marriage and his demise. No matter how slow the second hand turns on the clock, the time for punishment or reward always arrives. Time will always catch up.

You may have wondered while engaged in this tale, "Why is this the story Humanity has chosen to share? After all, you have been observing Humans since their creation. You have seen every depravity of Humanity. You have seen war, poverty, starvation, genocide, and the like. You have observed dictators and despots, men who needed to rule the world at any cost. There are hundreds of stories you could have told of men just as devious as Jesse, who by comparison, is a simple man. Why his story? Why now?"

Let me say, this story is specifically relevant to our time. Most of the despots, the abusive rulers over time, the cruelest of the cruel, burned a path through the history books as evidence of one man's attempt to rule the world, at any cost. Whether it was the physical destruction of a country or the murder of millions of people based solely on their religion, the goal was always to conquer. These men have been defeated by people who refused to be ruled, refused to yield, who stood up and fought for what was right. In the words of Abraham Lincoln, "right makes might."

I have observed in these times, unlike during the times of the dictators that I mentioned, that Man, and by Man I include both genders, has evolved in a most unpleasant way. The world today has become a generation of Humans that no longer wants what is in the best interest of Humanity. It is a generation that has been defined by one question; "What's in it for me?" That is the mindset of the dictator on a much smaller scale. It's not one man wanting to control millions for himself, it is instead millions of men wanting to control their own piece of the world for just themselves. In both cases...the rest of the world be damned.

On behalf of Humanity, including the hearts of generations yet to be born, I present what I see as the plague of the future. I am not suggesting that there is not hope, but the trend is concerning. Humanity has committed many generations to the service of others, lifting up our fellow man, treating others as we ourselves would want to be treated. There are still moments in pockets of the world where great charity is shown, usually on a grand scale after major catastrophes. I speak of the acts of charity in our day-to-day lives, the Good Samaritans of the world who act in silence with little or no fanfare. Those who pay it forward.

My hope is that this story has been able to illustrate that the person standing next to you, no matter their faith, or their color, or their gender, or their age, or their country of birth, or their sexual preferences has a story just as important as yours. You may not agree with the decisions that person made. You may have come to other conclusions or have at your disposal certain other factors, which would have allowed you to make different decisions. The point is that each person has a value as great as your own and deserves the same attention that you lavish upon yourself. Man has always glowed brightest when holding on to the greater good. When one man reaches out to the person next to him, simply to say hello, to lift them up, to let them know they are not alone in their struggle if only for the simple reason that what you give comes back to you. There will come a time when you will require a boost after a difficult day. Will you receive the encouragement you need in those times?

It is also noted in this story that you can be the subject of difficult circumstances at any given moment, as you saw with the wives and sons of this tale. Where do they go from here? Will they let the events described in this story turn them against the world, darkening their personal horizon, or alternatively, will they choose to overcome the decisions made by Jesse and learn from them...grow from them? Here stands the most vital lesson of this tale. In all my observations of Humanity, since the beginning of time to those walking the streets today, one truth rises above all others and that is this: Men and women are the captains of their ship. Each soul determines the direction their life takes. Nothing can alter your course unless you let it. No one can sink your ship unless you allow it to be sunk. Each charts their own course and each makes their own choices. No finger pointing or blame to be placed and no time for regrets. If a captain makes an error in setting his course, he simply takes hold of the rudder without looking back and regains his direction. It is only through the captain's hard work and persistence that he will bring his vessel safely to dock.

How do you think the wives and sons of this tale survived? Did they spend their lives singing, "Woe is me," or did they grow from the experience? Observe for yourself.

CHAPTER TWENTY-SEVEN
ADAM

———•———

The middle-of-the-night peace and quiet is destroyed by the wail of an ambulance siren, its light flashing to warn anyone still on the highway at this late hour. The tires squeal as the big red and white rig turns the corner and into the ramp leading to the ECMC trauma center. The brakes engage as the WNY Response vehicle comes to halt in front of the sliding double-glass doors leading to the waiting area. A large black SUV follows the ambulance up the ramp and two men who look like a security team jump out, most likely they've been sent to keep the patient in the ambulance from further harm. The two EMTs scramble from their seat and race around to the back of the ambulance and swing open its rear door, where they pull the gurney out onto the blacktop.

The hospital doors whip open and two nurses run out to assist. They had been forewarned about this arrival: A Buffalo political big-wig, shot outside a Chippewa Street bar.

"You had better hurry with this one, Lisa. I think he's circling the bowl," yells Devon, one of the EMTs.

"Is that your medical opinion, Dr. Devon?" Lisa yells back as she pushes the gurney toward the doors. "How about some facts instead, like vitals?"

The doors whip open again and they are joined by a new resident, doing his midnight shift duty like all the new guys. "Hey Devon," I call out.

"Well, hey there Dr. Adam. How's med school going?"

"I'll let you know in the morning, if I survive this night" I reply, glancing over at the security team. "This guy must be important."

"He's the current Deputy Mayor of the city. The mayor and commissioner are pulling out all the stops."

"Then I guess I better not screw up. What have you got?"

"GSW to the abdomen," Devon calls out as he rattles off all the current vital signs and how fast they are falling. The medical team reaches the inner doors as the nurses pull him into position in examination room one.

Just before the inner doors close, Adam turns back to Devon. "I gotta tell you, you're really getting good at this. Nice job!"

"Thanks, Adam...I mean Doctor," Devon stutters.

"Adam is fine for us," I assure him. The doors close as I enter the examining area and begin to pick up where the nurses left off. Snapping on the blue gloves, I start barking out directions to my staff.

I can't begin to tell you how strange it is to be back in this emergency room in my new role. I spent a few years in Devon's position, running in and out, doing my job trying to save lives. Now, instead of my job ending after delivering the patient to the ER, those lives are truly in my hands. This being only my second shift in trauma, I can't shake the memories from that night, eight years ago, as I rolled my father's gurney to this same examination room. So much has changed for me in those eight years.

All of our lives had been turned inside out. The night in the emergency room and the funeral that followed was simply the beginning. I gathered all of the records my father had left behind with both of his wives and studied them for days. The first thing I discovered was that my father was meticulous in his preparation for his demise. I wasn't surprised to find the names of an attorney and an accountant who had both worked diligently to make my father's estate iron clad. His earnings were far greater than any of us had imagined. He left behind two extremely generous life insurance policies, one for each wife as the majority beneficiary with a smaller piece of the pies left to his sons. He only had one social security number, with Mary Beth as the spouse of record, and a 401K that went to Annie. All very equal and all extremely significant. There was also a trust fund that he had set up for Will.

One of the bigger surprises was a set of papers my father had drawn up. They were adoption papers to make Will his son. They were about twelve years old but had never been filed. He wanted to do the right thing but for some reason, never got around to it.

It was only a week after my father's funeral that I sat down for lunch with my newly-found brother. After dissecting the complicated feelings each of us had about our departed father and filling in the gaps of our life to this point, Dylan asked me about my future and my plans. Well, that's the nice way of putting it. He actually said; "So how long are you going to ride out this EMT gig?"

"What do you mean ride out? The hours suck and the pay isn't so great, but it feels like I'm helping people. Is that so bad?"

"Adam, don't sell yourself short. I'm not saying this to be disrespectful of your job, but you are so much better than this. I have been watching you for a while. You are one of the best EMTs out there but you need to step up your game. You should be on the other side of the glass doing what I do."

"You really think so?"

"I really do. I think you should go back to school and get your degree. Then start looking at med schools. You have what it takes,

261

and I will be here to support you through it all. I never had a brother before, and now I'm looking forward to being a good one—through the good times and the bad. What are brothers for?"

"Can't really say since I never had a brother before."

That began my journey. It is utterly amazing how much confidence I felt by being lifted up by someone I respect—my brother Dylan. I decided to stay settled here in Buffalo and attend Canisius College for my undergraduate degree. I continued working for WNY Response but kept that mostly to weekends. I got a rather good financial aid package, and that, along with what Dad left me, made private school possible.

It was in my sophomore year that I discovered, through the attorney who was handling my father's estate, that my father had created a 529 savings account to cover my education costs. It got me through college with enough left to lessen the financial blow of med school at the University of Buffalo, Dylan's alma mater. My brother (that still sounds strange to say), was behind me every step of the way, even helping me prepare for my major exams. I'm not sure I could have made it through without his help.

That is just the tip of the iceberg of how much my life has changed since that fateful night. While at Canisius I met Carly, another pre-med student who was a year ahead of me. We have been exclusive since the day we met. We moved in together and have discussed marriage, but we both want to be done with med school before we take that step. I'm still remarkably close with my mom, but I don't speak to her as much as I did before. We have both created new lives since Dad's death. Dylan and I are as close as any brothers can be—we speak daily and get together at least once a week to share a meal or meet so I can kick his butt in racquetball. Will and I have drifted a bit as my free time is limited, making it tough to visit him as much as I would like. He begged for forgiveness for what he did, and I have given him that. I always considered him my brother and now, I know that will never change.

At the holidays, we have created a new family tradition of having Christmas Eve dinner together, with Carly and me joining Mom, Dylan, and Mary Beth. There will come a time when we will add Will to the mix but that is still going to be a little while.

As for my father, it is true that time does heal most wounds. I find it interesting that it was easier to forgive his transgressions against me than it was to forgive him for what he did to my mother. She was the direct victim while I was just the fall out. I have no hate for him, and the anger has certainly lessened, but no matter how much time passes, I will never be able to understand the choices he made. I will never get the contradictions in the man. He would have slapped me silly if I ever treated a girlfriend the way he treated Mom.

What I can't forget or minimize is just how much his death changed my life. That day was certainly a crossroads for everyone tied to his life. Just as I couldn't forgive Dad for the choices he made; I couldn't judge myself less for the ones I made. Dylan opened my eyes to that. He told me that my life is up to me, that I'm not a victim nor, he admonished me, can I blame Dad or anyone else for the choices I make in life. It is inevitably up to me whether I succeed or fail.

So, looking back to when Dad died, I did, indeed, have a chance to start over. It was the turning point for me. After seeing the mess he made of his life, I vowed to get mine on track. You can say he finally motivated me. I guess for that much, I can thank him. There are times I even think it's a shame he's not around to meet the new me. I think he would have been proud. My team and I just managed to stabilize the seriously injured Deputy Mayor. Two orderlies arrive to move him to surgery where they will try to remove the bullet and repair the damage it caused. As he is wheeled away, Lisa pats me on the back. "Nice job, Doctor."

I smile at her comment as I look up at the observation area above the trauma room. Dylan is looking back at me through the glass; he smiles and gives me a thumbs up sign. I wave back.

I walk slowly to the doctor's lounge. Dylan told me once that with all the improvements made over the years to the trauma center, they never touched this lounge. I believe it. I sit down on the cot and swing my legs up to try and catch a quick rest. I'm too wired to even try to sleep, so I close my eyes and watch a slow parade of the important people in my life. They turn and smile at me in approval; even Will waves. Trailing the pack is my father. He looks sad, as well he should. I believe that love is a sharing thing, that when you love someone, you give away a piece of your heart. That piece never comes back, always leaving a hole where it used to be. That hole is never missed when that person is in your life but when they leave, the hole is always there, reminding you of what was. I will always love my father, but I will never understand him and for me that's okay. My life is on the right track now; not despite him but because of him. I know when Carly and I finally decide to start a family, I will be the best, most attentive father, and husband in the world. That's the way it's supposed to be. Thanks, Dad, for that lesson by omission.

CHAPTER TWENTY-EIGHT
ANNIE

———•———

Waking from a sound sleep, I can see the first rays of light break through my French doors. I leave the draperies open every night so I don't miss one sunrise for the rest of my life. Having grown up and lived in Buffalo, New York my whole life, the sunrises seem pretty standard, how the sky lights up first, then the orange edges along the horizon, lighting up the jet trails that crisscross the Eastern sky. Finally, the sun begins to show its rim before breaking into full view. But I have learned how drastically different that whole process can be when living in a valley, how much longer it takes for the sun to show itself above the mountains that surround you. The light-show the sun provides as the land awakens around it is, quite honestly, breathtaking. Waking up to such a sight is one my new pleasures. I have been living like this for the past four years and loving it.

Of course, there are no mountainous valleys in Western New York, but I no longer live there. My French doors look out over the valley that beautifies Vail, Colorado, my new home. It is a thousand, six-hundred and twenty-eight miles from my old house in Amherst, but it might as well be light years away. It normally takes about twenty-four hours of driving, door to door, but the transition to my new life seemed to have happened over three years. Oh, how my life has changed, and I couldn't be happier.

I was faced with so many decisions and so many options after Jesse died that it took me a few years to work through them. The first area of concern was my job. I began to realize that the joy my career provided me had evaporated. Working in the medical insurance world could no longer provide the kind of fulfillment I craved, even if I was the CEO. Being on my own with no spouse meant that bringing home a paycheck didn't mean as much as it used to. I didn't have a family to take care of anymore; I didn't have a husband; I didn't have to work, but I liked to. I didn't want to do it another day. That led me to my first dilemma: I was ready for a change, but what kind?

Since the veil of my past life was lifted, I realized that I could be whatever I wanted to be. I looked at my beautiful home with new eyes. I designed and built it arm-in-arm with Jesse. His fingerprints were all over the design, right next to mine. It was way too big for the three of us when it was built, and it felt even more spacious with me living there alone. This decision was easy, sell. That led me to: "Where do I want to live?" That is where it got complicated.

After I became a widow, my wonderful son Adam was attentive, feeling it was his job to keep me entertained. Even after Carly came into his life, he still found the time to smother me. I love and adore him, but I didn't want him paying so much attention to me. He needed to live his own life and not be anchored to me. Together with my desire to sell my home, my thought of leaving town became more of a focus. I did not know where I wanted to go, so the location of a new home would depend on where work opportunities developed.

After I decided I would leave Buffalo, I began scouring the internet for business opportunities. Despite approaching sixty— I wasn't looking for an industry that was exclusively for my age group. I enjoy being around younger people. They energize me, help me feel alive. When I found my chance, I jumped at it. I found an operation for sale in Vail, called Higher Standards Dispensary. You guessed it. I went from the insurance industry to the world of legal cannabis. It keeps me busy, (probably too busy), and I love every minute of it. Owning my own business and being responsible for its success or failure was the kind of inspiration I needed to get me out of bed every day. And with the sunrise that greets me every morning, the earlier the better. I found a condo that I adore, and if anyone thinks the sunrises are great, wait till they see the sunsets from my hot tub. Do I sound excited? I hope so because I am.

Don't misunderstand me. I have not by any means left my friends and family behind. I'm back home every year for the holidays, although I'm trying to get them to come here for Christmas next year. Adam and Carly come out every year when they can create some away time from med school. Mary Beth has even visited twice with a third visit expected this February. We truly have become great friends.

I work hard and play hard. Living in Vail gives me ample opportunity to expand my leisure activities. I still play tennis and take skiing lessons from some the best instructors in the world. I have no interest in romance, nor would ever consider getting married again. It's not that I don't enjoy the company of a good man, it's just that there is zero chance it will ever get serious, at least for now.

That is probably the biggest impact my departed husband has had on me. It's the issue of trust. I trusted Jesse so deeply and believed every lie he told me that I question my ability to discern the intent of the men I meet. I'm not judging them; I simply don't trust myself to ascertain truth from fiction. It's not as big a problem in business or with my employees, just the affairs of the heart. So, for now, I'm laying low.

I know I sound confident and self-assured. However, it's mostly a façade, to be honest. That point in my life eight years ago, Jesse's betrayal and death, was personally devastating, and it took a while to heal. It is a tougher matter to clear the hate from my heart. It is one thing to trust someone and then catch them in a lie. It's totally different when you discover you have been lied to every day for thirty years and never suspected. As much as I hated him, I hated myself even more for being a dupe.

The visits I have with Mary Beth help us both in that we get a chance to talk about those events in our lives. It can be therapeutic for both of us.

"If you want my opinion," she said during her last visit as we sat in my hot tub overlooking the snow-covered ski slopes, "I think that you're hiding here in Vail, hiding from the pain of the past, hiding from the scene of the crime. You know you lived a full life back home even without a husband around."

"I know that," I replied.

"You dove into your job, got in close with Adam, and loved your friends. Now, you're skiing across the top of the snow and avoiding the deep white stuff."

"No, I'm not."

"You know you are, Annie. It's almost like you're playing at life instead of living it."

I was speechless after her last remark. She can be pretty honest with me, but maybe she's right. Maybe I am coasting to a degree, but who deserves to coast for a while more than me? I said after the funeral that I would never shed another tear over my ex-husband, and I haven't. That doesn't mean I have flushed all the hate from my system. I adore Mary Beth and Dylan. I have the best son in the world and now he has brought Carly into my life and she is a sweetheart. Even though I loved my husband and was loyal to a fault, my heart is dead to him now.

I haven't ruled out going back to Buffalo someday but for now the lifestyle I live here seems right for me. Maybe if Adam and Carly get married and start having kids, well, grandchildren might be the magnet that lures me back to Western New York. I suppose anything is possible.

Speaking of kids, that brings me to Will. I will always love him to pieces, and I try to see him when I'm home. Yet when I visit with him, he remains distant. I think he still thinks I hate him, and his guilt keeps him locked away from us. I really do not hate him. He did what he did out of love for all of us and that deserves to be rewarded no matter what the law books say. After all, would I be looking at this sunrise right now if he hadn't done what he did? I hope he is back in my life someday, whenever he is ready.

Thinking of Will inevitably leads me to thinking about his mother, Emily. I can't say I have made any headway in positive thoughts about her. She knew the kind of man Jesse was, how he was married to two women for all that time, and yet she still colluded with him. She disclosed she was Will's mother at Jesse's funeral, and then she ignored him. Add to that the fact that in the eight years since the funeral, she has made no effort to reach out to Will, and that makes her even more despicable. He could have really used having his biological mother at his side during these past eight years. All I can say is that she and Jesse deserved each other.

I slowly lift my head off of the pillow and get out of bed to meet the new day, stretching my arms high above my head, wringing out the kinks from my last skiing lesson. I ease my legs over the side and feel them settle into the plush carpet. I walk over to my French doors and look out over the mountainside. I crack the door open to feel the cool air across my naked skin. I lean against the door frame as the smell of the pine trees wafts into my home. Maybe Mary Beth is right, maybe I'm pretending to be this happy and care-free woman. Does she really think I don't know how deeply damaged I am? I do. Thoroughly cracked and broken inside this skin. Mary Beth and I have a bond formed by our brokenness.

Here is how I have survived. I have torn out all the rear-view mirrors in my life. I only look forward to the future and never back at my past. For the first time in my life, I have total control over the choices I make, and I plan to live by the consequences of those choices. I can't change the past so why live there and give it power over me? No one will have power over me again, ever. If that makes me broken, so be it. I'm alive and he's not. I have a future and he doesn't. In the game of life, I win; six-love, six-love. Now on with my day!

CHAPTER TWENTY-NINE
DYLAN

———•———

I know I said I liked working in trauma units, but I never said I wanted to be married to one. It seems like I never get out of here. If I knew then what I know now, I think I would have turned down the position of Assistant Medical Director of Emergency Medicine. I liked it much better when I was strictly working on patients. Frankly, when I was a resident, life was much better than it is today.

The view of the ceiling in the doctor's lounge hasn't changed much over the years, but I still prefer the lounge ceiling over the one at my apartment. Home is a place at the head of a trail I have little interest in traveling. I become too complacent at home. I am angry at the world, so much so that the distraction of the hospital keeps me from lashing out. Does that make me unreasonable and childish? Yes. Does it affect my life? In more ways than I care to list.

First the good things. I have a great relationship with my mother. She remains a remarkable woman; what she has done with her life leaves me speechless. I'm so envious of her ability to let the past go. She has wisely moved forward and forged new friendships and new relationships and seems genuinely happy. We get together for dinner at least once a week either at her house or at a restaurant. My apartment is not conducive to entertaining, nor am I the kind of cook who would endear

271

company. Our time is filled with her telling me the adventures of her week. I'm a dedicated listener, which is a good thing because my life wouldn't compare to hers. Really? It would bore the hell out of any human not already in a coma. My closest nexus to adventure is through my mother's stories.

Then, there is my friend and brother, Adam. We get together for either lunch or a night out at least once a month, not counting our weekly racquetball match. I think I'm the better player, but he is tenacious...he is able to hang back and wait until I am exhausted and then he finishes me off. He has become my best friend and confidant. Our evenings out are filled with heart-felt conversation. For my part, I have encouraged him to follow his dreams. Now that he is a resident in my department, I can guide him along that path. He is rapidly becoming an excellent doctor and will soon be the star of my department. To say I'm proud of him would be a huge understatement. I think Carly is amazing and I have also pushed him into making that relationship a priority and to prevent him from making trauma medicine the center of his life, like it has mine.

His influence in my life is no less a priority. He listens to me and asks me a lot of questions. He has become my conscience. Although that can push us apart at times, I know I need his input.

"You know, I have been watching you pretty closely our last few dinners together," Adam said one night.

"Oh, really?"

"Yes, really. Can I ask you a personal question?"

"Shoot."

"Can you taste the alcohol in those drinks?"

"What is that supposed to mean?" I ask, getting a little perturbed.

"I mean, you drink them so fast, I wasn't sure your taste buds get any idea what's going past them."

"Am I not drinking to your standards, Doctor?"

"I'm just saying, I am concerned, Dylan."

"About what?" I demand.

"About the way and the amount of your drinking. I think you're heading down a dangerous path."

"How about you mind your own business?"

"Like it or not, you are my business. You are both my brother and my mentor, so your well-being is my well-being. You do know that alcoholism has a genetic connection?"

"So, my mother is an alcoholic, therefore I must be one too? Well, genetically speaking, I already have a mother and am not in the market for another, so back off." I pause and look away for a moment, then reach for what is already an empty glass. Nothing but ice. A large part of me wants to dump what's left of his lasagna over his head then grab him by the throat and place him about a foot off the ground into the Roman column behind him. A larger part of me knows he is right. All I can do is nod.

It's just that…it's just that…I'm so angry so much of the time. I have to say, at least for me, the closure my mother was seeking is just a myth. The funeral, the family time, the days, months, and years since Jay's death have done nothing to minimize how furious I remain at the man I think of only as my mother's sperm donor. That's the best way I can describe him. Calling him a father is an insult to fathers everywhere. I hate any reminder of him, every memory that sneaks up on me. Every time I think about the battles my mother fought with her own demons because of him makes my blood boil. That man burned every life he touched, and I can't get past the thought that death and burial weren't enough punishment for him. When I tried to explain all that to Adam, this was what he said:

"I know Dylan, believe me I know. But here's the thing, every single time you get angry, every time you rehash your past and every time you lift a glass to his memory, he wins. You personally give him life again and you end up fighting the same battles your mother did for thirty years. He is dead and buried. Let him lie. This world...and that ER...and I...need you whole. Don't give up the best parts of who you are to a man who doesn't deserve it. The medical community needs you. Your mother needs you and I need you."

Adam took a big risk by gambling with our relationship and telling me his concerns, and I will forever be in his debt. It's been six months since his sermon and except for two lost weekends back in July, I'm doing pretty well. It's been forty-five days since my last drink. I have come to grips with what can only be described as my own alcoholism. I confessed my problem to my mother, and she has been a great support. She has even taken me to a couple of AA meetings. She is holding me accountable for my behavior.

I see nothing but good things for my future when I allow myself to look that far ahead. Don't get me wrong. Yes, I have stopped drinking, but I have not quite shed myself of my raging hate for my sperm donor, for what he did to me but mostly for what he did to my mother. She was such a delicate flower and all he did was lift his leg on her and force her to wilt. I'm happy to say she has blossomed into a whole new woman. What a loss it would have been for me and the world at large to not have experienced her at her best.

The walls of the lounge light up again as an ambulance bounces over the curb and glides to a stop in front of the sliding doors. In years past, that would have driven my feet over the side of this cot and into my waiting shoes. These days I'm in no such hurry unless we get overloaded with cases. Instead of heading to the examining rooms, I walk up the stairs to the observation deck to watch my young protégé at work. He really is impressive. In fact, he is a lifesaver for both his patients and for me. You don't have to be a doctor to be able to diagnose the path I would have been on without his intervention. Forget the "half" stuff. He is not my "half-brother." He is my brother by every definition of the word.

Looking down at his work, I can't help but revisit that night eight long years ago when another gurney got deposited in the same examining room. It was only ten short minutes of my life, but it may have been the most influential minutes I will ever live. As much as I fight it, those minutes have changed my life forever. It's only been recently that I can see that the changes have been for the better. I can see good things coming if I allow them.

Adam keeps trying to tell me he has someone he would like me to meet. I'm assuming she is a woman, but who knows? I have to admit, it would be nice to have someone in my life like Adam has Carly. For now, I want to enjoy my family and let my social life come as it will. No pressure. I have also been working on a dream of my own: traveling with a group of doctors to administer to the needy in poverty-stricken countries. I want to be able to give back more to the world as a payback to my good fortunes. Now I'm focusing on the good instead of the bad.

My path has had its share of speed bumps along the way, but the surface seems to be smoothing out. I can't say that I'm better because as it is with all alcoholics, the battle is never over. I have learned that as soon as you let your guard down, the enemy can sneak back in. As hard as my mother and brother will fight for me, my sobriety is up to me and I know it.

My name is Dylan and I'm an alcoholic.

275

Gary Friedman

CHAPTER THIRTY
MARY BETH

———•———

A single incandescent light bulb illuminates the crowded basement, the light fixture's combination chain-and-string hanging down to eye level. Along one wall is box after box after box of memories of years past: outdated women's clothing, more current men's suits, shirts, shoes and ties, furniture, tools, a relatively new set of golf clubs, and shelves of books. The contents of a common basement but all concentrated on one side of the room, pushed into the smallest space possible. The other side of the basement has been cleared of all boxed memories with the now-open space covered with drop clothes. The open ceiling has a variety of light fixtures; each offers illumination and ambiance for different settings. Spread across the room are five easels, each displaying a canvas holding partially completed works. In the farthest corner sits a small platform that will hold a wide range of displays from still life to human models, depending on the mood of the resident artist.

This morning, the lighting is just not perfect, so I have set up another easel on the deck behind my home, hoping to catch the sunrise just right to add new shades to the garden near the fence, which is one of my favorite subjects. I study my canvas with intense concentration, like a hound spotting a fox. Today's uniform is an old pair of sneakers that are covered with drips of paint, a pair of shorts and a man's dress shirt that has become my go-to smock. Who says my ex-husband hasn't contributed to my current vocation? I have a pair of reading glasses resting halfway down my nose. My hair is gathered into a ponytail and stuffed under a Buffalo Bills baseball cap. One would only need a quick glimpse of my face to see the peace that has enveloped my life.

Painting began as a simple hobby that has evolved into a life of its own. I painted because it helped me to relax, taking my mind of the day-to-day events in my life…and off drinking. It has blossomed into a full-fledged cottage industry. At the urging of my son and a few other friends, I decided to apply for a booth at the Allentown Art Festival in Buffalo. To my shock it was a huge success. I sold almost three-quarters of the canvasses I brought to the show. I also received two blue ribbons for my efforts. That was the beginning.

Since that first show, I have exhibited my work at three other shows around Western New York, and I have had single shows in Rochester, Syracuse, Cleveland, Pittsburgh, and Toronto. Living in the northeast, most of the art shows are concentrated in the good-weather months, leaving me lots of time in the off-season to create more paintings, but also to spend time with family and friends. I have found a new passion in traveling and have recently begun exploring opportunities to show my work in warm-weather areas to get me out of Buffalo in the winter.

I can honestly say I have never been busier or more content. Over the last eight years, I have worked hard at improving my life. My diet has gotten a complete healthy overhaul, and I have lost twenty-three pounds. I work out regularly, and I have a young male trainer who has actually asked me on a date more than once. Talk about flattering! Most importantly, I haven't had a drink of any sort during those same eight years. I still attend AA meetings on a regular basis. I have a sponsor and I personally sponsor four other women. I take my sobriety seriously; I am so appreciative of the program and my new life that I spend much of my time helping others get a grip on their addictions.

I never expected that part of my life to come full circle as it has, but it paid off when Dylan confessed to me his own issues with drinking. I took him to his first meeting and got him hooked up with an excellent sponsor. I have been there for him at every step, as has Adam. It really touches my heart to see those two guys together. It is easily the best thing to come out of all we have been through.

Having finished my painting, I lift it off the easel and carry it up to the balcony overlooking the living room where it can dry without being disturbed. I go back outside and close up my paints and easel and take them back down to my studio. I clean out my brushes and arrange them so they can dry uninterrupted. I hang my painter's smock and hat on their respective pegs and kick off my sneakers. I wash my hands in the utility sink, and while wiping my hands, I slowly turn and take in my entire studio. There are a few items I would like to add (they're currently in a virtual cart in an online store). Despite this, I'm pleased with what I have created and very satisfied that it was all designed by my own hands. I have accomplished something significant in my life and have done it all on my own. Coming from where I was not so long ago, the changes are nothing less than magical.

The greatest tool my sobriety has offered me is a different way to deal with my anger and in doing so dissipate my hate. I was terribly angry with Jay for the way he treated me and all the people who are so vital to my life today. Yet, the hate wasn't directed at him, my hate was inward. I hated the person I had allowed myself to become. I primarily hated that I made myself so dependent on my husband and allowed myself to drown my misery in alcohol. Jay never opened the bottles, never filled the glass, never forced me to drink a drop. I did that all to myself. What I had to learn was a sure-fire way to forgive myself for my weaknesses and vow to all of us that I would never walk that path again. I learned to stop hating myself, to forgive myself for my choices. Once I learned how to forgive myself, it was easy to follow the same steps to forgive others as well.

So, yes, I have forgiven Jay. I had to. I needed to move on with my life and that meant not wasting time with emotions from the past. Besides, had I not received the slap in the face that my ex-husband delivered that night eight years ago, none of my current life would exist as I know it. I suppose, in that sense, I should appreciate Jay, thanking him for changing my life. Many positive things have come from his actions.

Think about it. Jay's death brought my son back to me. Dylan and I have never been closer, and thank God I was there when he needed me, especially when he revealed his addiction. His death provided me with a new best friend; Annie and I have become remarkably close, and I was heartbroken when she decided to move away. She remained a major supporter of my artwork, introducing me to collectors she knew. These collectors critiqued my work and set me on my current path. I do worry about Annie and how she has chosen to deal with her losses, but I think she will be okay. At least I hope so.

Jay's death gave life to the new Mary Beth, to the better mother, to the artist, to the world traveler and to a supporter of people in need. His death introduced me to Adam who is one of the finest young men I have ever met. He calls me Mom-2, but sometimes just Mom. It's an honor to be called Mom by him. Jay's death also introduced me to Will.

With Annie in Colorado, I have taken over as Will's surrogate mother. We spend time together and talk whenever we can. I intend to be a supporting figure throughout his life. I understand the choices he made and the pressure he was under, and I will not desert him. When the time is right, I will do all I can to help him get his business back on its feet.

My reverie ends. I find my way upstairs and into the master suite. I have kept my home and probably will for a while. My finances are in order, and I feel no pressure to sell it anytime soon. Yes, it is too big for me, but it gives me space to wander, to work, to set up my own studio. For now, it fits my lifestyle. It is not filled with many memories as most of my time here was spent alone and in large part, intoxicated. Most of all, I'm comfortable here.

I reach into the shower stall and get the hot water flowing. I toss my shorts and sports bra into the hamper. I turn to brush my teeth while taking my physical inventory in the mirror. Where once my body was my enemy, now it is my close friend. I don't look a day older than the day Jay died, and maybe I even look a few years younger. I'm truly pleased with the image that looks back at me. I like who I have become, I enjoy my own company. I have no urge to add more to my life. I'm not interested in a husband or even a lover. I'm not opposed to the company of a man, but I'm not actively seeking a mate. If it happens it happens. If it doesn't, I don't expect that I will feel a sense of loneliness or loss.

I turn off the shower and pull the towel from the door to dry off. My hair is so much shorter these days that drying it takes only a few moments. I hang my towel over the door again and step out into my bedroom. I walk over to the window and draw back the curtains, taking in the sights and sounds of a perfect summer morning. When I think back to the hours and days I spent at this very window, waiting for any sighting of the man I had pinned my happiness on, the lost days, the lost nights, I want to cringe. Those days are gone and so is that woman. In their place are days filled with wonder, and the joy of people living their lives to the fullest. The woman standing here today has learned vital lessons on how a life is to be led. She embraces each day for what it offers, for the opportunity to give back to the world and to help those seeking the path she has discovered.

Gary Friedman

For me and mine, all is good…finally.

CHAPTER THIRTY-ONE
WILL

———•———

It's not a bad model, as riding lawnmowers go, but I much prefer the one I have sitting in storage. The suspension in this thing is just wrong. I can feel every uneven stretch of turf, every clump of dirt like they were ten-foot boulders. I tend to slow down to lessen the pain. Of course, there is no hurry. I've got nothing but time.

Eyes follow me everywhere. Grass cutting is a prime job here and it has taken me years of good behavior to earn it. Just the same, there are plenty of other inmates who would kill for the freedoms I have earned. Make no mistake about it, I have earned them. Two years of being the bottom of the barrel when it comes to privileges left me with lots of time in my cell to ponder my existence, reliving the mistake I had made. Most of the guys in here have made more than one mistake before getting sentenced to the Collins Correctional Facility. For me, it only took one. I have no complaints. I'm where I belong. Eight long years so far with two more to go before I'm eligible for parole. I have done everything asked of me here and have been a model prisoner. I can only hope I get my chance at parole the first time around.

The truth is, it feels like I have been in a prison of one sort or another my whole life. Except for building my landscaping company, every other choice has been out of my hands. I had adoptive parents who became bored with parenting shortly after my arrival. My biological father did what he could to help me but never admitted that he was indeed my father and a biological mother who kept herself a secret until the day of my father's funeral. She has made no effort to reach out to me ever since that day. It feels like I have never been a real priority in anyone's life, a fact I have had plenty of time to ponder over the last eight years.

I remember that moment like it was yesterday, hearing that woman publicly announce herself as my mother like she was ordering a coffee at a drive through. Not an ounce of emotion. Discovering I had a real mother in one second and realizing I had killed my real father in the next was more than I could stand. I raced across the cemetery and within minutes, with no plan to do so, found myself sitting in a pew of the church where the mass for my father had just occurred. Father Dominic was by my side before I sat down.

"Welcome back, Will."

"Thank you, Father." I sat quietly for what seemed like an eternity, making no effort to move, no effort to talk. Through it all, Father Dominic never left my side. I had a hard time catching my breath, taking deep sigh after deep sigh. My hands only left my lap to wipe away a tear before it became too obvious that I was crying. I wasn't thinking. I wasn't praying. I was just being, existing, taking up space. I wanted to be invisible...until I didn't. "Father, I have ruined my life and I don't know how to fix it. Can you help me?"

"I can try, Will. Do you want to tell me what happened?"

I spent the next two hours telling Father Dominic my whole life story, from my childhood to the afternoon I first saw Jesse in Mary Beth's driveway and the life-altering choices I made as a result. "Father, they have declared his death natural causes. No one is even considering that there was foul play. I know I'm free and clear of any punishment, but I can't live with myself, with what I have done. I am a free man with guilt as my prison cell. I don't think I can live like this."

"My son," Father Dominic began, "I'm not sure if you are ready to answer this question, but why? Why did you chance throwing your life away over your father's indiscretions?"

"Father, for me, it wasn't a simple indiscretion. It was like my life slipping away. My parents gave me up for adoption. The people who adopted me never really cared. To them, I was something to show off, a feather in their cap. Adam's family were the first people to accept me for who I am. When I saw Jesse in that driveway, I snapped. I didn't want to go back to being an afterthought. Maybe it seems like an extreme reaction to you, but to me, Adam was the glue that held my life together. If I lost that glue, my life would never be the same again. I saw no other way, yet I regret my decision. From the moment I left Jesse on that jogging path, I regretted it. Oh, Father, Help me! I have made such a mess of things."

I felt his arm pull me close as the tears streamed down my face.

"Will, there is only one medicine I know that will ease that guilt. You need to go to the police and make a full and complete confession and let the chips fall where they may. Please know that I will be by your side the whole way."

So, that's what I did that very same day. Gratefully, Father Dominic drove me to the Buffalo Police headquarters, and we asked to speak to a detective. After I told my story, they brought in the District Attorney and a stenographer and I told it all again. I told them I didn't need an attorney to confess and that I didn't want a trial. I wanted to plead guilty and do whatever the court decided. Father Dominic was there with me the whole time. He told them I wasn't a bad man, more that I was a good man who made a mistake, a crime of the heart. They offered me one phone call and I decided to call Mary Beth. She and her son Dylan arrived thirty minutes later.

Dylan explained to the detective and the DA that the cause of death was natural causes, that no autopsy was ordered and that the body was buried. He also stated that a full tox screen had been performed and that no drug had been found in Jesse's system. Even if I had given him an injection, Dylan stated it wasn't enough to kill him. That no murder had been committed. The DA wasn't convinced. He said that even if the injection didn't kill him, that was certainly my intent. He asked Dylan if the shock of being given an injection could have been a catalyst for coronary arrest. Dylan said he couldn't be sure.

I was assigned a legal aid attorney who said she was there to protect my rights. The negotiation led to a plea of involuntary manslaughter with a sentence of fifteen years meaning I could get out in ten with good behavior. I took it and immediately felt at peace, other than the fear of going to prison. Under the circumstances, all parties felt I wasn't an at-risk, potential repeat offender. I was sent to the medium security prison in Collins and here I am.

After two years of being a particularly good prisoner, I volunteered for and was given the job of cutting the grass. The fact that I had been a landscaper on the outside worked in my favor. After two more years of proving my worth, I asked for the privilege of cleaning up the beds and shrubbery, not an easy task considering the limited selection of tools I could be trusted with. Following one full growing season, I was given the chance to create a new bed next to the warden's office. I jumped at the chance. Most of the tool restrictions were waived for me. The warden, the administrators, the correction officers, the doctor, and prison psychologist all know me on a first name basis, and we smile and nod when we cross paths. A couple have said they will miss my talents when I'm gone. I tell them that I hope they won't be offended if I don't miss them after I leave. They just laugh.

The term "doing time" is wholly misunderstood. It's not just that you are spending days, weeks, and years in a six-by-eight cell. That's just the tip of the iceberg. The truth is that time is your jailer. The hours spent alone in your cell with nothing to do, no one to talk to is the hardest part of prison. The boredom, the anxiety, getting out of the habit of counting down every millisecond of your sentence are constant battles to fight. I spend much of my time reading, scouring the shelves of the library to find books to share my time with. Lying in my cell, I live vicariously through the characters of those books. When they walk on a beach, I walk on a beach. When they ride the Ferris wheel, I ride it with them. When they take the woman of their dreams into their arms, I can feel the moment, smell her perfume, experience her presence. Books have been my life preserver.

Then there's the visitors. Collins is about half-way between Buffalo and the New York/Pennsylvania border, making it about an hour's travel total, both directions. Adam makes a monthly visit. We talk a lot. I know he has forgiven me and says he understands why I did what I did. The part I got wrong, he said, was thinking he would have judged me for being the one to blow his father in. He would have never held that against me, ever. Dylan has come around a couple of times each year, always sharing the ride and time with Adam. They have both told me that we are three brothers, not just two. That brought tears to my eyes. They also said they plan on helping me get my landscaping business back off the ground and they're already generating contacts. Dylan arranged an interview with a Buffalo News writer who told my story from beginning to end. It was beautifully written and helped build a potential client list that Dylan continues to work on.

Annie came by a few times before she moved away, and they were tough visits. Seeing her, knowing what I took away from her, regenerates all my guilt. Those visits are the hardest of all. I did get a letter from her telling me she would be home for Christmas this year and wants to spend some time with me to put the past at rest and rebuild our relationship. I'm counting the days. I have become very good at that.

My most treasured visitor has been Mary Beth. She comes out as much as she can. Living in a southern suburb of Buffalo puts her closest to the prison. She comes out at least once a week, sometimes more. She has taken me under her wing, lifted me up when I needed it the most, and offered me a place to stay when I get released. She even told me she would adopt me if she could. She has become the mother I never had. Whenever I lose my temper in here, get close to wanting to get in someone's face, the vision of what that choice would do to her helps me to back down and take a deep breath. She has become the last person in the world I would want to disappoint.

I have made mistakes, big ones. I know when I put my time at the Collins Correctional Facility behind me, I will be ready to start my life over again. I don't expect to be mistake-free the rest of my life, but my mistakes will never be as life-altering as the one I made eight years ago. The biggest mistake I made that day wasn't killing Jesse, although that was certainly an unforgivable one. My biggest mistake was not trusting the love of the people around me, thinking I would be discarded just because I was the bearer of bad news. I have spent a lifetime questioning people's motives, second guessing the level of their commitment to me, and minimizing their love for me.

Finding a reason to smile in this place can be quite a challenge. I have found a way to overcome that challenge. It's knowing that I have one thing waiting for me when I get out of this cell that I never thought I would have in my life. One thing that would make the rest of the pain go away. A family to call my own.

Gary Friedman

EPILOGUE
ANGELINA

———— • ————

The bright sun crawls toward the Pacific Ocean as what's left of the small crowd pack up their coolers and lower their umbrellas to head home. The Marine Street Beach is never overly-crowded but today was more peaceful than usual. I'm certainly in no hurry to end my day in the sun. Two beach towels are spread out across the sand with one under my flat-to-the-ground beach chair and the other towel empty with a pair of sandals and some beach toys sitting on the sand nearby. Even the waves are calming down, causing what's left of the afternoon surfers to leave until tomorrow. Of the twelve miles of beach around San Diego, Marine Street remains my favorite. It has its share of palm trees and condos in all directions and some rocks that the kids love to climb, but it just doesn't attract the crowds that the nearby competition draws. That allows for early evenings just like this when I can count the number of beach-goers on my fingers and toes.

Half-way between me and the rolling surf is a young man toiling away on a sandcastle that has been his obsession for the last three hours. Ben has managed a few short breaks just to run up and give me a hug before returning to dig the moat just a little bit deeper and quite a bit wider. It might seem unusual to call a boy of seven a young man but in this case it definitely fits. He has been my young man since the age of four, having to take on many

291

responsibilities boys his age should never have to. Maybe it's my own weakness or the loneliness I have chosen as a lifestyle, but he seems to be aware of his mother's needs more than his mother. He never complains, never yearns for more friends to play with and is content to be by my side. I watch him intently as he works away at building a castle tower, which is tall enough to oversee his kingdom. He has such unusual concentration with an eye for the smallest detail, just like his father. Benny would have liked his father. Unfortunately, they never met.

I ease myself down on the sand and lay my head back on my beach chair, pondering the life I have made for the two of us. My job as a security technician for an internet provider allows me to work at home two days a week. That enables me to limit Ben's time in day care. Now that he is in school, I can manage with a babysitter a couple of afternoons after he gets home from school. Despite work, I consider myself a full-time dedicated mom. I'm only twenty-eight, and I feel no rush to build a social world outside of Ben and me. Having been in love once, I have no need to duplicate that moment.

That love isn't a dying emotion; it has only strengthened since Ben's father disappeared. I'm not certain I will ever get over him or that I would ever want to. The people who know me best, particularly my parents and brothers, think me a fool. I knew him for less than a year and he was over thirty years older than me, but he was everything I ever dreamed of in a mate or lover. He treated me wonderfully... and it was always with patience and understanding. He never pushed me into feeling one way or another about anything, but in the end, we always agreed upon most things. I felt loved, adored, and cherished.

Needless to say, when he called from across the country to tell me he was packing up all his worldly belongings and moving to San Diego permanently to be with me, well, I don't think my feet touched the ground for hours. I was so excited by his news that I never had the chance to tell him mine. He told me more than once that he never had the chance to settle down, and the one thing he missed in his life was having a son and watching him grow. At the time I didn't know Ben was Ben, but the possibility of giving him the son he wanted was a dream come true. Better I should tell him face-to-face. That next night would be my chance.

That chance never came.

He had given me the flight number and his arrival time. I took the sonogram image of our unborn child and wrapped it in a small box with a big red bow. I found a parking space in the Terminal One short-term lot and waited for the Southwestern flight to arrive. It was scheduled for 7:50 p.m. and was right on time. I waited patiently, gift in hand, as the passengers walked by. Finally, the flight crew approached. I asked if there was anyone still getting off the plane and the flight attendant said that they were the last ones to come through. I thought he might have stopped to use a bathroom so I waited a bit longer, but he never came. I checked my phone for messages but nothing. Slowly I walked back through the waiting area alone and in tears. I stopped at the Southwestern desk and told them my concerns. They checked the flight roster and confirmed that he was indeed scheduled for the flight, but that he was a no-show.

I tried to stay calm for the ride home but failed miserably. I tried to gather my thoughts as best I could. His flight was coming from Buffalo and his phone number was in the 716-area code, but other than his name and those two facts, I knew little else about him. Being so late on the East coast, I respectfully decided to wait until morning.

I left text messages and voice mails on his phone with no reply. I scanned the Buffalo paper but didn't see anything that might relate to him. I called all the local hospitals to see if anyone by his name had been admitted. I came up empty. I searched Google in the hope of finding more references to him but struck out. It was like he vanished into thin air. I continued my search every day for a month and found nothing. None of this made any sense. To say my heart was broken would be the understatement of the century. It's been eight long years since he disappeared and not an hour goes by that I don't see his face in crowd or in a dream. It doesn't help that Ben is an exact replica of him.

My eyes open again, and I watch Ben pat the sides of his walls smooth. His focus is so intense. The sun has cut the distance to the horizon in half since my eyes were last opened and the crowd has dwindled by a few more. My eyes fall to the ocean as the waves roll in. My mind wanders back one more time.

I was so in love with him, and I have no doubt that he was in love with me. I know I could have made him happy if I had the chance. It's the unknown that drives me crazy. Did something happen to him, an accident of some sort? Did he die? Why would he call me and say he was coming and then not show up? If he is alive, what kind of a man just goes *poof* like this, without a word? Did I ever really know him? Was this all some sort of a scam? Oh, Jesse, my Jesse. Where are you? What has the world done with you?

I call out to Ben and tell him to wrap up construction. He whines, of course, but doesn't fight me; he never does. I fold up the chair and the two towels and throw his tools in our beach bag. Ben grabs the bag in his left hand and I carry the towels and chair in my right. We hold hands as we walk slowly to our car.

"Thanks for taking me to the beach today, Mom."

"You are very welcome," I reply, smiling. He's so polite.

"I love you, Mom."

"I love you too, Benny, my little man."

"I like it when you call me that."

"I like it too!"

We lift the back of my SUV and slide the beachwear onto the carpet. I close the gate and kneel down and give Ben a hug. I do love him like crazy, mostly because he is my flesh and blood and a little bit because he is all that is left behind from the love of my life. Maybe someday I will fall in love again, but in all honesty, my ability to trust as well as my confidence in my ability to judge others has been deeply damaged and may never be fixed. For now, the love of—and for—my son is all I need. If only Ben knew the quality of the woman and son he left behind. He would be so proud.

Gary Friedman

HUMANITY

I am not me. I am more Us. Defined as a collection of Us, a collection that began as a population of one and has grown to cover the world. I represent the best of Us. I represent the worst of Us. I am the source of the greatest discoveries this planet has ever known yet I continue to disappoint: my artwork ranges from the most majestic masterpieces the world could imagine—to graffiti on the side of a railroad car. My music ranges from the great symphonies and evolves all the way to street musicians beating on empty pails. All meaning well and all for appreciating audiences.

I am no longer a physical being, more so a conscience, a soul, an observer of what I represent. I am beyond vision, sound, and touch; yet I have experienced every sensation, every emotion relished by those I observe...and I observe all, sometimes with great pride, sometimes with great sorrow. I am not a god, a deity in any form. I am more a history of what has been, a measuring stick against which change is arbitrated.

I am Humanity.

I do not judge, get involved or interact. I am known by all, but my legacy seems to carry little weight. The eyes of Humanity appear to have turned inward, focused on itself, while empathy dwindles to the status of lost art. During my existence, some individuals, some movements have come along that changed the view of me and altered my reputation. Those aberrations tend to be balanced out over time. Despots come and go; reason settles the score. History has less effect on my members than does their own misguided actions, fueled by a shallow heart or confused brain. The examples are endless.

The world that Humans inhabit holds many tales such as these. My ability to be surprised by the choices Humans make evaporated centuries ago. This tale came as close as any. It is my hope that the lessons learned by those who crossed Jesse's path will be meaningful to you as well. There were nine souls affected by his selfishness; affected in such a way that their lives will never be the same. They are genuinely good people who fell victim to the wants and needs of one damaged heart and in the process were damaged themselves. Whether they heal from their wounds is up to them. Know that I will be watching as is my want to do.

Know, as well, that nothing escapes my ever-watchful eye and as such, you too may be the subject of a story of Humanity. How will you be judged? What choices will you make that will bend your path into the way of others, obstruct their view, change their lives?

I have offered a story that may give you pause; a moment to recognize each man's impact on the world around him. I have always believed, and have seen in the daily walk of Humans, that each of them has a responsibility to the world in which they all live, to the air they breathe, the water they drink, the souls they touch. People can rarely be ignored; they are either raised or brought down by their own actions. Every Human affects the world at large, from the greatest leaders to the homeless in cardboard boxes. Give back; lift up; be a positive influence; make a difference.

Of all the creatures on this Earth, only humans have the power and ability to destroy it. The rest of God's creatures are at their mercy. That is an enormous power. I have not been impressed at the way Humans have wielded such power, either on the grand scale or in the smallest of ways such as how Jesse conducted himself. What kind of man was Jesse, indeed? From my lofty view, I see a world on the brink, teetering between good and evil with the outcome in doubt. Which side will you choose? My advice is to choose wisely, for you may not get a second vote.

I am not me. I am Us. I do not judge. I am simply a standard by which the world compares its current state of affairs.

I am Humanity.

Gary Friedman

ABOUT THE AUTHOR

Gary Friedman has traveled a long road, interacting with people every step of the way. He makes contributions to the betterment of the world every day. Whether in his role as a non-profit volunteer, business owner, coach, counselor, federal employee, or author, it has always been important to Gary to leave the community a better place than when he found it. His home in Western New York has been the backdrop for most of the poignant work he has accomplished so far.

In each of his careers, Gary has made people a priority by observing, listening, and reaching out to those in need and those who need direction. He has authored a series of three inspirational novels: *The Shepherd Chronicles*, asserting that one man can make a difference. He frequently speaks to audiences promoting that message. Gary's new novel, *Stones and Glass Houses*, demonstrates his intrigue with how humanity functions and interacts. His goal is to shake up the reader's perspective and invoke curiosity... this book does not disappoint.

Enjoying his retirement from the Federal government, Gary spends his days enjoying time with family and friends, traveling and writing. Be sure to visit his website to find out more about Gary and *The Shepherd Chronicles*.

www.garyfriedmanbooks.com

Gary Friedman

BOOKS
BY
GARY FRIEDMAN

Book One of The Shepherd Chronicles

The
PROMISE

One man can make a difference

GARY FRIEDMAN

The Promise is the first book of The Shepherd Chronicles trilogy. It tells the story of David, who quietly returns to his hometown after failing to establish his musical career in Nashville. He avoids all contacts from his past except for his mentor Jacob, who helps David rise to the top of Buffalo's club scene. With new success and reconciliation with his family on the horizon, tragedy suddenly strikes, and David finds himself lying in an emergency room, nearing death. While on his death bed, David makes a promise that proves to be life altering. After a miraculous recovery, he finds himself being held to his promise. Thus, begins a journey that will take David from New York to Georgia and back again, discovering that one man can make a difference, not only in the lives of others he encounters but in his own destiny.

David Hynes is dutifully following the path laid out for him by a mysterious messenger. He now travels without a map, a star to follow, or a plan. Open to all possibilities, David is led only by the seed planted in his heart, nurtured by faith and a possible destiny. Armed with only a shepherd's staff, David's journey intersects with others who have either lost their way or have reached an impasse. As his travels lead him to Ohio, David is confronted with his own crisis that threatens to end his journey and change his path forever. As David ultimately discovers the rules that govern his journey through life, he becomes a symbol of hope and reassurance to all. But as his future waits, only time will tell if David will ever be able to find inner-peace and an important sign from above that will allow him to continue his mission. In this inspirational tale, a young man continues on a quest to help humans in trouble, guided by a messenger from God.

David Hynes is torn between continuing on the path created for him by a mysterious messenger or supporting a grieving family and starting a life with his beloved, Peggy. After deciding to move forward on his journey, David strikes out once again to bring his message to those that have lost their way. With his flock growing, David finds his way from national politics and battles with terrorists to rescuing an elderly man from a fate that does not belong to him. Along his path, he discovers the greater depth of his mission and a new mentor to guide his way. His mysterious messenger takes on a new form as

David begins to define his future. Through it all, David proves that one man can make a difference not just for himself, but for every life he touches, while encouraging all of us to do the same. In the conclusion to the Shepherd Chronicles trilogy, one man continues an inspirational quest to take the focus off himself and make a difference.